## Praise for Katerina Diamond

'Diamond is the master of gripping literature'
*Evening Standard*

'A terrific story, originally told. All hail the new queen of crime!'
*Heat*

'A web of a plot that twists and turns and keeps the reader on their seat . . . don't read it before bed if you're easily spooked!'
*Sun*

'A page-turner with a keep-you-guessing plot'
*Sunday Times Crime Club*

'Packed with twists until the last page'
*Closer*

'Deliciously dark, keeps her readers guessing throughout as she leads us on a very secretive, VERY twisted journey'
Lisa Hall, bestselling author of
*Between You and Me*

KATERINA DIAMOND burst onto the crime scene with her debut novel *The Teacher*, which became a *Sunday Times* bestseller and a number 1 Kindle bestseller. It was longlisted for the CWA John Creasey Debut Dagger Award and the Hotel Chocolat Award for 'darkest moment'. Her second novel, *The Secret*, became a number 1 Kindle bestseller too and received widespread acclaim. Her third novel, *The Angel*, published in 2017 and again hit the bestseller lists. *The Promise* published in 2018 and went in at #7 on the *Sunday Times* list. Katerina has lived in various glamorous locations such as Weston-Super-Mare, Thessaloniki, Larnaca, Exeter, Derby and Forest Gate. Katerina now resides in East Kent with her husband and children. She was born on Friday 13th.

By the same author:

# Woman
## in the
# Water
## Katerina Diamond

avon.

Published by AVON
A division of HarperCollins*Publishers* Ltd
1 London Bridge Street
London SE1 9GF

www.harpercollins.co.uk

A Paperback Original 2020
2

First published in Great Britain by HarperCollins*Publishers* 2019

ISBN: 978-0-00-828295-0

Typeset in Sabon LT Std by Palimpsest Book Production Ltd,
Falkirk, Stirlingshire

Printed and bound in UK by CPI Group (UK) Ltd,
Croydon CR0 4YY

MIX
Paper from
responsible sources
FSC
www.fsc.org
FSC™ C007454

This book is produced from independently certified FSC™ paper to ensure
responsible forest management.

For more information visit: www.harpercollins.co.uk/green

For Pat and Kitty

# Prologue

*It's so cold out here. I stare up at the ink blue sky above me, not a cloud in sight, and focus on the stars, a passing airplane twinkles and blinks as it crosses. I hear my name being called, but aside from shivering, I can't move, my whole body numb. I don't want them to find me.*

*I'm as close to death as I have ever been, but I still hang on. I don't know why when I have wished for the end so many times before. I need to stop fighting it. I need to let myself just slip away.*

# Chapter One

DS Adrian Miles soaked in the sunrise as he drove home along Glasshouse Lane after a few days away with his partner, DS Imogen Grey, far from local prying eyes. They had barely noticed the relationship creeping up on them. They had gone from strangers to good friends within weeks of meeting each other, then things had blossomed and grown between them until the chemistry was undeniable. They were still in the early stages, not enough to announce anything, not enough to tell anyone.

He smiled to himself as he thought about the last few days, weeks, months. Every moment was a countdown to the next time they could be alone together.

It was always so quiet on these suburban streets, especially at this time in the morning, and the calming effect of the River Exe seemed to ebb into these surrounding neighbourhoods. Something about living near water makes people generally more relaxed. He must have driven past at least ten people out for a morning stroll with their dogs. Maybe getting a dog would be a good way to get out of the house more; these days, he mostly just drove anywhere rather than walk.

More often than not, as he drove he found himself thinking about Imogen and missing her when she wasn't beside him, in any capacity. These feelings had crept up on him and he found himself completely losing himself to her, as though he had no choice in the matter. He'd also sometimes find himself smiling, without realising. Was this happiness?

It was certainly difficult with Imogen wanting to keep it a secret. Although relationships were allowed it definitely complicated things at work. The DCI had expressed in the past that she wasn't overly keen on relationships within the unit. It was a mess for sure, but worst-case scenario one of them could transfer to a different division. He wouldn't let work get in the way of this. Adrian had never felt like other people in as much as he had never thought himself capable of a meaningful and grown-up relationship. If that's what this was then he would rather lose his job than her. He couldn't lose her, not after all the pain of losing his previous more serious relationships. Jobs were replaceable, people weren't.

He spotted a group of women gathered by the riverside wall. As much as anything, it was a strange time of day for this kind of gathering. The sun was barely up. They were looking over towards a small muddy offshoot of river that ran through the thickets. There

4

was something about the way they were talking to each other that made Adrian pull the car over. Brows creased, they turned towards him, eyeing him suspiciously before turning their attention back to something on the other side of the wall.

'Everything all right?' Adrian said, pulling his warrant card from his pocket and showing the women.

Their faces lightened immediately and one of the women stepped forwards. She scrutinised his ID before speaking.

'There's something in the water. The kids were out playing on that patch of grass last night. They kept saying how there was someone in the water and this morning my two maintained they saw a dead body down in the water before they came home – had nightmares because of it. We thought it was part of their game last night, you know what kids are like. We can't really see from here and none of us want to climb the wall to go and check. There's something there but it's in the shadow of those bushes. It could be anything.'

'Why didn't you call the police?' Adrian asked.

'I don't know if you've got kids, but they can be known to tell the odd porky. I asked the girls if they would come with me and look, but there are so many bushes we can't see anything clearly.'

'Where?' Adrian said, walking up to the wall and looking over into the riverside shrubbery.

The light was terrible and so he would have to climb over to take a closer look.

'Can you see that blue thing?' The same woman

who had spoken pointed towards the left side of the greenery.

Adrian put his card back in his pocket and hoisted himself over the wall, trying to make it look effortless – he had an audience, after all.

The drop on the other side was a little lower and he just managed to save himself from embarrassment when he fell by placing his hand on the ground as though he were a superhero who had fallen from a great height. Anything over four feet was a bit too high for Adrian. It wasn't like he was trying to impress anyone, but he wanted to avoid any humiliation, as this could all end up in a police report, depending on what he found in the river.

He took his phone out of his pocket and switched on the torch; the sky had adopted a grey-and-orange hue as the sun hid behind the houses. The blue thing in the bushes looked like denim. It was obscured and could just as easily be a discarded denim jacket or plastic bag from a newsagent as anything else. He tried not to think about the anything else. As he got closer it became clear that whatever it was, it wasn't a discarded item of clothing. *Please don't let it be a child.*

Holding his breath, Adrian edged closer to the pair of legs that lay in the undergrowth, the top of the body still obscured by the bushes. Forced to climb into the river, he put his phone between his teeth as he walked around the legs into the water. It was cold and muddy; he tried not to slip on the mud banks as he made his way to the top of the form. After taking the phone from his mouth, he shone the light on the legs, gradually moving upwards until he found a head.

It was a woman. She wore a baggy cream Aran jumper and jeans. One of her boots was missing. Her right arm, hips and backside were submerged in the water, but her body was contorted in such a way that her head, legs and left arm were out of the water. Her face was dirty, one eye swollen from a possible fracture as the bruising had closed it, but her other big blue eye was staring at him, fixed.

He turned the torch off on his phone and dialled DI Matt Walsh.

'We need a team down on Glasshouse Lane. I've sent over my location. I've found a body in the water.'

'A body in the water? A dead body? How?' Walsh responded.

'Well, I was driving down the road when I saw a group of women by the riverside wall. I approached the women and they said that last night their kids were playing outside and this morning told their parents they saw something that resembled a body.

'Description of the victim is: female, Caucasian, maybe twenty-five years old, blonde hair, blue eyes. Looks like she was assaulted beforehand. She's been here at least the one night, not sure how much longer.'

Suddenly, Adrian felt a hand grip his calf. The kind you half expect when you step out of bed in the middle of the night. He froze. He took a deep breath before turning the dim light of the phone screen towards the woman to illuminate her face. She blinked slowly.

She was alive.

'Adrian?' Walsh said.

'She's alive, Walsh, get an ambulance! She's alive!'

# Chapter Two

Adrian immediately removed his jacket and threw it over the woman to keep her warm. He stuffed his phone into his back pocket and knelt down next to her, gently removing the muddy hair from her face. She was younger than him, mid twenties at a guess.

'Can you hear me? I'm Detective Sergeant Adrian Miles; I'm going to help you. Can you move?'

She nodded her head weakly. How long had she been here? She must be freezing. Even in the summer the river wasn't warm.

'Can you tell me your name?'

'I'm so c-c-cold,' she said faintly.

'We have to wait here for the guys with the stretcher, OK? I don't want to move you in case anything is broken.'

He went to stand again but she grabbed his hand, this time with more strength than before.

'P-p-please get me out of h-h-here,' the woman whispered.

DS Miles could see she had tried to pull herself out of the water, which is why only part of her was still submerged.

'We really should wait for the paramedics.'

'C-cold . . . P-please,' she rasped.

'OK, I'll try. But you tell me straight away if I hurt you.'

Lying next to her on the bank, Adrian got as close to her as he could, the chill of the water against his thighs inconsequential. She groaned as he tilted her enough that he could slip his shoulder underneath hers and gradually slide his arm under her for support as he tried to pull her from the brambles. She was weak and completely limp, with barely enough strength to lift her head. The left side of her torso was supported by the right side of his. Some of her blonde hair had become entangled in the spiny branches that protruded from the hedge. Adrian gently tugged at the hair to dislodge it, leaving some of it behind.

As soon as she was free, he put his arm around her waist and tried to move with her away from the hedge. Her head thumped against his chest. He felt her sigh heavily, her weak heartbeat gently beating against his arm. He pushed his legs against the floor of the muddy bank and as he moved up onto the safety of the grass, she moved with him. He sat up and she lolloped forwards, weak from exhaustion. Adrian didn't care to think how long she had been lying there. He moved her onto his lap and put her arm around his shoulder.

'Can you put your arms around my neck and hold it? I need to use my arm to leverage myself to standing.'

Fingernails dug into his skin. He could feel that she

was using everything she had to hold on and probably wouldn't be able to keep it up for long, so he pushed himself up before quickly making sure both of his arms were securely around her. He heard the gasps of the women as he emerged from the bushes with the woman lying against him.

'Oh my God!' one of the women cried.

'Is she alive?' another shouted.

'Could you get some blankets or something to warm her up quickly while we wait for the medics?'

In situations like this, it was instinct and training that carried Adrian through, but at some point, there is a moment where you get to think about what is actually going on and that's when the reality of the situation hits home. Who was this girl? How had she got here? Who had done this to her? She was petite and her injuries were not the result of an accident. He could see fingermarks on her neck and he clenched his jaw to suppress the rage that threatened.

Adrian lay her on the grass and stroked her forehead. She began to tremble and Adrian hoped the medics would appear before she got hypothermia.

'Thank you,' she said, her voice breaking as she spoke, and a guttural moan followed soon after as she began to cry.

The ladies from the houses opposite the wall appeared holding blankets. He noticed one of them was filming with their mobile phone, which ignited the anger that he was fighting so hard to suppress.

'I'll be back in a moment. I'm just going to grab those blankets, see if we can warm you up a bit.'

She tried to grab at his shirt, to stop him from leaving. She mouthed as if to speak but nothing came out.

'I won't be a second. I'm coming back, I promise.'

He stood and walked over to the woman holding the phone.

'Can I ask you not to share that video until we have had a chance to identify the woman and inform her family. It would be horrible to find out something like this from a video on the internet, wouldn't it?'

'Oh, I wasn't going to share it,' she said, her cheeks flushing.

'My colleagues will be here any second to take all of your names. Please just wait here.'

'I got you these blankets; they are my kids' blankets; it's all I had. Sorry.'

'Thank you.'

Adrian took the blankets and walked back to the lady on the ground. He was starting to feel cold himself. He was thankful that the area was poorly lit, so at least the video would be poor quality. He covered her with the kitten-patterned blankets and waited for the ambulance; the sirens were getting closer.

In the back of the ambulance, Adrian stayed with the woman. It felt wrong to leave her at this point. She must have been terrified and hopefully, she knew she could trust Adrian by now. The paramedics had cut off her wet jeans and covered her in a thermal blanket to help bring her temperature back up.

'What happened?' one of the paramedics said.

'Some kids found her; I just pulled her out. I'm hoping the doc can tell us more about what's happened to her.'

'What's her name?'

'I don't know,' Adrian said, realising she hadn't answered him when he had asked her before.

'What's your name, love?' the paramedic asked the woman, leaning down to hear better.

The woman winced and closed her eyes as the ambulance went over a pothole. She squeezed Adrian's hand weakly.

They pulled up outside the hospital and Adrian saw that Dr Hadley was waiting outside the emergency department's bay doors. Adrian had texted her to come and meet them. Dr Hadley had worked with the police on numerous occasions and Adrian knew she specialised in women's cases, especially where sexual assault was a probability. The clothes the victim was wearing were intact when he found her, which was unusual in cases of sexual assault. But whatever had happened to her, this was a horrific attack that she wasn't going to be getting over anytime soon. If she made it, that is.

'I'm going to go now, but I will be back.'

'Please don't go,' the woman said.

'This is my friend Dr Hadley and she is going to look after you, OK? I'll be back before you know it,' Adrian told her.

The woman nodded.

'Thank you, DS Miles. I'll give you a call after I've done a thorough examination,' Dr Hadley said with a heavy sigh as she appraised the woman's condition.

Adrian watched as they wheeled the trolley into the

hospital through the emergency doors, two uniformed officers following behind. The ambulance doors closed and the vehicle drove out of the bay.

Pulling his phone from his pocket, DS Miles texted Imogen to come and pick him up. Still covered in mud, his clothes still damp, Adrian needed to get changed before the last half an hour got a chance to creep under his skin. Someone had hurt this woman and discarded her. He was going to find out who.

# Chapter Three

Imogen put a towel down on the passenger seat of her car before Adrian sat down. He had that look in his eye, that angry, determined look he got when he was well into a case and it wasn't going their way. Whatever he had seen had obviously affected him; he seemed anxious and slightly haunted.

'What happened? I only saw you a couple of hours ago,' she asked.

'That woman I found. She was completely fucked up, thrown away like rubbish. It was awful. I thought she was dead. She looked dead.'

'You found her in time, though. You got her to the hospital.'

'Who does that to another person? Sometimes I feel like we are swimming against the tide with this job, I really do. Every day it's something else; it never stops.'

Imogen knew that this was about more than the woman he had rescued today – it was about the woman he grew up with, about his parents. Adrian rarely talked about his mother, but Imogen knew that his father had been violent and that Adrian struggled to accept aggression towards women on any level. She knew what it was like to grow up in challenging circumstances, but not a day went by when she wasn't grateful that there was no kind of abuse in her own childhood; she had seen what it had done to friends. Working in the police, she knew how demoralising an abusive childhood was and how massively it impacted who people became.

'You'll feel better after you get cleaned up,' she said. 'We can go straight back to the hospital as soon as you've showered.'

'What if she dies?'

'Whatever comes next, we are going to find out what happened to her. She's not going to die. I know it. You saved her, Adrian.'

Imogen parked the car near Adrian's house and he jumped out immediately. He didn't want to hang around, she could tell. He unlocked his door and went inside, leaving it open for her to follow.

Imogen made herself comfortable on the sofa and waited for Adrian to return. She was at home in his house now, maybe even more at home here than in her own place.

There was an old cookery show on TV; it was one she hadn't seen since her mum was alive and she felt a pang of sadness as thoughts of her mother crossed her mind. They used to watch Keith Floyd together regularly; her mother loved his vibrancy and authenticity. She would wink and say that she had met him once, and Imogen wondered if it was code, a clue that he was her biological father. The mythical bio-dad who was everything from a prince to a crack addict – it seemed silly now to think that she thought this TV celebrity might be her father. There again, her mother had a way of doing the unexpected, so it wasn't completely out of the question.

It had been almost a year since her mother had died and she had barely allowed herself time to think about her. Once she gave herself that permission, there would be no stopping it and so she preferred not to start. Imogen had always felt as though crying was a weakness in some way and so she was loath to succumb. She switched channels until she found something less emotionally challenging.

Her eyes became heavy as she focused on the screen, the Northern accents a refreshing change from the Devonshire twang that she was used to.

Adrian's lips woke her, pressing against hers gently; she wondered what she must look like and hoped she wasn't drooling.

'I forgot to say thanks,' he said before kissing her again.

She kissed him back.

'Feel better?' Imogen said.

'I'm sorry if I was a shit,' Adrian said, perching on the sofa next to her.

She moved to accommodate him and nestled in his arm as he drew her closer.

'You weren't. I get it. That must have been a traumatic

experience for you. Sorry you had to go through it alone.'

'I'd better get back to the hospital,' Adrian said.

'Can we just stay here for a minute?'

'DI Walsh is already there. She hasn't woken yet, but I'd like to be there when she does eventually wake up. I offered for us to do the night shift. He just phoned to tell me the doctor ruled out sexual assault.'

'Well, that's something at least,' Imogen said.

'Is it? I don't see how anything could have made it any worse. She was as near to death as anyone I have ever seen. When I felt her hand around my leg, I thought I had lost my mind. She looked so . . . she just looked gone. I should have checked her pulse straight away.'

'She's in good hands now. The doctors will take care of her. We just need to find out who she is and how she ended up there. How about you? Are you OK?'

'I don't know if OK is the right word for it.'

'I can see your brain ticking over. You can't overthink this one; you're going to do your head in. You acted quickly and now that woman is in hospital getting treatment thanks to you. You did absolutely everything you could. This isn't on you. This is on whoever did that to her, OK?'

'This is going to be a messy one, isn't it?' Adrian sighed.

'Let's hope we have seen the worst of it. Whatever happened to her, she's got us now. And we can make sure it doesn't happen to anyone else,' Imogen placated but knew his mind was already swimming with the ghosts of his own past.

'I wish I shared your optimism.'

'If I had been through what she had been through then there is no one else I would want on my side. You saved her life, Adrian. Remember that.'

# Chapter Four

*I am in a hospital bed, everything hurts and I don't know how I got here. Various nurses and doctors come and go – I haven't opened my eyes yet, but I hear them speaking. I know from their conversation that I have no identification on me and they have no other way for them to identify me. I wonder if this is all a dream – am I really asleep? Or maybe I'm really dead and in some kind of celestial waiting room. I can't say I would be devastated if that were the case. I feel no pain – I am grateful for the drugs they've given me. I fade in and out of sleep, undecided on whether or not I even want to wake. Maybe this time I can disappear. I have a head start and he thinks I'm dead.*

# Chapter Five

Adrian watched the numbers and lines on the heart monitor. He had no idea what any of the information meant, but it was steady and so he assumed that was a good thing. They weren't in intensive care either, which also boded well for the mystery woman. The easy chair in the hospital cubicle was comfortable and he had volunteered to stay until the woman woke. He had sent Imogen home after a couple of hours; there was no point in both of them losing the night.

Adrian was shaken by what had happened. He had seen plenty of horrific cases in his time as a DS and he wondered if there would ever come a time when he wasn't shocked by this kind of thing. But being upset was the right reaction. The moment you stopped being upset was the moment you should go and do something else. It's normal to be afraid or angry. It's normal to feel frustrated or powerless in some situations. You had to keep it inside, though. You had to stay strong, not just for yourself, but also for the people around you. One chink in the armour and all of your defences were compromised.

A nurse came in with a small basin and a cloth. She smiled uncomfortably at Adrian then gently wiped the woman's face and hair, trying to soften the mud that had now dried on her skin and clumped together at her roots. They had already scraped under her fingernails and taken photographs of any abrasions or bruises. But legally they couldn't take blood samples or test her DNA without consent and she would need to be awake for that. The nurse rinsed the cloth and dabbed at a cut across the woman's eyebrow.

As he watched the nurse, Adrian remembered his mother, a fragment of time that they shared together. In a conscious effort to block out his father, Adrian's mother had also disappeared into the back regions of Adrian's memory, but it hadn't worked and his father now became more prominent than ever.

The moment he thought of now was of his mother sitting with him at the kitchen table, remnants of a shattered plate on the floor as they played Connect 4. Adrian's father had thrown the plate across the room and it had glanced off his mother's temple before smashing against the terracotta floor tiles. She steadied herself against the counter and, in order to distract Adrian from the argument, she smoothed her skirt and suggested he run upstairs and get a game for them to play.

When he returned, she had a plaster over her eyebrow and it was as if nothing had happened. They played the game over and over until bedtime, presumably just to avoid any kind of conversation or acknowledgment of what had transpired. Until weeks later, that is, when there was a fragment of blue-and-white willow china lodged under the corner of the washing machine that his mother had missed. The rest of the memories of his mother then faded and reappeared with little clarity; she was an extra in his childhood with barely a speaking role.

Outside, the light faded as the machines bleeped and blinked at regular intervals. Who was this woman? Why had no one reported her missing? Was no one missing a daughter? A sister? Wife? No one even remotely matching her description was in the recent additions to the missing persons database. This was highly unusual and Adrian considered all the questions he didn't even know to ask yet. Already unnerved, Adrian folded his arms and settled in for the night.

Troubling dreams woke him – bruised faces of women he had questioned over his years in the police. Whether it was a husband, a father or a stranger, the assailants were almost always men and more often than not they were known to the victim. He knew that domestic violence wasn't purely men against women, but in his experience that was much more common, or at least women coming forward and reporting it was. People warn you about strangers, but no one warns you about the people you love, the people who say they love you.

He looked over at the woman and saw something different about the way she was breathing. It was shorter, shallower – more controlled than before. His eyes adjusted to the dim lighting and he stood slowly so as not to startle the woman who was almost certainly now awake. Her one good eye opened and she looked across to him; the swelling in the other had reduced significantly since he had found her. She started to breathe faster.

'Hey, I'm a police officer. My name is DS Adrian Miles. I found you by the river. Do you remember?'

She blinked away a tear and he felt her fingers brush against his hand.

'Water,' she mouthed.

He couldn't hear her, but he could see the formation of the word on her lips.

'I'll get a nurse.'

'Wait,' she whispered again, the faint noise coming from her. Then she wrapped her fingers around his. 'Thank you.'

Out of nowhere, Adrian felt a weight in his throat. What if he hadn't found her when he did? Adrian leaned in and spoke softly to her.

'Can you tell me your name?'

She closed her eye again, although this time it stayed closed tight as a tear rolled down her face.

'I don't remember,' she said weakly.

# Chapter Six

*The police officer is sitting by my bed. I have the smallest memory of him pulling me out of the water. I open my eyes and he rushes over. He asks my name again but I tell him I don't remember.*

*Maybe I could get away this time. Couldn't I? He has that look in his eyes; I have seen it a million times before. He tells me I am safe now. He thinks he saved me. I can't be saved.*

# Chapter Seven

Imogen stood by the wall and looked over the crime scene. She hadn't been able to relax, so she took Adrian to the hospital last night and got down to Glasshouse Lane as soon as the sun came up the next morning. They needed to figure out what had happened to their Jane Doe. Best-case scenario, they would find some kind of identification that the woman dropped. Imogen knew the scene hadn't been fully processed yet and so there would be people there.

It was a huge area to cover. The woman could have got to the river from several access points and they would need to check all of those as well as the routes from the access points to where she was now. Not to mention the fact that the river itself posed a massive problem in terms of processing evidence. Even just getting hold of the correct equipment took time, as it had to be shared with the whole constabulary. Water and forensics didn't mix.

Imogen climbed the makeshift step that put her on the other side of the wall. She saw the techs working meticulously beside the riverbank, pulling snagged hair and fabric from the branches that overhung the water. The inhabitants of the houses surrounding the area gathered back by the road to try to catch a glimpse of the crime scene technicians at work. DI Matt Walsh was already there when she arrived and he surveyed the river, trying to work out where the woman could have come from.

The forensics team were spaced out along the riverbank looking for any evidence that pertained to the woman Adrian found. Imogen looked on at the chaotic hedgerows that enclosed the water and was glad at least that this part wasn't her job. She didn't have the patience for something as meticulous as forensics.

'They've got another one!' someone called.

It took a few moments to realise what that meant. No one moved and then suddenly everyone sprang into action. There was someone else in the water.

Imogen walked as quickly as she could to the technician who had called out, careful not to step on anything that could later be determined as evidence.

'Got another what? A person?' Imogen asked.

'Yep, about a mile upriver.'

'Alive?' Imogen said.

The technician shook his head as Matt Walsh got to him.

'What's going on?' Walsh asked.

'There's another body, but according to the technician at the scene it's difficult to discern anything. Male this time. He's in a pretty bad way, apparently. He's been beaten, by the sounds of it. They are just securing it now. There's no real riverbank up that end and so they will transport it straight to the morgue.'

'They can't tell anything else?' DI Walsh asked the tech.

'Late twenties at a guess, but we will know more when we get him back to the pathologist.'

'We'll need to set up a tent before the news cameras get wind of this. Dead body adds to the news appeal of this case and we need to find out who it is, first. Did you speak to DS Miles? Is the woman awake yet?'

'Yes, DS Miles called to say she's awake but she hasn't said anything meaningful yet. She claims she doesn't remember anything. Including her name.'

'Get over there and see if you can find out anything about this man. The DCI is going to want a briefing ASAP with both you and Adrian. See if you can drag him away from the hospital. He seems to be taking this case rather personally.'

'He did pull her out of the river. He feels responsible for her. That's all. I'll do my best to get her to talk.'

'They must be connected and so she must know something. Tread lightly, but see if you can push for information on who did this to them and who the other victim is.'

Imogen trudged back to the car. As awful as it was, a body would at least tell them something – it was a break in the case. But then, what could the motive be? Revenge? Hatred? Punishment? A message? Over her time in the police, Imogen had realised that when it came to murder, there weren't that many possible motives; figuring out who these people were was key to finding out why this had happened to them.

# Chapter Eight

Imogen handed Adrian a coffee she had picked up on the way over. He hadn't left the hospital all night; he had barely slept since she had been discovered yesterday. He was a mess.

She looked at the woman. She could see instantly why Adrian was so affected by this case. Who wouldn't be? The cuts and bruises across the woman's face looked angry against her pale, shiny porcelain skin. Imogen could see the weave line of the woman's hair extensions – not cheap ones, either. The nails she had left were acrylics, a French manicure. Her clothes were folded on the chair by the bed – Stella McCartney jeans that run at three hundred quid a go. Imogen wondered how much they would be worth now they had been cut into several pieces. There was also a gold ring, a wedding band, sitting on the bedside table. Presumably, it was hers. Whoever this lady was, she wasn't destitute and yet still no one had reported her missing.

'Hey,' Adrian said, standing and stretching out of his hunched seated slumber.

Imogen waved Adrian over to the corner of the room, as far away from the woman as they could get without actually leaving the room.

'We found another body in the water, about a mile from where you found the woman. Male, similar age – dead, though; much worse injuries than her. They must be connected. I'm going to have to ask her about it,' she said quietly.

'Why didn't you call and tell me?'

'I thought it would be better in person. DCI Kapoor wanted me to question her, so I thought it best just to tell you when I got here.'

The truth was, she wanted to check on Adrian. He had refused to leave until the woman had woken. Well, she was awake now.

'Maybe he will have some ID on him. We still don't know her name; she said she doesn't remember.'

'Do you believe her?'

'I don't know what I think, to be honest. I don't know why she would lie. Do we know anything else about the body?'

'No, but hopefully the pathologist will be able to tell us more. It's possible he is your woman's boyfriend but we don't know that either. The DCI wants us back at the station to brief us after we have spoken to her.'

'I don't want to leave her.'

'What did the doctor say?'

'Dr Hadley said she is going to be fine – sore for a while, but fine. She was beaten quite badly, possibly

31

with the intention of killing her. Now that we have found the other body, that seems quite likely. Whoever did this, I get the feeling it was personal. It must have been someone who had something against her, or him. She still had valuables on her so robbery wasn't the end goal, and according to the doctor, neither was sexual assault. Most of the damage to her was on the surface, no internal injuries. I guess we need to figure out if they were both the target or if it's something that's only connected to one of them.'

'It's already been on the news that she's in hospital,' Imogen said.

It was almost impossible to keep a lid on any kind of news these days.

'Do you think she could still be in danger?' Adrian asked.

'I don't think we can know anything for sure at this point. That could be why she isn't telling us her name. We need to speak to her.'

'She woke briefly but she hasn't said much about anything. It's entirely possible she really doesn't remember what happened, given the state of her and the injuries she sustained.'

'Or she doesn't want us to know what happened. Maybe she is still afraid. Whoever did this is still out there,' Imogen said.

The truth was they could speculate all they wanted at this point. Until she gave them information, or they managed to identify the man whose body they found, they might as well just be pissing in the wind. Imogen could already see how invested Adrian was; he wasn't

32

about to walk away from this case. Imogen shuddered involuntarily, a chill at the nape of her neck. She had a bad feeling about this woman, whoever she was. Adrian was already well and truly hooked.

# Chapter Nine

They found him. They think I am asleep, but I hear them whispering. Their words drift in and out of my head as they pass my bed. That's what happens when I try to get away, people get hurt. He warns me and yet still I persist.

When will I ever learn?

I am both glad and disturbed that I can't remember what happened that night. I have the tiniest ember of hope left. If he thinks I am dead, then there is still a chance that I can get far enough away before the truth comes out.

# Chapter Ten

In the briefing room, Adrian had his phone on the table, waiting for Dr Hadley to call and update him on the condition of their Jane Doe. She had promised to message when the woman woke again. While violent attacks were on the rise by almost twenty per cent in the last year across the country owing to a multitude of factors, including government cuts and a mounting feeling of general hopelessness among the populace, this was something else. This was personal.

He thought about the body they found. He should have checked the area to see if there was anyone else. He didn't even think to do that. Maybe he could have saved that man if he had just walked a little further downriver. What if the man heard him? What if he tried to call out? Adrian waited for any small piece of information that would release him from the weight of his guilt.

DCI Mira Kapoor walked into the briefing room with

DI Walsh and nodded at Adrian before putting her mug down on the desk. Gary Tunney followed closely behind and opened his laptop. Gary was the district forensic computer analyst and all-round genius; they relied on him for a lot and he seemed more than happy to oblige. He was one of those people who was constantly thirsting for knowledge, always doing a course of some kind or other. At present, Gary was doing a part-time degree in forensic psychology. Adrian was a little in awe of Gary's capacity to learn things.

'First, great job, DS Miles. That must have been a very upsetting situation and I'm very proud of the way you dealt with it. You're a credit to the station.'

Adrian was slightly taken aback by this comment, as it wasn't like Kapoor to heap the praise on quite so thickly. *Just take the compliment*, he thought.

'Thank you, Ma'am.'

'Also, thank you for staying with the Jane Doe at the hospital last night. Now, we don't have an ID on the male victim, is that correct?'

'Nothing as yet,' Imogen said.

'And she still hasn't said who she is?' DCI Kapoor added.

Adrian looked at the DCI and shook his head.

'Has anyone been reported missing?' she asked.

'Not in the last week,' Gary said.

'Well, they came from somewhere and so someone is missing them. When the woman spoke to you, did you notice an accent? Was she British?'

'I believe so. She hasn't said much, but it seemed to be an English accent.'

36

'Gary, do you have anything?' the DCI said.

'I haven't managed to find anything through the CCTV; there's not a whole lot of cameras down that way,' Gary said sheepishly.

Adrian watched and waited as DCI Kapoor sucked in a breath. It was always tough when there were no leads. All they could do was hope that once the crime scene was processed and the autopsy had been carried out, they would have more to go on. It wasn't a given. Some investigations required a little more investigating than others.

'Do we know the time of the death of our John Doe? Was he alive when I got her out of the water?' Adrian asked.

'I spoke to Karen Bell. She was heading the forensic team down there and she said he had been dead for more than twenty-four hours. Likely, he died some time before you found her on the Saturday morning. You couldn't have saved him,' Imogen said.

Adrian could see she wanted to reach out across the table to reassure him, but with all the prying eyes, she settled for giving him a comforting look. He wondered if anyone noticed these affectionate glances between them. It was mostly her decision to keep the relationship a secret, though he was happy to go along with it for now, until they were comfortable enough to go public.

'There was nothing you could have done,' Walsh added, which was uncharacteristically comforting.

Adrian could tell Walsh's opinion of him was, at best, on the fence.

'So, we have nothing? Nothing at all?' DCI Kapoor

said with a prominent tone of disappointment in them.

'I can check with other constabularies re MisPers. It's possible whoever they were that they were just visiting the city,' Adrian said.

'Is that likely? That would make this an opportunist attack and it certainly doesn't feel that way,' DCI Kapoor said.

'It's got to be worth checking. I don't mind doing it,' Adrian said.

'Thank you, Adrian, that would be great,' DCI Kapoor said. 'The preliminary report from the pathologist records that he died from multiple blows to the head. Definitely deliberate, definitely with the intent of killing the young man. He will have a more detailed report for us in a few days.'

Gary raised his hand. 'I know someone at the university who may be able to help. He's the professor of forensic anthropology and archaeology on the Streatham Campus.'

'How is an archaeologist going to help us?' Adrian said.

'He does skull reconstruction and can get a good likeness of John Doe for us to work from. He is superfast. I don't have any decent facial reconstruction software here and if we send it off to London or one of the other constabularies with the program, it's likely to take a week minimum because of backlog. It's actually two separate programs run by two different people.'

'Why don't we have this software? Can't you run it?' DCI Kapoor asked.

'I can run it. It is, however, several grand. I put in

for it a couple of years back but was denied owing to budget constraints. My guy at the uni is a fast worker and he would prioritise it; he lives for this kind of thing.'

'OK, brilliant. Has he worked with us before? Is that how you know him?' DCI Kapoor said.

'No. He's in my guild. He's the Healer.'

'Your guild?'

'Warcraft. It's a computer game thing. We have a local guild and we meet up occasionally. Anyway, he is kind of a big deal. In the real world, I mean, but also in the game.'

Denise Ferguson, the duty sergeant, knocked on the door of the briefing room and walked in with a piece of paper, which she handed to Gary. When Denise looked up, her eyes widened at Adrian and she had a smirk on her face.

'This was just on the local news Twitter feed.'

Gary put a video up on the big screen. Bloody mobile phones. Adrian knew before it even started what it was going to be. He watched himself pulling Jane Doe from the bushes and then carrying her to safety on the bank, to the soundtrack of gasps from both the women in the video and his colleagues in the room, followed by a round of applause when it ended on a freeze-frame of him walking towards the camera. He blushed.

'I see they cut out the bit where I asked her not to share this with anyone until we identified the woman,' Adrian said.

'Well, DS Miles, I think you are probably going to have a few questions to answer as soon as the press learn your name. It's always great to have some good PR for a change and so it would be nice if you would issue a statement, even nicer if we had any good news with regard to Jane Doe's progress.'

'Do I have to?' Adrian said.

'It's better if you do, then it's over and you can get on with things. Trust me, I learned this lesson a long time ago. If you cooperate then you control what information they get hold of. They are going to talk about you anyway,' DCI Kapoor said.

'Are we going to give them a picture of the woman's face? Like a proper one. You can't see who she is in this video. It might help us to identify her,' Adrian said.

'I think we should get an ID on the man first. Until we know the circumstances of this attack then I don't want to risk it. She could still be in danger and I don't want to advertise her location at the moment. It's annoying that this video is out there; it makes our job a little harder by forcing us to deal with the bloody newspapers,' Kapoor said. 'Let's just give the press a statement for now.'

'Fine,' Adrian said.

'I'll set something up. You never know, maybe someone saw something and we might even get a lead out of this. You're unusually quiet, DS Grey,' Kapoor added.

'Sorry, Ma'am. I can give Gary a hand checking out missing persons in other constabularies,' Imogen said.

'OK, then. When you're done, could you check with the pathologist for any updates on the autopsy of John Doe?'

'Of course.'

The DCI picked up her mug and left the room. Gary put the video on again.

'Look at those strong arms and that pretty face. The press are going to love you, don't you think, Grey?'

'Irresistible,' she said flatly, standing and turning to Gary. 'I'll meet you in your office so we can go through the missing persons files.'

Adrian couldn't tell if she was upset. What could she possibly be annoyed with him about? Gary took the hint by shutting his laptop and leaving.

'Is everything all right?' Adrian asked as they left the room.

'You tell me.'

'I don't know what you're talking about.'

'I'm just concerned that you are too emotionally involved in this case already. That must have been tough, finding her, pulling her out of the river like that.' Imogen's voice softened.

'It's not something I particularly want to experience again. It was horrible.'

'Do you think maybe you should go and see the counsellor? Might be good to talk it through properly.'

'No, thanks. I just want to find out what happened.'

'I know. We will.'

'I genuinely thought she was dead. How could anyone do this?'

'If there is one thing we have learned, it's that people are capable of anything. Look, I know you found her and that you're invested in this case, but I really have a bad feeling about this whole thing. I can't explain it,

Adrian, and you know I am not superstitious or anything, but I want you to promise me you try and stay level-headed about it.'

'It's sweet of you to worry, but I am fine. Let's just find out who Jane and John Doe are, then we can figure out who did this to them. I'm not some ticking time bomb waiting to explode. Have a little faith in me.' Adrian squeezed Imogen's hand.

They were at work and had promised to keep their relationship out of the office as they knew the DCI didn't really approve and it could affect the way the DCI treated them. Neither one of them had a particularly stellar reputation for following the rules and so they needed to be careful not to piss the boss off. Adrian had promised himself that he would stop walking that line between what he was obligated to do and what he thought he should do. The law existed so people like him didn't get to decide other people's fate, he needed to remember that.

# Chapter Eleven

It was amazing how much the woman's appearance had improved since she had come in just a few days ago. She wouldn't be winning any beauty competitions just yet, but the swelling on her face was almost gone, and she was sitting upright in the bed when Adrian and Imogen arrived at the hospital. But her face was still a patchwork of pinks and purples.

Imogen noticed the way the woman smiled at Adrian. She wasn't threatened by every female who spoke to Adrian, but she had come to realise he was more naive than she had first thought. He didn't seem to notice when he was being manipulated by a woman, or even flirted with, which was refreshing. Probably because he didn't have a manipulative bone in his body.

Maybe he deserved more credit than she was giving him, but she was concerned that someone might take advantage of his good nature. This woman was obviously just expressing her gratitude again and yet there was still something about her that Imogen had a problem with. She was off in some way.

They had to tell her about the body of the man, they had to ask her who he was, and Imogen had a feeling they weren't going to get the truth. But they at least had to try.

'Hello. I am DS Imogen Grey. I need to talk to you about something.'

'OK,' the woman said, sucking in a breath, bracing herself for the conversation.

'There's no easy way to say this. We found the body of a young man near where DS Miles found you. We are in the process of identifying him. Do you know who he was?'

'I'm sorry, I don't,' she said too quickly, reaching for her glass of water.

She gulped it down. She was clearly trying to obscure her face for a moment, just enough to compose herself. It was obvious the question wasn't a complete surprise to her.

What had happened to her? Why wouldn't she tell them? Imogen didn't have a medical degree, or in fact any degree at all, but she felt sure this woman was lying about not remembering. Why wouldn't she want them to know who she was? Or who the man she was with was? Could Adrian see past what was happening to her? Could he see she was lying to them? Imogen wasn't sure.

'So, you have no recollection of him? Of what happened?' Imogen said.

'I'm sorry, I wish I did,' she said. 'Was it quick? When he died, was it quick?'

'We don't know yet. He sustained some very serious injuries,' Adrian said.

'I'm really tired. I would like to be alone, if it's all the same to you. I really can't tell you anything useful.'

*Can't? Or won't?* Imogen thought.

'We'll be back again if we learn anything about your situation. Do you have any idea as to why no one would have reported you missing?' Imogen asked.

'None, I'm sorry.' Their Jane Doe lay back and folded her arms, closing her eyes.

'It's highly unusual,' Imogen said, hoping to catch the woman's eye. She wanted her to know she was on to her, in case there was anything to be on to.

But Jane Doe wasn't going to say anything that might give an indication as to who she was, that much was clear. They were wasting their time talking to her. They could come back when they had more information on the body – maybe then they would find something they could press her with. They could run a DNA sample on the dead body, something they couldn't do to Jane Doe without her permission, which she hadn't granted. At this time, she was an obstruction to finding the truth and they had to treat her as such. After the forensic anthropologist had reconstructed the man's face, they would come back and question her further.

'If you need anything, get the nurse to call me,' Adrian said.

'Thank you, Adrian. I really appreciate everything you've done for me,' the woman said, reaching over and taking Adrian by the hand.

Imogen had to walk away; she didn't like thinking

the things she was thinking. This woman was vulnerable and needed both their protection and their help. So why did Imogen feel like they were being sucked into some big black hole of a mess? She wouldn't ignore her instincts. Every time she had in the past, she had kicked herself for not listening to that little voice inside her head that told her something was wrong. Right now, that little voice was screaming.

# Chapter Twelve

*They asked me who he was. I couldn't tell them; they can't find out who I am. If they do, then he will find out I am here.*

*I heard the nurse talking about how there is a video online of the detective pulling me out of the water. I can no longer disappear. Maybe he didn't mean it when he said he was done with me and wanted me dead.*

*Who am I kidding?*

# Chapter Thirteen

Dr Forrester was placing an eyeball in the socket of a plaster mould of a skull when Adrian and Imogen entered his office on the Streatham Campus of Exeter University. The office was a cornucopia of dusty old books and curios, the way you imagine a professor's office to look. There were several clay skulls at various stages of development around the room. Adrian had seen plenty of dramatisations of this kind of thing on the TV, but it was fascinating to see in person.

Gary stood up excitedly as they approached. 'Imogen, Adrian, this is Dr Carl Forrester.'

Dr Forrester nodded hello to them. 'I would shake your hands, but I'm a bit mucky at present.'

'The doctor is reconstructing our John Doe's face,' Gary said.

'Already?' Imogen asked.

'What is it you're doing? How do you do that? How do you know what his eyes were like?'

Adrian fired a series of questions at the professor. This kind of thing seemed like magic to Adrian and yet he had seen the results with his own eyes before. It worked. What was it they said? Magic was just science we don't understand yet, which, in Adrian's case, was almost all science.

'I spoke to your pathologist last night and she sent me photos and measurements. From the body, I would say that we are looking at a Caucasian male in his late twenties. He has brown hair and brown eyes, and would have stood around five foot eleven, which we know because the pathologist told us; that's not information we normally have when reconstructing.'

'How did you get the skull so quickly? Is pathology done with it?' Adrian asked.

'We did an MRI of the head and then used a program to create a 3D image of the skull from the source material. We were then able to print a 3D replica of it, so we didn't need the actual skull,' Gary said excitedly.

'When that was ready, I began to attach the markers and the eyeballs. Next, I will start to build muscle up to the marker lines,' Dr Forrester said.

'How do you know where the marker lines are?' Adrian said.

'There's a lot of measuring and maths involved, plus decades of research and other people's work to pull from. We measure the skull and construct markers of varying depths, which we place in specific points on the skull that will in turn guide us when creating the flesh and muscles out of clay.

'We already have more to work on than usual, because

the actual skull is still . . . well, fleshy. The eyeball that I have just inserted is on a bed of clay to bring it to the right depth, which is where the flat part of the front of the eye is flush with the socket around it. Next, I will be adding clay to the chin and jaw. Then I fill the spaces in between the markers and smooth it all out until we have a face. You are welcome to stay and watch.'

'Thanks, Doc,' Adrian said. 'When do you think he will be ready?'

'Give me 'til the end of the day. If I work through, I should have it done.'

Adrian and Imogen stood and watched as Dr Forrester rolled the clay carefully into tiny balls and placed each one in between the markers on the face – small foam tubes of varying lengths. He started on the jawbone, filling the space slowly with the small lumps of clay until they reached the required height, then he smoothed it over until you could barely see the markers anymore.

Adrian would have loved to stay and watch the man work all day, but they had to go and speak to the woman again. All this could be completely unnecessary. She might change her mind and give them the name of the man whose body they found floating in the River Exe. Even as he thought it to himself, he knew it wouldn't be that easy. Whoever had hurt the woman had scared her enough to keep her mouth shut. Nothing they could say would change that. They had to keep trying, though. Someone was missing this man and they deserved to know the truth.

# Chapter Fourteen

They were soon back at the hospital. Imogen had grown to hate this place: the smell, the noise, everything about it set her on edge. She had been here too many times already, not only with her own injuries, but also visiting Adrian, victims, witnesses. She had never been to hospital for a happy occasion. She didn't have many friends, certainly none who were interested in having babies, and given her history, she wasn't sure she would be that happy in that situation, anyway.

The injuries that Imogen had sustained in a previous case made the likelihood of her being able to have a child unlikely. She still thumbed at the scar that ran the length of her torso, given to her by a suspect of that case. The doctors at the time hadn't completely ruled out having children, but she got the feeling they were just trying to spare her feelings. It wasn't something she was preoccupied with at the moment, as she wasn't ready to have kids of her own, but she knew that there might come a time when she might feel differently.

She had never talked about it with Adrian, nor any of her previous boyfriends, either. Adrian had a son, but Adrian was still young enough to have more children, younger than a lot of first-time parents these days. Hospitals made her think about these things and that was annoying; the rest of the time it barely crossed her mind.

They walked towards the ward Jane Doe was on and already could feel tension as people bustled about. Even from this distance they could see the uniformed officer they had left with her now walking in and out of rooms, looking for something or someone. They didn't even need to hear it before they broke out into a run – their Jane Doe was missing.

'What the hell happened?' Imogen called, startling the young PC.

He stood bolt upright and she saw him fumbling for words.

'Where is she?' Adrian said.

'I really needed the loo and I told her I would be back in five minutes. When I got back, her bed was empty,' the PC said nervously.

'When exactly did this happen?' Adrian asked.

'About twenty minutes ago,' the PC said sheepishly.

'You've called this in, right?' Imogen snapped.

'I thought I would be able to find her.'

'Have you told hospital security?' Imogen said.

'I was just about to,' PC Milbourne replied.

'Twenty minutes? She could be anywhere by now.'

'I'm really sorry.'

'Call it in. We'll see if anyone saw her leave,' Imogen said to the PC, whose face was the colour of a raspberry.

She had wanted to add a few expletives, but time was of the essence and, realistically, aside from making her feel better momentarily, it would be completely pointless. The young man looked distraught enough as it was; he had learned a lesson. DCI Kapoor would have a few words for him, anyway.

'Maybe she didn't leave of her own accord. I'll get them to pull up the CCTV and see if anyone was with her. Maybe whoever did that to her found her after that sodding footage got out,' Adrian said.

'Hey, this isn't your fault,' Imogen said, knowing that Adrian would already be blaming himself for allowing the woman at the riverbank to film him. 'She probably just left on her own. Let's find out what happened before we freak out.'

'I'll go check with security, you go check the main entrance,' Adrian said to her and rushed off.

Imogen peered into rooms as she walked briskly towards the main entrance to the hospital. The buses ran quite frequently past the hospital and so she could be on a bus, or she could have walked into the residential area. Given that they knew nothing about her, they had no idea where to look.

It wasn't just about her, either. They had a body they needed to identify and she was the closest thing they had to a witness. Imogen accepted that the woman had probably lied about not remembering anything and if she did, then she knew the who and perhaps the why.

There was no reasonable explanation for her to run away if she genuinely couldn't remember anything about her situation. Was she afraid of getting in trouble with the police? Was she afraid of a person? Was the man who died her husband? So many more questions . . .

Imogen knew before she got to the exit that she wouldn't see the woman, that there would be no way to find her. This case was feeling like one door slamming in her face after another. She pulled her phone out and called Gary to check for any CCTV of the hospital and surrounding neighbourhoods. He could put someone on it while they searched the area. She should get him to make that young PC who was supposed to be watching the woman to do it as punishment, but she wouldn't trust him not to miss anything.

'I heard,' Gary said as he answered the phone. 'The DCI has already asked me to look for CCTV and she has dispatched a couple of cars to look for Jane Doe. DI Walsh is also on his way to the hospital to speak to PC Milbourne.'

'We are going to look here as well. Adrian has alerted hospital security in case she is still in the building, but she's had plenty of time to get away. He said twenty minutes, but I reckon we can add at least another ten minutes to that.'

'There are cameras on the exits to the hospital, so I should be able to get an exact time for you soon enough. I've got the head of hospital security on the other line. I'll text you when I know,' Gary said before ringing off.

Imogen reached the exit and went outside. She

surveyed the surrounding area, but it was desolate. The bus stop was empty and since they had banned smokers from congregating outside the main entrance, there wasn't anyone to ask. Why would the woman run? *Did she run?*

Since the video had hit the internet, they couldn't be sure at this point that whoever had hurt her the first time hadn't come back to finish the job. Staring at the car park wasn't doing her any favours, so she went to find Adrian.

What if they couldn't find the woman? Was she in danger? Was she dangerous? They had no idea. They had less now than they had this morning, significantly less. Maybe the DNA would come back on John Doe, but she didn't want to admit to herself how unlikely that was.

# Chapter Fifteen

Sitting in the incident room waiting for a reprimand felt a lot like being on detention. Imogen knew the DCI wasn't going to be happy, but Adrian was more stressed about the missing woman than worried about what the DCI was going to say. She knew he felt personally responsible because he left her bedside and Imogen felt partially responsible for making him do that.

The truth was, no one was to blame except the woman herself. She wasn't under arrest but just saw an opportunity to leave and left. There were obviously too many questions that she didn't want to answer. No one could know what she had been through – only she knew that. It was pointless being annoyed with her; she was the victim in this. One of the victims, anyway.

DCI Kapoor walked in and folded her arms.

'I've just spoken with PC Milbourne and he said she gave no indication that she was going anywhere. One second she was there and when he looked again, she was gone. It's happened now, anyway, so we need to make sure the newspapers don't find out that we lost her.

'The *Echo* have been asking for an interview with you, DS Miles. I said you would give them a call today, so do that before you go home. The last thing we need is them poking around the hospital. Remember: careful, measured answers. Reporters are always looking for an angle, that's their job. Your job is to make sure they don't get it.'

'What if they ask me how she's doing?'

'Say she's up and walking about. You wouldn't be lying,' Imogen said.

'Please, someone tell me we have something else? Any new information on John Doe?' Kapoor asked.

'No match on his DNA and his fingerprints aren't on file with us, either. Dr Forrester will send a photo over when he is done. I have compiled photos of all current male MisPers within a hundred-mile radius. We can expand further if that doesn't pan out.'

'How many are there?' Imogen asked.

'Too many,' Gary said.

A brief silence descended over the room as Gary's words hit home. A person goes missing every ninety seconds in the UK, almost two hundred thousand are reported missing a year. The amount of people who return to their families or home are few and far between. Most families never got any closure, left to assume the worst for ever.

'Adrian, you go with Gary and see if, together, you can rule out some of those missing people until you get the reconstruction of John Doe's face.'

'Yes, Ma'am,' Adrian said, shooting a glance at Imogen as he left the room.

*Separation anxiety*, she thought.

'Imogen, I would like you to speak to Dr Hadley who was treating Jane Doe. She is in the liaison room; she was called in for something else, but I thought it would be good if you could have a little chat while she's here. She spent some time with the patient and may have some information that doesn't violate the patient's confidentiality. Maybe she mentioned a person or a place. Also, she might know if Jane Doe made any calls or if anyone suspicious in general was hanging around the hospital.'

'Yes, Ma'am,' Imogen said.

'Go on, then,' DCI Kapoor said, shooing Imogen out of the office.

Imogen walked towards the liaison room to speak to the doctor, hoping she could give them a lead of some kind. At the moment, they were flying blind.

## *Chapter Sixteen*

Someone had already given Dr Hadley a drink when Imogen arrived in the liaison room. She was occasionally the on-call doctor for the station and so she was friendly with many of the staff. Dr Hadley had even been out on a date with Adrian once, which Imogen couldn't help but remember every time she saw her. It wasn't jealousy, more an acknowledgment of the fact, which her brain liked to jab her with.

'Dr Hadley,' Imogen said.

'DS Grey. Mira, DCI Kapoor, said you wanted to speak to me about the patient.'

'Yes. Is there anything you can tell us about her that may help us locate her? I am sure you are aware that we found the body of a man near to where she was found. Down on the riverbank.'

'Yes. And I saw the video of Adrian pulling her out of the river online.'

'Do you have any information?' Imogen said, ignoring her comment about Adrian.

If she told herself she wasn't jealous enough times then maybe she would believe it.

'I can tell you that she was terrified. She was calm and even-tempered when other people were around, but when she was alone, she was quite distraught. I walked in on her and saw her sobbing more than once. I got the feeling she was in some kind of untenable situation, as though a difficult decision needed to be made. She seemed to be unsure of what she should do.'

'Well, she had been through a terrible ordeal.'

'Yes, of course, but she was so determined to keep it hidden, that's what concerned me. She didn't ask for advice, or help. I've seen this kind of thing before.'

'What do you mean?'

'Those injuries that she sustained, they weren't the first. Not by a long shot. There was evidence of injuries and breaks going back a long time. Without saying too much, I think you are looking for a very vulnerable individual.'

'Did she use the phones at all? Did you see anyone else hanging around the hospital? Did you see her speaking to anyone who wasn't staff?'

Imogen fired the questions without giving Hadley the opportunity to respond. Hadley was so guarded with her responses and Imogen didn't have all day.

'She was very jumpy whenever someone walked into the room, expecting someone to come for her, I think. I don't think she is running from the law, she is running from someone else. Pure speculation, of course, but I work predominantly with women who are either sexually assaulted or in domestic abuse situations. The marks I saw on her body are consistent with those I have seen on women who are in abusive relationships. As she didn't tell me directly and as this is conjecture on my part, I don't feel like I am breaking confidentiality in this instance.'

'Thank you, Doctor. We'll contact you if we need to speak to you again.'

Imogen showed Dr Hadley out of the liaison room and walked back to her desk. Finding Jane Doe seemed more pressing than ever.

# Chapter Seventeen

Adrian clicked through all the images Gary had compiled. As they had barely any information on John Doe, he could have been reported missing at any point from anywhere. The things they knew were that he had naturally brown hair and brown eyes, and was no younger than twenty and no older than forty. He was five foot eleven and Caucasian. Anyone who didn't fit those criteria was immediately removed from the list.

'Dr Forrester said he would have something for us in less than half an hour,' Gary said as he returned to the room with two hot coffees from the secret coffee machine in his office.

'I'm down to under three hundred now, much better than what we started with,' Adrian said. 'I feel like we should be investigating all of these, anyway.'

'It's definitely depressing.'

'I don't know what we'll do if he's not one of these men. Back to CCTV from the quayside, I guess, see if there is anything. There must be something we are missing.'

Adrian looked through the faces one more time, thinking about the faces he had already discarded. Who was going to look for them? The idea that every single one of those people had someone who cared about them enough to notice they were gone, to report them missing, was distressing. Growing up with an addict for a father meant Adrian was no stranger to living with someone who was in and out of your life. Charlie Miles came and went as he pleased, and they never reported him missing. Maybe it was the same for some of these people.

He couldn't get bogged down in what their stories might be, though. They might not all be sad stories. The truth was, he didn't know and it was no use speculating; he couldn't think about them right now. They weren't all dead – some were probably homeless, some may have just felt suffocated in their lives and needed a new start elsewhere. It was common for people to disappear after a bad break-up. Sometimes the police would track them down and the missing person wouldn't want to be found; it was their right to leave in the first place. Occasionally, they were fleeing abusive situations.

Adrian couldn't imagine that, just dropping everything and moving away, but then he had his son, Tom, to think about, so he was tethered. Even when things had got really rough with his ex – Tom's mum, Andrea – Adrian wouldn't have thought about leaving; it didn't even occur to him.

A notification sounded on Gary's personal laptop and he rushed back over to the seat next to Adrian with it under his arm. Within seconds, Gary had the image on the screen of the reconstructed face.

The man looked quite young. He had the slender, angular face of a man under thirty. His cheekbones were prominent and he had a fairly square jaw. He didn't quite have superhero looks, but there was something so everyday and inoffensive about him. Even Adrian could see that he was a decent-looking guy, the right side of average, symmetrical in all the right places.

Adrian started at the beginning of the MisPers list again. It was easy to see which faces didn't belong to the man in the clay reconstruction. As he looked through, he tried to commit each face to memory so that if he ever saw them in the street, he would be able to remove them from the list. He knew he wouldn't remember, though. Each face was replaced immediately with a new one before he really had a chance to study it. They went through the faces over and over again, whittling them down further and further each time until they had just seventeen faces left.

Some of the photos supplied by the people who had filed the report had been less than clear, but Adrian found himself drawn to one particular image. The man was smiling in the photograph, standing on a jetty overlooking one of the major lakes in the Lake District. He had his arms outstretched and was wearing an orange beanie. Simon Glover.

Simon Glover was reported missing from Charmouth in Dorset just a week earlier by his sister, Fiona Merton.

The more Adrian compared the image of Simon to the clay model, the more he was convinced they were the same person.

'It's this guy. Simon Glover. Can we get any better images of him?'

'He's probably got some form of social media profile; most people have. I'll look him up,' Gary said as he opened various tabs and typed into each one at a speed that seemed inhuman to Adrian.

'Well?'

'This is him, I think.' Gary said, spinning the screen towards Adrian.

A Facebook profile, current job listed as working in Weymouth. It was him, though; a more serious picture of his face, but it was uncanny how much he looked like the clay sculpture. It's not as if Adrian didn't believe in the science of it, but this confirmed it in a way that couldn't have been done any other way. He could see it with his own eyes. Simon Glover was John Doe.

'Gary, I could kiss you.'

'I'm sorry, mate, I'm taken.'

'Talking of which, is he married? Is our Jane Doe his wife?' Adrian said, remembering the wedding ring Jane Doe was wearing.

'His relationship status on this is listed as single.'

'So, whoever Jane Doe was, she wasn't Simon Glover's wife. What was her connection to him, then? How did they end up in the river together? Are there any pictures of Jane Doe on his profile?'

'In all of his public photos he's alone. We can put in a request to gain access to his account, but Facebook

65

are notoriously slow for granting these requests, so I wouldn't hold your breath.'

'Do you have an address for his sister? I'm going to grab Imogen then we can head on over there.'

'I'll send all the details to your phone.'

Adrian rushed out of the room. Finally, a break in the case. It was horrible to think of unclaimed victims, that somewhere out there their unsuspecting family members were just carrying on with their lives. Simon Glover was the first real name they had. Even though Adrian wasn't relishing telling his sister the news of her brother's passing, it was worse when you couldn't find the family to notify them. Now that they had somewhere to start, it was only a matter of time before they got the whole picture, a matter of time before they found the woman again and made sure she was safe.

# Chapter Eighteen

Fiona Merton lived in a modest bungalow at the top end of a shallow hill in Bridport, Dorset. The low-level buildings allowed the vista of the patchwork hills behind them to be seen in all directions, broken only by the square orange roofs peppered in between. She opened the door as Imogen and Adrian walked up the driveway; they obviously looked like police.

'Are you here about my brother?' she said, arms folded as though cold, even though the summer heat was starting to build.

'I'm DS Imogen Grey and this is my colleague, DS Adrian Miles.'

'Is this about Simon?'

'Can we come in?' Imogen asked.

Fiona Merton walked back inside the house, leaving the door open for them to follow. Inside, it felt like a home that belonged to a much older woman. The curtains were mustard-and-terracotta stripes, very dated, and they looked like they had been there as long as the house. The sofas were large and almost cartoon-like, with a floral chintz in autumnal colours. Fiona Merton was no older than thirty and so Imogen assumed that she must have inherited the property.

'Well? Where is he? Have you found him?'

'I'm going to show you a photograph,' Adrian said, pulling out his phone. 'I want you to prepare yourself.'

'Prepare myself for what?' she said, clutching herself even tighter.

'We recovered the body of a male who matches your brother's description and we have reconstructed an image of his face to show you. Maybe you can identify him from it.'

'Reconstructed? What was wrong with his face?'

'If you wouldn't mind taking a look at this. Are you ready?' Adrian said, avoiding the question.

Fiona nodded and Adrian showed her the clay recon-struction. She looked confused at first, but then her face settled and the tears came.

'Yes, that's him, that's Simon. He's dead? What happened?' Fiona said, crying but still somehow composed, cold even.

'Was Simon in a relationship?' Imogen said.

'No. He works a lot; doesn't have time for a rela-tionship. His time's divided mostly between the construction site and an evening class. Didn't want to work on a building site for ever.'

'What was he studying?'

'He wanted to be a teacher. He's been studying English literature so he can teach English in secondary school.

He was a bit of a romantic.' Fiona struggled to speak, her breath shortening as the impact of the situation hit her.

Imogen put her hand on her shoulder to try to impart some kind of empathy.

'Do you recognise this woman at all?' Adrian said, showing Fiona a picture of their Jane Doe.

She shook her head.

'We're sorry for your loss,' Imogen said as Fiona looked up at her. What else was there to say?

'How did it happen?' Fiona said, wiping her cheeks, clearly unaccustomed to vulnerability.

'That's what we're trying to find out,' Adrian said. 'We recovered him from a river last Sunday morning.'

'What was he doing in the river?'

'I'm afraid we don't know that yet,' Adrian said.

'Did he drown? He was a really good swimmer. He's the only family I have . . . had left,' she sobbed.

'We are investigating what happened to Simon. At this point, we don't believe he died of natural causes. If possible, would you be willing to give us a DNA sample so that we can confirm the person we have is in fact your brother?'

'Why can't I see him? Why won't you answer my questions? Where did you say you found him?'

'We really don't know anything yet. The body was recovered from the River Exe in Exeter.'

'What was he doing there? You don't think he died of natural causes. So, you think he was murdered?'

'It seems your brother sustained some serious injuries before he died, probably from a physical assault.'

'Who would do that to him? Everyone liked Simon; he was a good man. Honestly, you would be hard pushed to find anyone who had a bad word to say against him.'

'We don't know who yet, but we will find out. Did your brother have a mobile phone?' Adrian asked.

'Of course he did. What kind of question is that? Who doesn't have a bloody mobile phone these days?'

'It would have been on him?' Imogen said.

'More than likely.'

'Your brother lived in Higher Sea Lane in Charmouth, correct? Do you have spare keys for his property?' Adrian said.

'Yes, I'll get them for you.'

She stood and walked over to a sideboard, where she opened the drawer and pulled out some keys, which she held in her hands tightly. Imogen could see the woman's knuckles whiten as she squeezed.

'I was close with my brother; he came here every week for Sunday dinner. When he didn't turn up last week, I knew something was wrong. He was secretive and I know there was a lot he never told me about himself, but he wasn't a bad person. I don't know why anyone would want to hurt him.'

'Can you think of any reason your brother would be in Exeter?' Imogen said.

'He used to work there until about six months ago.'

'Where does he work now?' Imogen said.

'He's an Assistant Site Manager for the Sigma construction company. He's working on a flat development on the front in Weymouth.'

'Does he have any close friends we can talk to? Someone who might be able to shed some light on your brother's activities?' Imogen said.

'He's worked with a guy called Leon Quick for the last couple of years; Leon got him the job at Sigma after he left the last place.'

'Thank you very much, Miss Merton. Again, we are sorry for your loss and we will let you know as soon as we have any information for you. Is there anyone you need us to call to come and be with you?' Adrian said.

'Thank you, DS Miles, I can call my neighbour, don't worry,' she said, arms folded as they walked to the door.

# Chapter Nineteen

I gain entrance to the house by the patio door, which is always left unlocked. I go to the shower and wash the smell of hospital off me. I add make-up and put on a dress. Then I go into the kitchen and start dinner. He gets home and hangs his coat up. When he smells the food cooking, he'll know I am back. The table is laid and there is a cup of tea waiting for him, his newspaper to the side of it. Everything is just the way he likes it.

He walks in and kisses me on the forehead. He tells me he knew I would be back before sitting at the table with his cup of tea and the paper. I tip the carrots into the pan of water and we both carry on as though we live a perfectly normal life.

# Chapter Twenty

Imogen and Adrian walked into Simon Glover's flat. It was a nice place looking out towards the horizon, probably quite pricey. But it was empty. Bed stripped, no electricals or soft furnishings, no sign of human habitation. The walls had been freshly painted, the doors and woodwork, too. It smelled clean, too, but not polish clean, bleach clean, ammonia clean, sterile and medical. Unnatural. It looked like it had just been built.

'We should call this in before we look around,' Imogen said.

'Presumably, Fiona Merton has no idea that Glover's flat is like this. She would have said something if he was moving out.'

'Unless he didn't tell her,' Adrian said, shrugging.

He could be right; they already knew Glover kept secrets from his sister.

'Where are all of his clothes? His things? Did *he* do this?' Adrian said.

'You think this is the crime scene?'

'I would put money on it.'

'If that's the case, then this has been professionally cleaned, which is concerning,' Imogen said.

'Concerning, how?'

'Who cleaned it? I'm going to assume there was some blood, which would correlate with Simon Glover's murder having taken place here. And who painted this place? It's not as if Glover was disposed of particularly carefully. But this level of work and attention to detail means that more than one person was involved. Cleaners, painters, movers.'

'This seems highly organised. Is this something they have done before? Something they do regularly. Not to mention the distance from the original crime scene. We are at least an hour away from where the body was found.'

'Maybe you do need to do a TV appeal for information. They love you at the moment.' Imogen smiled, knowing Adrian hated being the centre of attention, but she loved to watch him squirm.

'Seriously, though. If they have done this before then why was this job so sloppy? Why haven't we been finding bodies in the river for years? Are they trying to send a message to someone else?' Adrian said.

'Sloppy, how?'

'You know, body in the river, which is basically a trail of evidence. Not to mention the fact that they didn't finish the woman off. Not quite professional, more confusing. I'm telling you, it's a message. Judging by the way the woman behaved, I think she was

74

probably the intended recipient of that message. She wasn't beaten as badly. I reckon Glover was beaten as a lesson to her.'

'You've been watching too much TV. People don't do that in real life.'

'Maybe not in your life. We're missing something.'

'That's an understatement,' Imogen said.

'So, what now?'

'Let's go and see this co-worker of his and see if he can shed any light on what might have happened to Simon Glover.'

Adrian pulled out his phone and called Karen Bell, the lead crime scene investigator and recently promoted head of the forensics department. Imogen knew that she and Adrian alone wouldn't find anything here – not a fingerprint, a strand of hair or a speck of blood that would confirm it as the crime scene. They needed to call the crime scene technicians in to work their magic. Even the cleanest rooms aren't forensically clean.

They waited outside for someone to come and secure the scene; the smell inside was too chemical and over-whelming to stay there.

'Do you think we will get any answers from the friend?'

'I'm going to go with no. The secrecy and silence around this case is not only bizarre, it's already pissing me off. There's no reason to believe it's going to get any easier.'

'That's the spirit,' Adrian said.

'So far, we have a dead guy and a missing woman

who would rather risk her life and her health than tell us what's going on. My guess is this guy we are going to see now is going to be equally unhelpful. We just need to figure out why.'

# Chapter Twenty-One

The summer temperatures were starting to kick in after another unpredictable cold spell and Dorset was a real suntrap. Leon Quick lived further away from the coast than Simon Glover, in a studio flat above the garage of his parents' converted barn house. It was hot and stuffy inside and you could hear the clatter and clink of Leon's father tinkering with something in the garage below.

The flat itself consisted of a bed and an armchair, plus a small side table and a TV, with built-in cupboards either side of the dated tiled fireplace. In one corner were three kitchen units with a microwave and a kettle. He also had a small fridge. There was nowhere to sit, really, so Imogen just folded her arms and waited for him to speak.

Leon looked shaken when his mother showed them upstairs and introduced them as police. Mrs Quick had given Leon a scathing look as she went back downstairs.

'Leon Quick? I'm Detective Miles and this is my

colleague, DS Grey. We are here to speak to you about your friend, Simon Glover.'

'Is he OK? Did you find him?' Leon said.

Imogen noted he was tense, his eyes darting around nervously as he spoke.

'You knew he was missing?' Imogen said.

'Fiona called me and I've been calling him. He hasn't been at work and everyone's really concerned about him. I told the boss he had flu, but I knew something was up.'

'What do you mean, you knew something was up?' Imogen probed.

There was a twitchiness about Leon – she wondered if he was an addict of some kind.

'He had been acting weird the last few weeks; he had a week off and when he didn't come back I suspected something.'

'Why would you suspect something? Was he in some kind of trouble?' Adrian asked.

Leon's anxiety had spiked when they had turned up and Imogen noticed it growing by the second. He started to chew on the skin around his thumb.

'Just tell me what happened to him. He's dead, isn't he?' he said.

Imogen could see he was shaking. Was it nerves or maybe withdrawal? For some reason, she suspected the former. Why was he so uneasy?

'Why would you think that?' Adrian said.

'Why else would you be here?'

Imogen took a deep breath before speaking. 'His sister has positively identified a body we recovered from the River Exe as Simon Glover.'

Leon shook his head and exhaled deeply before sitting on the edge of his bed. 'What did they do to him?'

'Tell us why you don't seem surprised,' Imogen said.

'He told me. He told me this might happen the last time I spoke to him.'

'He told you he might die?' Imogen asked.

'Yes. He gave me a letter to give to his sister in case anything happened. He gave me some other stuff to look after, as well. I guess you want it?'

'Yes, please,' Adrian said.

He got up and went to his cupboard before pulling out a small correspondence envelope and an A4 Jiffy bag. He handed the envelope to Imogen. She opened it and looked at the letter, though it felt wrong to read it. There were no explanations, just an expression of love from one sibling to another. It was a goodbye letter, but there was nothing sad about it. It certainly didn't read like a suicide note. Leon then gave Adrian the Jiffy bag.

'He asked me to hold onto this for him, too. Said he was going to swing by and pick it up on Friday. He was going away for a while.'

'How do you guys know each other?' Imogen asked.

'We work together.'

'Fiona Merton said you worked together at your last place of employment, too. Is that where you met?'

'Yes,' Leon said, shifting his gaze uncomfortably.

'And where was that?'

'Corrigan Construction. In Exeter,' he said quietly, as though he didn't want to say the words.

The name was familiar. Corrigan was one of the

larger construction companies in the town and their vans were everywhere. They handled a lot of the re-developments in the city and most of the roadworks. It couldn't be a coincidence that the construction company was in Exeter. *Is this a lead?*

'DS Grey,' Adrian said.

Imogen looked at him. He was holding the contents of the Jiffy bag: two spanking new passports sealed in a vacuum-packed bag. Even without opening them, Imogen knew it was possible one of the passports was Simon's and the other belonged to Jane Doe; perhaps they were running away together, and *from* something, judging by what happened to them.

'Did Simon have any enemies?'

'No. Not really. Not before working there, anyway.'

*What does that mean?*

Imogen could sense by Leon's increasingly agitated manner that they were skating closer to the real issue.

'How come you both moved from Corrigan Construction? Did you get fired?' Imogen said.

'I had to move out of my flat and back in with my parents. My mum's not been well and I needed a job closer to home, that was all. I was trying to help my parents out a bit. They need some building work doing around the place and I thought it best if I moved in here and did it,' he said, scrambling for words.

Imogen wondered if any of them were true.

'And Simon?'

'I just told him there was a space for him if he wanted to move and he decided to take me up on it.'

Imogen exchanged a look with Adrian. It was clear

to both of them that Leon was uncomfortable with this line of questioning. He had become evasive and couldn't meet their gaze.

Adrian pulled his phone out of his pocket and showed Leon a photo of the Jane Doe they had found near the spot where Simon was discovered.

'Do you know this woman?' Adrian asked.

Imogen studied his face for a reaction. It was momentary, but it was there. He recognised her.

'Sorry, no. I don't know who she is.'

'We are trying to locate this woman as we are concerned for her safety. Any information you can give us would be greatly appreciated.'

'I wish I could help you, but I can't.' He stood and walked over to his kitchenette in the corner, flipping the switch on the kettle. 'Can I get you a drink?' he asked.

'It's clear to me that you aren't telling us something,' Imogen said. 'I don't know what that is, Leon, but it's going to come out. You could save us all a lot of time and energy if you just tell us what you know.'

'I can't,' Leon said. 'You don't understand. You should just drop it and walk away.'

'Are you scared of someone? Is that what this is?' Adrian said.

'I've told you everything I can. I'm sorry. I can't say any more.'

'Leon, what happened at Corrigan Construction? Why did you leave?' Adrian said.

'We just wanted a change,' he said, leaning against the counter for support, a hint of desperation in his voice.

'Come on, Leon. Tell the truth. We can take you down to the station and ask you questions there on tape, if you want. Or you can tell us right now what the issue was. Why did you leave Corrigan Construction? Did you have a problem with someone there?' Imogen asked.

Leon took a deep breath, then another. He was considering his options. Whatever he wasn't telling them was weighing on him. He went to speak more than once then thought better of it each time. His eyes were glassy and bright.

What wasn't he telling them?

'It was a nightmare,' Leon said, tears falling.

'In what way?' Imogen said softly.

He was on the brink of telling them – all he needed was a little push.

Leon turned away from them, his eyes streaming. He wasn't just crying, he was distraught.

'Tell my parents I'm sorry,' he said, his hands flat on the worktop as he breathed heavily.

A *panic attack*, Imogen suspected. She was no stranger to them.

Imogen saw the knife in his hand too late. She rushed forwards as he raised it in the air, but she couldn't reach him in time. He plunged it into the centre of his chest and collapsed to the ground.

*What the hell was going on?*

Imogen was on the ground with him seconds later then she heard Adrian on the phone requesting an ambulance as she frantically clutched at his chest and tried to stop the blood from pouring out. He spasmed and struggled for a few seconds but no more than that. She felt his heart labour then stop. He was gone. The pained look on his face was also gone and she could see the peace wash over him.

Imogen's hands were covered in blood and she didn't know what to do. She looked up at Adrian, who was on the phone but staring at the body on the floor. What was it that Leon hadn't wanted them to know? What was he afraid of? Who was he afraid of? For all the questions Leon had answered, with this latest action he had opened up a whole load more. Too stunned to think, Imogen sat back on her heels and just watched the red stain on Leon's shirt get bigger. Who would answer their questions now?

# Chapter Twenty-Two

'What the hell happened?' DCI Kapoor snapped at Adrian and Imogen as they sat in her office.

Imogen could see the dark line of blood under her fingernails. Even though she had scrubbed her hands, she could see it and feel it. She clenched her hands into fists and tried to forget what had just happened.

'We were just talking and he . . . he just stabbed himself,' Imogen said.

'That's highly unusual behaviour, isn't it?' DCI Kapoor seemed just as baffled as them.

'Well, yes,' Adrian said, nodding.

'And there was no indication before then that he was going to do that?'

'He was agitated, but we had just told him that his friend was dead,' Imogen said.

'What did he say about Simon Glover?' DCI Kapoor said.

'They used to work together. As soon as he brought

up the old job at Corrigan Construction, his demeanour changed completely. He became jumpy and anxious. I got the impression that he killed himself to avoid having to divulge anything else. He had secrets and it was all to do with that job they had together in Exeter. Something must have gone on down there,' Adrian said.

'You should have brought him in for questioning. I wish we had the exact words he said on tape. He never should have had that knife,' DCI Kapoor said.

'With all due respect, Ma'am, we speak to people in their houses all the time; this is not something we have ever witnessed before. It's not as if we could have anticipated he was going to do that. It came from nowhere,' Imogen said.

'Well, I want both of you to see the counsellor and talk this through.'

'We're fine,' Imogen said, huffing.

'Then it shouldn't be a very long session, should it?' DCI Kapoor replied, conversation over.

'Yes, Ma'am,' Adrian said.

'What did he say then, before he died? What the hell was he hiding?' DCI Kapoor said.

'He gave us an envelope with a letter for Fiona Merton inside. A goodbye letter from Simon, saying he was leaving and not to worry about him. We've handed it to Gary to match handwriting samples. Quick also gave us a Jiffy bag that had two brand-new passports in there. They were vacuum-packed, but we got one of the forensic techs to open it. They belong to Simon and the woman from the hospital, Jane Doe, but with a false name for him, so we assume for her also.

'There were also train tickets into London, then Eurostar tickets to Paris, France, and then a flight to Montreal, Canada. Judging by what happened to them, I would say they were running away from someone. When we asked Leon Quick about their time at Corrigan Construction and why they left, he got more and more anxious. That seemed to be the trigger for . . . what he did. We were in there less than ten minutes,' Imogen said.

'Well, brace yourselves. The family liaison officer has been speaking to the Quicks. They are obviously very distressed, said he was fine before you got there but obviously dead when you left. The parents were understandably upset by the whole thing and so the FLO is trying to make sure they are OK and also advise them against lodging a complaint, which they had mentioned. She's very good, so I am sure it will be fine.

'Walsh is already looking into Leon Quick to see if he has any history of mental health issues or suicidal tendencies,' DCI Kapoor said.

'I just don't understand what happened. Something we asked him provoked that extreme reaction in him. He looked terrified of something. Then he picked up that knife and stabbed himself. How do you even do that? How do you push a knife into yourself like that?' Adrian said.

'I've never seen anything like it,' Imogen said.

'I just don't understand what could have been so bad that he would rather kill himself than talk about it. And kill himself like that, too. To just make that decision in that split second like that. I feel sick just thinking about it,' Adrian said.

'Do you think he was involved in Simon Glover's death? Maybe he felt guilty,' DCI Kapoor said.

'It didn't seem so. It wasn't guilt, it was fear,' Imogen said.

'Although he wasn't surprised, I got the impression he was genuinely upset when we told him what happened to Simon Glover. I don't think he was involved in his death. No, he was afraid of something or someone. I imagine it's probably connected to what happened to Glover,' Adrian said.

'I can't be certain, but I think he recognised the woman as well, even though he pretended he didn't. Our Jane Doe,' Imogen said.

'I don't suppose he told you who she was before he offed himself?'

'I'm afraid not. It wasn't long after we showed him the photo that he took his own life,' Adrian said.

'Right, well, it's too late to do anything else today. At least we got the passports; although the chances of us finding out where they came from are pretty slim. Go and write up your reports about what happened, then tomorrow morning go to Corrigan Construction. Maybe you can find out something more,' DCI Kapoor said.

'Thank you, Ma'am,' Imogen said and stood up.

They left DCI Kapoor's office and went back to their desks. Still shocked. The anguish on Leon's face played over in Imogen's mind. The DCI was right; he never should have had that knife. This case got more complicated with every passing moment.

Imogen pulled up the report form onscreen and stared for a moment, unsure where to start.

'We've got two dead bodies and a missing woman,' Adrian said, breaking Imogen's trance.

'But at least we have a lead. Something happened at their last job; you could see it in his eyes. I've never seen anyone go from mildly uncomfortable to such extreme agitation so quickly. He was beside himself. Was he distressed about something he had seen? Was he afraid of someone? Whatever it is, the answers are at that construction company.'

'He was fine when we got there, a little on edge maybe. I just don't understand what happened,' Adrian said. 'Maybe we need to look at why he moved back in with his parents, too? Did he lose his flat, or did he choose to move back home to look after his mother, like he claimed? Was it a financial decision or something else?'

'We definitely don't have all the pieces to the puzzle at this point,' Imogen said, staring at her hands again.

'Are you OK?' Adrian said.

'I just . . . I don't understand how anyone could do that. That wasn't a cry for help. The force he stabbed himself with, he wanted out.'

'It was crazy.'

'What could be that bad that he would rather end his life than talk to us about it? He was terrified.'

'We'll get the answers eventually. At least we have someone else to work on,' Adrian said.

'Where the hell is that woman?' Imogen said.

In all this, that was the part Imogen had the most trouble understanding. Neither Jane Doe nor Leon Quick would speak. She risked her own life by leaving the hospital to avoid any questioning and Quick ended his for the same reason. Who were these people and how were they connected?

'Gary said he checked MisPers against her photo; there was no one matching her description reported missing.'

'How is that possible? Does she not have a mother or father? We assumed she was married, but maybe the ring was something else.'

Adrian leaned closer to Imogen and lowered his voice. 'Stay at mine tonight? I don't think either of us want to be alone right now.'

'You're not wrong.'

She stayed at his most nights; in fact, she rarely went home. After a couple of months seeing each other in secret, they were on the brink of being in a serious relationship, she could feel it. It was exciting but at the same time, as usual, it came with a whole host of other complications. She hadn't felt this way about anyone before. It wasn't the crazy-making irrational lust she usually felt for someone when she thought she was in love with them. It was something much calmer, much more grounded and dependable. Was this the real deal? Did he even feel the same? Adrian was the kind of person who said what was on his mind and she still wasn't sure how he felt.

Imogen started typing, filling out the fields on the form as succinctly as possible. Before she had joined the police, she didn't fully understand how different people react under pressure and she had seen all sorts of things before – but this? This was a new one on her. More than anything, she wanted to know what had caused Leon Quick to do that to himself. The worst thing was accepting that she might never find out.

# Chapter Twenty-Three

The head office of Corrigan Construction was in Matford Business Park just outside Exeter city centre. The building itself was more substantial than Adrian was expecting. A large red-brick-and-grey structure the length of several houses, with windows stretched across the front so you could see the staff inside at their desks. The lobby was a wide-open space with a high glass ceiling and a reception desk in the centre. The walls were a dark slate grey and the wall facing the entrance had an enormous painting on it, which must have been over twelve foot square.

Adrian stared at the painting as they both approached the desk, a contemporary swirl of reds and browns; even with his non-existent knowledge of art he could tell this was an expensive piece and not just something off the rack. He turned to the young woman behind the counter, who looked up and smiled. The smile dropped when Adrian held up his warrant card.

'Can I help you?' She returned her eyes to the computer screen.

'I'm DS Miles. My colleague over there is DS Grey. We need to speak to someone about a former employee of this company.'

'Do you have a name for this employee?'

'Simon Glover. Do you know him?'

'Vaguely. I saw him around. Is he in trouble?' she said with uninterest, continuing to tap away on her keyboard.

Adrian couldn't tell if she was actually busy, or if it was just a pretence.

'Is there anyone here who did know him?' Adrian asked.

'I'm just checking out which projects he was on and which crew he worked with,' she said as she hammered away. 'He worked our biggest contract last year, that new multistorey in town, which means he knew most of the guys.'

'Who is the person in charge, then?'

'Do you mean the gaffer on site, or the head of the company?' she asked before adding, 'Actually, on that project it was the same person. The big boss. Mr Corrigan isn't in just yet. Jimmy Chilton is in, though; he's the next most senior member of staff on that project. He's just in a meeting at the moment, but if you wait over there, I'll get someone to call him out.'

'Thank you.'

Imogen and Adrian moved to one side and waited as the girl on reception carried on with what she was doing. Imogen turned to face her and put her hand on her hips. No one was better at passive aggression than Imogen. When the girl looked up again and saw Imogen, she finally picked up the phone and called through to someone, rolling her eyes at the same time.

'We're in the wrong job. Look at this place!' Adrian said.

'Pretty fancy; there's obviously a lot of money in construction,' Imogen said.

'I wonder who or what in this place spooked Leon Quick so much,' Adrian said.

'Officer?' A man in his late forties with a scruffy peppered beard and a red baseball cap walked towards them with his hand outstretched to Adrian. 'Jimmy Chilton. What can I do you for?'

He turned his hand to Imogen, who reluctantly shook it. Jimmy Chilton looked out of place in this grand lobby, as though he had just clocked off after a long-distance lorry trip.

'We're here to talk to you about two former employees of yours,' Adrian said.

'Two?' Jimmy Chilton said.

He ushered them to the far corner of reception, away from the receptionist's earshot.

'Simon Glover and Leon Quick.'

'Ah, right. Yes.'

'Are you familiar with them?'

'Yes, of course.'

'What can you tell me about them?' Adrian asked.

'They were often late; sometimes their work was sloppy. Spent more time chatting than working. We had to let them go.'

'We were led to believe they both left of their own volition,' Imogen said.

'I don't know where you got that information from, but it's incorrect. They were both fired. Why do you want to know why they left?'

'Who let them go?' Adrian said.

'Probably me or Reece. Reece Corrigan. We do most of the hiring and firing. I'm afraid I don't remember exactly which one of us did the actual firing. You'd be surprised at the sheer volume of turnaround in staff within the construction industry.'

'When was the last time you saw either Simon Glover or Leon Quick?' Imogen said, unconvinced by his vague response.

'Oh, it's been months. I haven't seen either one since they left.'

Adrian noted that Chilton hadn't asked why they were asking questions about the two men. People usually ask, curiosity getting the better of them. It could just be that Chilton didn't actually give a monkey's, or maybe it was something else. Maybe he already knew.

'What time does your boss get in?' Imogen asked.

'Today, he won't be in until after lunch.'

'We'll need to speak to him. Could you tell us his address?' Imogen said.

Jimmy shifted uncomfortably, his calm, collected look turning to one of unease.

'Ruby on the desk can give it to you. I need to get back to my meeting, if that's all?'

'Thank you, Mr Chilton. Don't leave town; we may need to question you again.'

Chilton nodded and walked over to the desk, instructing Ruby to give them Reece Corrigan's address. She gave them a suspicious side-eyed look as Chilton spoke.

'What do you make of that, then?' Imogen asked Adrian, her eyes fixed on Chilton as he went up the stairs.

Adrian had noticed that his behaviour wasn't right. It was obvious just from speaking to him that Jimmy was lying and keeping secrets. He didn't seem to be afraid in the same way that Leon Quick had been, but there was something weaselly about the man.

Adrian turned back to Imogen when Jimmy had finally disappeared from view.

'God knows. I don't know what's going on anymore.'

'Let's go get this address and visit the big boss.'

'Maybe he can shed some light on this situation,' Adrian said.

'What are the chances of that?'

# Chapter Twenty-Four

I should have known better than to think I could escape, that there was any chance for me to have a normal life. I don't even know what that is. Everything has been so twisted for so long now that I really think I am where I belong. There is no Hail Mary for me, no last-minute reprieve.

Being back home is like riding a bike with a broken seat or slipping into an uncomfortable pair of shoes that you can't remove. I wish with every fibre of my being that I had died on that riverbank, and yet I survived and here I am, back here again. Groundhog Day.

Every day is the same, I wake up and then I pretend to be the person he wants until it's time to go to sleep again. I may as well be a doll or a robot. I am barely human at all.

Slipping out of the hospital was easy enough; no one thought I would go. People are always underestimating *me and that's fine. I don't really care. I wonder if I really care about anything, anymore. I used to want to get away, but now I think I have used up nine lives and not all of them were mine. This is where I belong, uncomfortable shoes and all.*

# Chapter Twenty-Five

Since Imogen and Adrian had started dating, things had definitely changed at work. As they drove out to Reece Corrigan's home address, Imogen found her cheeks warming as she watched Adrian drive. She had never really thought about how attractive he was, as if the mere fact of her thinking about it might inflate his ego. He was a more cautious driver than her, didn't seem to wander off in his own head as much as she did. He was definitely more at peace than he had been in a long time. Since his last girlfriend, Lucy, was murdered in connection with an investigation they were conducting last year.

She remembered when they'd met, how she had assumed so much about him and yet within just a few hours they were completely at ease with each other. You don't get that every day. Imogen knew that this could get tiresome at some point. That one day she might not want to spend the day with the person she spends her nights with, but for now it was easy, it felt right. These moments together in the car were her favourite, she had no idea why.

'Do you think the DCI knows about us?' Imogen said.

'No, I don't, do you?'

'I can't imagine her not pulling us up on it. What would you do if she does?'

'Then we deal with it, I guess. I'll move, if she wants, to another department, another team or something.'

'You would do that?' Imogen said, taken aback by the very idea.

'Why not? Wouldn't you?'

'I feel like I'm just getting settled here and don't really want to change again. I like the way things are.'

'I like it too, but I think I like you more. I've been here since I started, maybe a change would be good for me.'

'I wouldn't want to feel responsible for that.'

'I know, but you wouldn't be. I have thought about this before. After losing Lucy and now finding myself with you . . . I know I hadn't been with her long, but it was the first time in a long time that I thought I was capable of a real relationship. When she died, I thought that was it for me. No more chances. Sometimes you just have to decide what you want most – and I know you're more important to me than this job.'

'Where would you go?' she said, surprised that he had given this any thought at all.

'I have no idea. Maybe I could train new recruits for a while, or maybe I could move to canine division.'

'Dogs?'

'What's wrong with dogs?'

'Nothing. You've just never mentioned it before.'

'It could be time for a change, anyway. I don't want to piss off the DCI and who knows, maybe you'll like me even more?'

'Not sure that's possible.' She smiled.

He put his hand on her knee and squeezed. This felt like an unusually mature approach to the situation from Adrian, Lord knows he wasn't usually so level-headed and measured when dealing with matters of the heart. They had been through a lot together over the last couple of years and she had seen him at both ends of the spectrum, high and low. There was no doubt that he had grown and changed into a different person. She liked to think she was at least partially responsible for that.

# Chapter Twenty-Six

It was obvious from the moment they arrived at the house that it was worth well over a million. This area and this view alone were both assets, but the real gem was the property itself. An eco house, white and wood with large metal beams, the back of the house was overlooking the Blackdown Hills on the border. Green upon green upon green. The house was detached, although they had neighbours either side with just a short distance between them. Enough not to be bothered by loud television sets or even louder parties.

Adrian pulled the car into the large driveway next to a white Lexus. He had never been one of those men who was preoccupied with cars. If it worked, that was enough for him; he only used it to get to work and back, anyway. Corrigan's driveway could hold at least six cars. The second floor of the house had much larger windows overlooking the drive.

They knocked on the door and waited patiently.

'Would you want to live in a house like this?' Adrian asked Imogen, who was looking through one of the windows, studying the inside.

'God, no. It would freak me out, all these windows, everything on display like that. I know it's set away from the road, but it's still weird. And just so cold and impersonal. The only thing I can tell about these people is that they have an interior designer.'

'I wouldn't like this, either.' He smiled to himself, reassured.

He was paranoid about his own financial attractiveness after the mother of his child left him to be with a man of means. His lack of money was one of the things that made him feel a little inadequate. Probably just a residual chip on the shoulder from being poor as a kid.

The large wooden front door opened and an older gentleman stood in front of them. He was in his fifties, no hair and a very ruddy-coloured skin. He must have been around six foot three and physically he was a robust man, not exactly fat but not exactly muscly, either. He wore a wax Barbour jacket, Timberland boots and a Hackett rugby shirt. He wanted people to know he had money. There was an air of intimidation about him and that was before he even spoke.

'Are you the police officers who were at HQ earlier?' Reece Corrigan asked, shaking Imogen's hand, then Adrian's.

He had a strong, confident grip and seemed completely unfazed by their appearance on his doorstep.

'That's correct. I wonder if we might speak to you

about your former employees. Simon Glover and Leon Quick,' Adrian said.

'Yes, Jimmy told me you were asking after them. I believe he already told you everything. They were rubbish, so I sacked them. There really isn't anything else to say.'

'Can we come in? Maybe you can remember some more details about the men.'

'I'm afraid now isn't a good time. My wife and I are just off out. Why are you asking me about those two no-marks, anyway?'

'We are investigating their deaths.'

'They're both dead?' he said, genuinely surprised.

Adrian noticed the emphasis Reece put on the word 'both', as though that was the part that was unexpected. Did he already know about Simon Glover's death?

'Can you tell us where you were last Friday night?'

'Friday night is poker night. Me and a few of the boys at work get together once a week.'

'Which boys? We will need some names.' Imogen said.

'Jimmy and some other lads. I'll call Ruby and get her to send you over names and contact details, save you some time.'

Behind them, a woman, presumably Reece's wife, appeared at the top of the stairs. At first, all they could see were her bronzed legs and white patent heels. It was immediately obvious before they even saw her face that she was significantly younger than him.

She descended slowly, trying to put her gold hoop earrings in as she walked. A tight dress clung to her toned thighs. There was something of the Hollywood Barbie doll about her. She had long blonde layered hair, big blue eyes with heavy black mascara and a golden powder dusted over her cheekbones. She looked at Imogen and Adrian then faltered for a moment in her descent. The perfect porcelain-toothed smile dropped almost imperceptibly before she continued to walk down the stairs.

It took Adrian a few moments, but his body prickled with goose bumps as she stood on the bottom step. It was her – it was Jane Doe.

Reece spoke again. 'This is my wife, Angela.'

## Chapter Twenty-Seven

Angela Corrigan had immaculate hair, blonde and bouncy with loose, tumbling curls just past her shoulders. Imogen barely recognised her. It was her, though, the woman Adrian had saved.

Imogen shot a look at Adrian. He met her gaze immediately, the tiniest nod of his head confirming she wasn't imagining what she was seeing.

Angela Corrigan was at most half the age of her husband. She took a deep breath and approached the doorstep. She wore a polo-neck knitted dress in cornflower blue, which made her eyes even bluer. Imogen noticed that aside from her lower legs, she was almost completely covered.

On closer inspection, there was a thick layer of foundation on her face, good foundation but still an unnecessary amount for a woman as young as Angela Corrigan – no doubt to hide the bruises she had sustained. Perfectly composed and immaculately dressed, she didn't look the same as the woman they had seen almost completely broken in that hospital bed.

Angela's smile reappeared, a strained look in her eye, which clearly asked them not to mention what they knew, wanting to keep up the charade of a first meeting. The tension in the air was palpable as no one spoke for a moment, each unsure what to say.

Imogen decided that now wasn't the time for this confrontation; they didn't know enough. She thought about what Dr Hadley had told her about the woman's injuries and the possibilities of a prolonged campaign of physical abuse against her. Imogen would let the woman dictate how this introduction was going to go.

'Who's this?' Angela said, walking forwards and slipping her arm through Reece's, looking up at him.

Imogen could see that whatever was going on, she didn't want her husband to know about it; she wanted them to pretend they had never seen her before.

'The detectives just came over to ask about a couple of former employees.'

'Oh. Will you be long?' She looked at a slim, expensive-looking gold wristwatch. 'I have an appointment with the salon at eleven.'

Corrigan kissed her on the forehead before turning back to them.

'Listen, I'll give Ruby at HQ a call and she can email over their personnel files for you. It's been a few months and so I really can't remember anything particularly insightful about them off the top of my head.'

Imogen looked at the couple in front of her. She wondered why he hadn't reported his wife missing. She also wondered why Angela was pretending she didn't know them. Their charade was well-rehearsed and if Imogen didn't know what she did, then she wouldn't even question it. What this did tell her was that she couldn't trust a word that came out of Reece Corrigan's mouth.

'Just a few more questions,' Imogen said. 'Was there a specific incident that led to their dismissal, do you remember?'

'It was cumulative, you know? Sloppy work and insubordination. It will be in the files. We got sued a few years ago by a disgruntled employee that we let go, so now we log every single altercation and incident. The employees have to sign a form for every single incident or accident that occurs on site.'

Imogen noticed that Adrian was unusually quiet beside her. A part of her wanted to reach out and hold his hand. She wasn't sure why, but this interaction confirmed some kind of domestic abuse to her. Even if Reece didn't do it himself, he knew. Corrigan knew she had disappeared and he knew what kind of state she was in when she got back home. Reece Corrigan was not an innocent bystander in this.

'I'll just go grab a bagel or something for breakfast while you finish up.'

Angela smiled and disappeared into the back of the house, presumably where the kitchen was.

'Were there any other employees you got rid of for similar reasons?'

'Loads. Over the years we've got through a large volume of staff. I like to give people a second chance, so I employ some ex-cons. I also employ a lot of young 'uns who think it's going to be an easy job, but when they start, they find it too much for them physically. Ruby can compile a staff list for you, if you think that will help. I'll get her to send it over with those other contact details. Unless there's anything else you need to see?'

'We may need access to your accounts. We'll get in touch if and when we have enough for a warrant,' Imogen said.

'No need for a warrant; I am happy to provide you with them. I've got nothing to hide,' Corrigan said.

'Give us a call if you think of anything else.'

Imogen wanted to move away from the door for now. There was more going on than a conversation about Simon Glover and Leon Quick. The lies and secrets surrounding this case just kept getting bigger and harder to understand. She wanted to regroup with Adrian and discuss what their next step needed to be. She wanted to check he was OK.

'Glad to be of service,' Reece smiled and closed the door.

Imogen and Adrian walked away from the house in silence. They got in the car and it wasn't until the house disappeared from view that they actually turned to each other.

'What the fuck was that?' Imogen said.

'That was her, right? That was Jane Doe.'

'Angela Corrigan. I almost didn't recognise her, she looks so different.'

'She acted like nothing had happened, like she had no idea who we were. Why would she do that?'

'So did he. Why didn't he report his wife missing? Dr Hadley implied to me that Jane Doe . . . Angela Corrigan was a vulnerable person. I took that to mean an abusive situation,' Imogen said.

'And we're just going to leave her there?' Adrian said, his jaw tightening.

'We can go back when he is at work, speak to her and see if she can shed any light on anything. If she is still in a dangerous situation then we don't want to make it worse.'

'She went back to him? If, indeed, he was the person who did that to her,' Adrian said.

'Which means he is probably the one who killed Simon Glover. I don't like jumping to conclusions, but the conclusions are right there. She lied to us about not remembering who she was.'

'Wouldn't you?' Adrian said.

'What else did she lie about? I wonder.'

'Do you think we did the right thing? Not letting on that we knew her? Leaving her there?' Adrian said.

'I think for now we need to get more information on Reece Corrigan and then we can show our hand.'

'Let's go back and tell the DCI that we have identified the woman. That's a huge break,' Adrian said.

'Yes, and then we need to find out everything we can about Reece Corrigan and that construction company. Maybe bring that Jimmy Chilton guy in for questioning, see if we can't get him to tell us something useful. Find any other employees who have left and see what they have to say about the place. Maybe Fiona Merton will know someone else that her brother used to work with over there who we can speak to. Maybe Simon spoke to her about Corrigan,' Imogen said.

'Reece Corrigan just became suspect number one.'

# Chapter Twenty-Eight

I dust the blusher on my cheeks and hope that it's enough. I wash my hands in the sink, the residual foundation on the back of my hand running into the drain, then I inspect my face again as I dry my hands. I have my mask on again. My white privilege, my hundred-pound Christian Louboutin lipstick and Moschino dress, coupled with my white Blahnik shoes. Who wouldn't want to be me?

I didn't choose any of these things myself. I have a personal shopper who consults with R. She has a luxury boutique in the city and keeps a clothes rail just for me at the back. I can choose from that rail, but that's hardly a choice at all. It's not that I don't appreciate the things I have; it's just what comes with it. Most people would give anything to have everything that I have. At least they think they would.

I take several deep breaths with my eye on the clock – ten seconds of deep breathing before I go downstairs to meet R – we are going out. He likes to be seen out with me, likes people to know how much he has. I am nothing but a possession to him. He owns me.

I grab the gold hoop earrings he took out of the safe and told me to wear today. I head towards the stairs.

At the top of the stairs I hear R talking to someone. I can't tell who at this point, but I am glad of it – he behaves much better in front of other people.

I brace myself for a social interaction; they are always hard. The more I speak to people the more lost I feel, the further inside the lies. Do I even know who I am anymore? Always acting, always pretending to be someone I am not. I must pretend to be the doting wife, the perfect woman. I must make him look good. If anyone even gets a whiff of the monster he is inside, without him wanting them to, then I have to face his wrath. Something I am more than accustomed to. This is me. This is my life. To be a mark of his success, his virility, his desirability, his power.

I gulp in a breath before treading on the first step down. I must keep my composure. I put my earrings in as I take each step – it gives me an excuse not to make eye contact – but I glance up and see them there. I'm tense anyway, I'm always tense, but seeing the police at the door knots my spine immediately. I recognise them. They are the ones who tried to help me. Did they find me? I thought I had got away without anyone knowing who I was. I mustn't let R know that I know who they are. I hope they play along.

They both look up at me, initially a little confused, probably because of the age difference between R and *me – it always makes people uncomfortable. I see them totting up the cost of my clothes as they look me up and down, wondering how much it costs to keep a girl like me around. Then came that spark of recognition that I was dreading.*

*They continue their conversation without skipping a beat and I hear them talking about Simon. Poor Simon. I thought there was more distance between R and Simon, but apparently not. R is smiling and he moves his elbow a little, signalling for me to play my part. I oblige.*

*I walk forwards and slip my hand through his arm. I kiss him and I can feel the judgement from the female detective, or maybe I am projecting, maybe it's me who's placing judgement on myself. I hate myself for playing along with his game, but every time I try to break away I get hurt, or I get someone else hurt. Or worse, killed.*

*DS Adrian Miles looks at me in a way that reminds me of so many people before him, people who have tried to help me, people who paid a price for that. It's always men, which I find annoying. Do women just think I made my bed and I should lie in it, or is it more sinister than that? Is it because the men want me, is that all I am? Is it a hero complex? Is it because I am pretty, or is it because I remind them of someone else?*

*I hate them for recognising that weakness in me, I hate them for wanting to help or maybe exploit that weakness, I hate them for giving me hope that they can free me from this gilded cage. I know they can't. I hate myself for not knowing who or how to trust anymore.*

*I want to go with them, but I know R knows how to get me back, he always knows. An image flashes in my mind. I don't react because I never do, but it's Simon, broken and bloody, begging for help, a split second and that's it. My mind cuts instantly to lying in the river and praying for death but still somehow fighting to stay alive by pulling myself from the water, feeling both relieved and disappointed when DS Miles came to rescue me. I wish I could remember more, but it just won't come. That whole night is a blur, I didn't lie about that.*

*I smile, make my excuses and go to the kitchen. I breathe out and suppress the urge either to scream or throw up. I pour myself a gin; I'm not driving today, not that that would stop me. I hear the door close a few minutes later and drink to another lost opportunity as the police walk towards their car.*

*Bracing myself yet again for a moment alone with R, I finish what's in the glass and hear R on the phone to someone from the company, chastising them for something. At least it wasn't me who disappointed him this time – I would hate to have to do my make-up again.*

# Chapter Twenty-Nine

There was a plethora of information on the rise of Corrigan Construction. Adrian had found article after article online about contract bids won by the company, including many of the bigger construction jobs in the county and beyond. Over the ten years they had been in the area, their profile had increased exponentially. The head office building Adrian and Imogen had visited had been constructed when the company moved into the area, bringing with them hundreds of job opportunities.

Adrian couldn't stop thinking about the difference between the woman they had seen in that hospital bed and the polished Angela Corrigan with her *Dynasty* looks. They needed to speak to her alone, without being under the watchful eye of her husband. A husband who had never reported her missing, even though she was in the hospital for several days. Adrian could only imagine what kind of state she had been in when she turned up back at home.

There was something else bothering Adrian. Something that had just occurred to him. Adrian had been all over the news when he rescued Angela Corrigan from the river, so unless Reece had been living under a rock then he would have seen that footage. Granted, Angela looked nothing like the woman they had seen at Corrigan's house, but at the same time, if Reece had been involved in what happened to her, then surely he would have been paying attention when the news said she had been fished out of the water, that Adrian had pulled her out. This was the point that Adrian was stuck on. How much did Reece actually know?

He obviously knew his wife was missing from their home, but did he know where she was? Did he know what had happened and why? When he opened the door and saw Adrian standing there, did he know that Adrian had pulled her from the river?

More secrets. More lies.

'Find anything interesting?' Imogen said, putting a coffee in front of him.

'Lots of stuff about the business, not much about the man. Literally pages of results online about Corrigan Construction. Charity things, building jobs, but they all seem to be kind of impersonal and distant. There's got to be more to him than this.'

'I was thinking about that, actually,' Imogen said. 'He said they got sued by someone a couple of years ago. Who was that? I bet they have a story to tell.'

'Good thinking. I'll see if I can find out who it was.'

Adrian typed in the buzzwords and looked through the results. He found a small article four pages into the search engine in an old local paper about an accident that had happened on one of the Corrigan building sites. A man lost his arm owing to a faulty piece of machinery.

'This guy lost his arm on a Corrigan building site two years ago. The timing fits. If nothing else, we know this guy used to work for the company. Maybe even at the same time as Simon Glover and Leon Quick.'

'I just keep seeing it repeatedly. Leon Quick was a bit tense when we got there and then minutes later, he decided to take his own life,' Imogen said, preoccupied by what had happened the day before. 'Did we do that?'

'I don't think he was fine when we got there, to be honest. Did you see how jittery he was?'

'I thought he might be on something, or you know, in withdrawal, but the preliminary path reports say he was clean.'

'Just anxious; scared of something or someone,' Adrian said.

'Do you think Angela Corrigan knows why he killed himself?'

'If she does, I don't think she will tell us. No one seems to be telling us anything.'

'You think Reece Corrigan is the one who gave her those injuries and left her in the river?'

'He didn't report her missing. He must have known where she was or thought she wasn't coming back. Did he even care? But then, why would she go back to him?'

'Is it a money thing? That house, that car, don't come

117

cheap. Is that why she stays with him? I always used to struggle to understand why a woman would choose to stay in an abusive relationship, but with the things I have seen in this job, I am just thankful for everyone who gets out. If he did think she was dead she could have been home free. She could have disappeared without a trace.'

'I don't think either of us are in a position to judge other people for their relationships. Maybe she's too scared to leave. We need to speak to her alone,' Adrian said.

He would be lying if he said he didn't hold some resentment towards his mother for not getting out while she could, for staying with the person who made their life hell. He wouldn't hear anyone else say that, though; she was as much a victim as he was.

'How are you with all this?' Imogen asked as if reading his thoughts.

'Right now? I'm really angry. I want to get her out of there.'

'Until she confirms what we already think we know then we are powerless. She didn't give us any fingerprints or DNA at the hospital, so we can't even prove that she is Jane Doe. They will have top lawyer money and they could explain their way out of it. Say it was a lookalike or something.'

'But it is her.'

'So, we wait until he leaves for work and then we go and speak to her. We'll brief the DCI today and we can go in the morning. If we blow this, then we put her in even more danger. Not to mention the fact that we have absolutely no proof that Reece Corrigan is to blame for Simon Glover's death and Leon Quick never specifically named him. It could just as easily be someone else at the company. Corrigan himself said they employed plenty of ex-cons. We have nothing.'

'It was him. I can feel it. I'd rather keep an eye on him. A violent man like that, he is bound to step out of line. I saw it time and again with my father. It didn't matter how many times he claimed to have changed, he always resorted to that closed fist again.'

'What are you suggesting?' Imogen said.

'I'm suggesting a romantic evening in the car with a chip butty and couple of Tizers. We can brief the DCI in the morning.'

'You want to stake out the house?'

'I feel responsible for that woman, Imogen. Isn't there some old proverb that says if you save someone's life it then becomes your duty to protect them? I feel like I have to make sure she is OK.'

'How do you know that the violence is not the compromise she is willing to make for that lavish lifestyle?'

'That doesn't make it right. Besides, she was trying to leave, remember? At least that's what the passport suggests.'

Adrian tried not to sound as annoyed as he was. His words were clipped and his jaw clenched to stop himself from snapping at Imogen.

'Of course not. I am not saying it's right at all. I'm just saying, she might not thank you for getting involved.'

'That's our job, to get involved. Do you know how

119

different my life would have been if the police got involved once in a while, how different my mother's life would have been? Thankfully, we don't have the same insane domestic abuse laws that existed when I was a kid. Did you know that up until 1991 it was legal to have sex with your wife without her consent? Can you imagine that? It wasn't considered rape if you were married.'

'You're taking everything I say the wrong way. We're both responsible for Angela Corrigan, but what's happening to her isn't our fault, though. It's Reece Corrigan's – we think.'

'It has to be him,' Adrian said, blowing the air from his cheeks, trying to calm himself.

'And we'll get him, we will. But we can't go about this half-cocked. If we want to nail that shitbag then we have to do it by the book.'

Adrian admired Imogen's optimism, but he knew from experience that domestic abuse was so much more complicated than that. He saw his mother get hurt time and again, almost as many times as she defended his father's behaviour to Adrian. Even when people tried to help, she would push them away.

He wasn't angry at Imogen, though. How could she understand? How could anyone who hadn't been in that situation? It was hard to explain that it was possible to love someone who hurt you. That it was fear that kept you in line, not just the fear of what they might do to you when you were there, but also an amplified fear of what they would do to you if you tried to leave. And then there were the things they told you: that you would never make it without them, that you were nothing and that you deserved everything you were getting. How could you make someone who hadn't lived through it understand?

# Chapter Thirty

The smell of chips saturated in vinegar was less appealing after you had finished eating them. Imogen and Adrian had parked among some other cars on a hill behind the Corrigan house, the remnants of their takeaway tossed onto the back seat of the car.

The back of the house was different to the front. It was almost completely windows and you could see everything inside. Fortunately, their position was fairly obscured by greenery. It felt like they were watching a TV show, a big glass box with little people moving around inside. Angela Corrigan sat on a chair in the lounge reading a book. She didn't look relaxed or even engaged – it looked like a pretence, but then why would anyone keep it up when they were alone in a room? Reece Corrigan was upstairs in an office on the phone. He seemed angry, certainly not the personable man they had met earlier that day, but then they already knew that was a facade.

'You wouldn't like to live in a house like that, then?' Adrian asked again, drinking the last of his can of Coke before stuffing it into a carrier bag full of rubbish.

Was this a discussion about living together? Like proper grown-ups? Imogen wondered. They had so many things to think about before that could happen. He hadn't even told his son, Tom, they were dating and she didn't want him to, didn't want to jinx it. They hadn't even said the l-word to each other yet. Not that she was playing a game or anything, but Imogen didn't want to be the one to say it first. Self-preservation, she imagined, especially when she considered how much more complicated that made things. When love comes into play the stakes get much higher.

'It's like a fishbowl. I have always seen myself as a cottage-by-the-sea kind of a girl,' Imogen said.

It was true; she had always imagined that kind of future. There was something decidedly un-Imogen about it, but that's what she wanted. That was the dream.

'Not in the city, then?'

'It's convenient, but if I didn't have to go in to work every day, I would rather be looking at the horizon. I mean, this is pretty and all, but there is just something about the sea that fills me with wonder. Do you know what I mean?'

'I do know what you mean. I've always lived in the city, though. Couldn't imagine living anywhere else. What if you want a cheeky kebab in the middle of the night or something?'

'They have kebab shops in smaller towns, you know?'

'Yeah, but they are usually shut by eight o'clock.'

'How would you know? So, no midnight kebab shop is a deal-breaker for you?'

'At this stage in my life, I feel like it is. I'm a simple man, Imogen.'

'You can say that again.'

The office light turned off and they watched Reece go downstairs into the lounge where his wife was sitting. Although she didn't stop what she was doing immediately, her posture changed. She seemed more alert. Something about the way Angela had tensed made Imogen feel a little nauseous. Reece said something, a command maybe, and Angela put her book down on the coffee table before standing.

They spoke briefly and he brushed the side of her face with the back of his hand, bringing it down and gently holding her chin as he kissed her forcefully on the mouth. She recoiled, but he just pushed further. He moved his hand down further still, putting his fingers for a moment around her throat until she kissed him back, opening her mouth and accepting his tongue. He removed his hand from her throat and started to undo his trousers.

Imogen's stomach turned and she looked across at Adrian, who had the beginnings of a grimace on his face. From this distance it was hard to tell how Angela really felt about all of this. Maybe this was just the way they did things. No one knows what goes on inside a relationship except the people involved.

She walked over to the sofa and lay down. He climbed on top of her. Imogen was grateful that from this aspect they could only see the back of the sofa, Angela's fingers gripping the top for several minutes until Corrigan eventually stood up and buttoned his flies.

Everything about it made Imogen's skin crawl. She had, of course, been in relationships that weren't healthy before. Possessive or jealous boyfriends who couldn't appreciate that she wasn't theirs to control, and she certainly wasn't their property. But this? She couldn't imagine this.

'What do you think Angela's connection is to Simon, then?' Imogen said to Adrian, desperate not to address what they had just witnessed.

'Were they lovers? Do you think she was having an affair with him and Corrigan found out? That certainly would explain the extent of the injuries,' Adrian said.

'That's the obvious connection – they are much closer in age than she is with Reece. The passports certainly suggest they were running away together. But, when she found out that Glover was dead, she didn't seem particularly heartbroken.'

'Maybe she's just broken altogether,' Adrian said.

Imogen reached over and held his hand, pushing her fingers through his and squeezing tight. She knew this case was making him think about things he didn't like to think about. She wanted him to know that he could talk to her if he needed. The trouble was, he really wasn't good at sharing, neither of them were. She just hoped the case didn't drag on too long. The longer they were in it, the longer Adrian would have in which to fall apart.

As they watched the house, Imogen found herself tensing when the Corrigans were in the same room together, afraid that he was going to hurt Angela, afraid that they would see it and they still wouldn't be able to get to her before any real damage was done. She flashed back to the memory of Leon Quick plunging the knife into himself and how quickly his life had ended. How helplessly they had watched it happen.

Angela walked into the kitchen and Reece grabbed his coat and left. Imogen looked over to Adrian. They saw Reece's car lights disappear up the road.

'Looks like we won't have to wait 'til tomorrow, after all,' she said, starting the car.

# Chapter Thirty-One

Sitting in the Corrigans' living room, Imogen couldn't help but wonder what kind of things went down in this house. Every surface was spotless, every cushion plumped and placed strategically. She avoided sitting on the sofa, knowing what had just taken place there.

Imogen had seen Angela's injuries and she wasn't healed when she left the hospital, so her husband must have seen them, too. Added to that was the fact that she most likely wasn't wearing make-up under those clothes. There was no getting away from that fact – whether he was involved or not, Reece knew something awful had happened to his wife.

Since Reece Corrigan had left, Angela had got herself a glass and a crystal decanter with some honey brown liquid in it. She poured herself a generous measure.

'You shouldn't be here,' Angela said.

'Neither should you,' Imogen said. 'Why did you leave the hospital?'

'If you're here when he gets back then we'll all be in trouble.'

'What kind of trouble?' Adrian said.

'You don't want to know,' Angela responded.

'We're police officers,' Imogen said. 'He can't do anything to us.'

Angela scoffed and saluted Imogen with her glass. 'If you say so.'

'Were you lying the whole time when you said you didn't know what happened?' Imogen said.

'I don't remember that night. I did know my name and who I was, though.'

She drank the contents and poured herself another.

'The bruises you had in hospital don't just appear, someone did that to you.'

'I don't want to talk about it. Please go.'

'We can help you. There are shelters for women in your situation,' Adrian said. 'Why don't you let us help you?'

'I doubt there are many women in my situation. You have no idea what he is capable of. He doesn't care that you're police. If he wants to hurt you, he will. If you know what's good for you, you'll get out while you still can.'

'Like you said, we're the police. Getting out while we can isn't really the way we operate. We can protect you,' Adrian said.

Imogen could feel how much he wanted to save this woman. It wasn't about her, though – it was almost a selfishness on his part. If she got hurt again then Adrian would feel bad. Maybe that's what things like this were always about, maybe that's what their entire job was – just making sure the police themselves didn't feel crap.

Angela smiled and took another swig of the liquid in her tumbler.

'You think that, but you can't. He always wins. Always.'

'Can you tell us about Simon Glover?' Imogen said.

'Simon?' She took another swig. Still emotionless, still cold.

'Were you having an affair with him?' Imogen said.

'Kind of, I guess, but it was more of a friendship. I don't have many friends; I'm not allowed. He was one of Reece's favourites and so he used to spend a lot of time here. He has a few favourites, for a while, at least. We became friends in secret. It never went any further than that. I wasn't sleeping with him.'

'You had feelings for him?' Adrian said.

'I think so. I don't know. I was too scared to have feelings for him.'

'Did he know that your husband was hurting you?' Imogen asked.

'At first, no. Everyone loves Reece. Believe it or not, he can be quite the charmer when he wants to be. *Reece*'—she spat his name—'is really good at making people like him, until they see who he really is. Usually, if that happens, if he lets you see who he really is, then you need to be scared.'

'So, what happened to Simon?' Adrian said.

'He was helping me to leave. New name, new passports and tickets to Canada. I thought I was finally going to be free thanks to Simon – and now he's dead.'

'Are you saying your husband killed him?' Adrian said. Imogen shot him a look; he shouldn't be putting words in her mouth.

'I'm saying it's not safe for you here. If he thinks you are trying to help me to leave, then he will stop you. Somehow, he will stop you. I have to be here. I can handle it.'

'Do you love him?' Imogen said.

'It's complicated.'

'Why is it complicated?'

'I guess I'm just fucked up. You shouldn't waste your time trying to help me. After what happened to Simon, I am not pulling anyone else into this. You both seem like good people. You should leave.'

'What about Simon? Doesn't he deserve justice?' Imogen said.

'You won't get any justice here, just more pain,' she said, swigging the last of her drink.

Imogen watched her face. This coldness wasn't an act. She wasn't pretending. She was broken. For someone so young to be so completely resigned to this fate was incomprehensible to Imogen. Angela knew what the man she was living with was capable of, *they* knew what he was capable of, but they were powerless to stop him without her testimony.

'Is there anything you can tell us that would help in our investigation into Simon Glover's death? If you know what happened to him then you need to tell us. We should bring you in for questioning anyway. Just tell us what he did. How did you end up in the river?' Imogen said.

'I have no idea what you're talking about.'

'Are you just going to wait until he succeeds and kills you?' Adrian said.

'I can't have anyone else getting hurt because of me. Now, please leave. I'm tired and he could be back at any moment. I'd like to have a bath and be asleep before he gets home.'

'You're not safe here,' Adrian said.

'I know my place. As long as I do what I'm told then no one else gets hurt. I can't have anyone else on my conscience.'

'Have there been others?'

'There won't be from now on.'

'Did you know Leon Quick?' Imogen asked.

'A little. Reece told me he took his own life; I was sorry to hear that. I didn't know him well, but I know he helped Simon out, got him away from Reece. For a little while, at least. I don't know why Leon killed himself. I promise.'

'Do you think the suicide was anything to do with your husband?' Imogen said.

'It wouldn't surprise me, but I honestly don't know. I didn't know Leon but to say hello. I know Simon and he were close friends.'

'Why didn't you ever call the police?' Adrian said.

'I did call the police. Not long ago, actually. They did nothing and so I asked Simon to help me leave and now he's dead. He got away from all this and now, because of me, he's gone.' Angela sighed heavily.

'You spoke to the police? When?' Imogen asked.

'Goodnight, detectives.' She stood up and walked through to the front door.

131

Imogen waited for Adrian to go first, but he wasn't going to let this go. He was projecting a lot of energy. She could feel his agitation as he had asked questions and see it in the way he looked at Angela. She had become a symbol to him for the mother he had neglected to protect when he was a child. A mother he couldn't have protected even if he wanted to. A child can't fight off a full-grown man.

One thing Imogen did know was that people in these situations needed to help themselves. Angela needed to make the decision. They couldn't do it for her. In other cases, if the wife wasn't on board then she just lied and protected her abuser. They needed to show Angela that they *could* help.

They stepped out of the house and Angela closed the door.

'You need to stop taking this so personally, Adrian. Look at you! We are doing everything we can,' Imogen said quietly as they walked towards the car.

Imogen reached to take Adrian's hand, but he pulled away and got in the driver's seat. She climbed in and folded her arms, knowing if she said what she was really thinking it would only make things worse. She knew he felt responsible for this woman. As though it was somehow his fault. That by getting away from his situation at home he was somehow just as culpable as his father was, as Reece Corrigan was. Adrian was pulling away from Imogen and she didn't know how to stop it.

# Chapter Thirty-Two

*I lie down for him and let him do what he needs to do. That's how it's always worked. It's never been any other way. When it's over he stands up and I am relieved when he tells me he is leaving, he is working on winning a contract and needs to schmooze some client or other. I zone out as he speaks; I don't care where he is going. All I can think about is getting clean and sleeping until morning. First, I need a strong drink to burn away the taste of his saliva in my mouth.*

*I knew they would come and speak to me alone. I suppose they have to, it's their job. I see them park the car outside just as R has left; I never know how long he will be gone for and so them being here makes me very nervous. I wish they had waited a little longer. I would like to have a shower and maybe a few more drinks before I have to pretend some more.*

*Maybe they know enough already, maybe they have figured out all the different ways in which R has hurt* me. If I were them, I would assume the worst of R. It all depends on what you think is the worst a human being can be. They have no idea.

I doubt any one person knows the full extent of R's malevolence; he is evil. I wasn't brought up religious or anything and I know that word comes with religious connotations, but if there is a devil, then R is the human representation. I know he will be the end of me one day.

I open the door and the police officers both come in and follow me to the lounge, where I have left my drink on the coffee table. They sit down. I notice DS Imogen Grey glance at the sofa and realise they were probably watching from the roadside and could see inside the lounge. I doubt they can see me blush through my heavy make-up – what does it matter, anyway? Humiliation is not something that particularly bothers me anymore; if I do experience it, it's fleeting.

It must seem strange, a woman in my situation, with a house that's ninety per cent windows, but it's all part of R's game. He likes to make sure I am always switched on, always playing my part of doting wife. There are a few rooms in the house where there isn't a view – those are usually the rooms he picks to teach me a lesson.

I see no point in lying to the officers about anything they already know. They saw me at my absolute worst and so it's silly to pretend that everything is peachy. I can feel the concern coming from DS Miles and I know that he's already too involved to let go. Maybe I need to be completely odious in order for him to walk away. I don't want him to get hurt.

*They ask me about Simon. I don't remember the night that we ended up in the river but even if I did, I wouldn't tell them. I remember what we arranged, but after I left the house that day everything is a blur. I have blacked out before and the doctor explained to me at the hospital that I had experienced head trauma and that it could affect my memory, maybe even permanently.*

*I can't imagine R dumping us both in the river to be found; that seems far too clumsy for him. I just can't remember. All I see when I try is that one image of Simon, begging for them to stop. I shake it off again. It's my constant companion these last few days and part of me hopes I never regain the memory of the hours surrounding that moment.*

*The female officer, DS Imogen Grey, seems angry with me. I think there are several reasons for this. First, because she feels powerless to help me. She wonders why I am protecting R, but I am not protecting him, I am protecting her. Also, because my weakness reflects on her, on our gender, I know there are women out there who can't imagine themselves in this situation – they are lucky. I didn't go looking for this. This is the life that found me.*

*They ask me their questions and I bat away the ones I feel will help them in any way. I am purposely cold and obnoxious. I don't want them to pity me; pity is the last thing I need. I don't want their help.*

*I tell them what they already know about Simon and I don't know anything about Leon Quick to explain why he killed himself. I have absolutely no doubt that*

R is involved in Leon's death; there was a certain look of accomplishment on his face when he told me about the suicide. If any one person could have that much influence over another person's life, it's R. God only knows what R did to him.

The police have been to this house several times in the past, once quite recently, back when I still had the tiniest sliver of hope that I could maybe one day escape. I watched R talk the police constable around with ease – a few choice words and my call was explained away as a prank of sorts. We all laughed, and I watched on hopelessly as he left me to face yet another round with R.

I can fake any mood thanks to my years of experience playing the role of dutiful wife. Knowing that the police could no longer help me, I decided to contact Simon. I wish I had never made that call. Maybe he would still be alive. Maybe I would still have hope for some kind of future. That one phone call was the beginning of the end. There is only one way out of this and that's in a wooden box.

I see both DS Grey and DS Miles' frustration. Part of me wants to tell them it's nothing they are doing wrong, they are saying all the right things to make me want to speak to them. I wish I could. I wish I believed that they could help me, but I have been here too many times before. They are too late. I have no faith in the system. The only thing I believe in is the fact that this is my life. There is no way out.

# Chapter Thirty-Three

Adrian was already at his desk when Imogen arrived at work. He'd been awake for hours anyway and so he sneaked away before she woke, leaving a coffee and clingfilmed marmite sandwich on the bedside table. He wanted to find out as much as possible about Corrigan and he didn't need Imogen there second-guessing his motivations all the time. Had he told her too much about his past? Was she reading into things? Seeing things that weren't there. Would things be different if they weren't together?

She was waiting for him to snap, he could see that. It made him feel like she had no faith in him and what bothered him the most was that she was right. Being level-headed was admittedly not one of his strengths. Occasionally, he let his emotions get in the way of critical thinking. Yes, he was determined to stop Corrigan from hurting his wife, but that was literally their job – it wasn't him going off half-cocked on some personal vendetta. It's what he was paid to do.

The fact that he was going to enjoy nailing this shithead was neither here nor there. He had found the information on the man who sued Corrigan Construction and he'd also contacted dispatch to find out if there had, indeed, been a call received from Angela Corrigan.

'What time did you get here?' Imogen asked as she put her bag in the bottom drawer of her desk.

'A couple of hours ago; just wanted to get ahead of this. I've got a name and address for the disgruntled employee.'

'Is he local?'

'Yep - ten minutes' drive, tops. Lives in one of those nice flats by the river.'

'We should check in with the DCI before we go. Give her a heads-up of what we're doing.'

'Why not wait until we actually have some information?'

'Remember what I said yesterday. By the book. Adrian, we can't take any risks with this case. There is too much at stake.'

'Fine. But I'd appreciate it if you stopped treating me like I'm overreacting and taking it all personally.'

'That's not what I meant. We've been burned before by not following the rules. It always comes back to bite us on the arse. I just want to make sure that we are both protected from any repercussions and that when we put this fucker away, he stays away and doesn't get off on some technicality because we fucked up.'

'OK,' Adrian conceded. 'Sorry I snapped. I am not

trying to dodge the rules, I just want to get this done as quickly as possible, she can't stay there much longer.'

'Then let's work together and get it done. I want him put away, too. We keep the DCI informed every step of the way and that way, we are covered if it all goes Pete Tong.'

'You're right.'

'Always. Remember that.'

Imogen walked over to the DCI's office and knocked on the door. Adrian followed.

He noticed that DCI Kapoor looked braced for bad news. As though that's all they ever seemed to deliver.

'We've identified our Jane Doe,' Imogen said.

'How? Who is it?'

'Simon Glover and Leon Quick's former boss, Reece Corrigan – it's his wife, Angela,' Imogen said.

'We went to see Corrigan and she was there, like nothing had happened. Made a point of not acknowledging the fact that we had met before, either. It was very strange. She's got to be half his age, easily. They live in some million-pound house over the Blackdown Hills.'

'Well, tread carefully. We need to understand her situation fully before we wade in there,' DCI Kapoor said.

'We are about to go and see Rajesh Baqri, a man who sued Corrigan Construction in the year 2017. So far, no one is willing to tell us any specifics on what is so bad about the company, but given the way Leon Quick reacted to the questions we put to him, we think it's something we need to get a clearer picture of. At least we know Corrigan is at the centre of whatever this is now,' Imogen said.

DCI Kapoor nodded then said, 'DI Walsh spoke to Jimmy Chilton again, but he said he kept his resolve. If he knows something then he isn't talking. Hopefully, you can get something out of this Baqri man.'

'Also, we hung around the Corrigan house last night and waited for Reece to leave. When he was gone, we spoke to Angela, but she is too scared to turn against her husband. She thinks he is some kind of all-powerful being who can get to her anywhere, get to anyone. She pretty much admitted that he did it, but right now there is no way she will testify.'

'Well, at the moment it's all on her and without physical evidence, it's possible he won't get sentenced. She's possibly right to be concerned. Let's get some independent evidence to support a testimony if you can eventually convince her to give one.'

'There's plenty of physical evidence. She *is* the physical evidence,' Adrian said.

'I mean without witnesses. A man with his means could get off. It happens. They could argue she is after a payout and that she injured herself. They could argue that someone else did it. As frustrating as it is, we can't just go on what we believe happened. There needs to be some kind of corroboration. At the moment, it's he said, she said. Are you willing to take that risk? Her life could depend on it.'

'Maybe Rajesh can give us something, then,' Imogen said.

'Bloody well hope so. So far, apart from some names, we really don't have anything,' Adrian said.

'We have a suspect,' Imogen said.

'I spoke to Gary this morning, as well, to see what public information he can dig up on Corrigan Construction,' Adrian continued. 'Maybe we can get him on something else. My main concern right now is making sure Angela doesn't get hurt any more than she has been.'

'That's what we all want, DS Miles,' Kapoor said. 'Continue to keep Corrigan in the dark about us connecting Angela to our Jane Doe. If he is a danger to her, we don't want to put her at further risk. Some good news is I have heard that the Quicks decided against legal action, so you're in the clear there. They acted out of grief. I think we can all appreciate how hard it must have been for them. Now, go on. Let's nail this bastard.'

'Thank you, Ma'am,' Adrian said as he left the room, annoyed yet again that they wouldn't be getting Angela out of there.

He had forgotten about the Quicks' threats to press charges. All he could think about was protecting Angela Corrigan. He just didn't feel like they were doing enough, he didn't feel like *he* was doing enough. What pained him most was that maybe Imogen was right and he was spiralling. He couldn't think about that right now, though. All he could think about was helping Angela.

# Chapter Thirty-Four

'It's been two years since this happened.' Rajesh Baqri pointed at his arm. 'I thought someone would have caught up to him sooner.'

He gestured towards the sofa; Adrian and Imogen sat down opposite him.

'What happened?' Adrian asked, unsure if he wanted the answer or not.

'I signed a non-disclosure agreement in exchange for a decent settlement. I can't afford to give the money back, so I'm afraid I can't talk to you.'

'A non-disclosure agreement is not legally binding if its purpose is to cover up a crime,' Imogen said.

'Well, I had no proof anyway, so there isn't much to say. Machine malfunction and then zap, my arm was gone. I sued the company and got a nice lump to live on for a while. Better than nothing.'

Rajesh Baqri had a strange optimism considering his situation. His flat was nice, probably funded at least in part with whatever money Reece Corrigan had paid him off with.

'Did you suspect that it wasn't an accident?' Adrian said.

'I've given it a lot of thought over the last couple of years and in all honesty, I don't know. The timing of it? The fact that he paid up leads me to believe that it probably is true. I got lucky, though. I could have easily been killed in that accident.'

'Would you be surprised if it was planned?' Adrian said.

'No.'

'Why would Reece Corrigan want to hurt you?' Imogen asked.

'The man is nuts. I once saw him pay a man five hundred quid to eat a bowl of wet cement.'

'Jesus. Did the man do it?' Imogen said.

'He tried, but he couldn't keep it down. Puked everywhere. It could have literally killed him.'

'Why would Corrigan do that?' Imogen said.

'He gets off on humiliating people and playing God. He thinks he is above everyone else. Total narcissist.'

'Anything else you can remember? What about his wife?'

'Oh, yeah, when he brought her to the site you had to keep your eyes down. If he thought you were looking at her then you were in trouble. And God help you if you tried to help her out in any way.'

'In what way?' Imogen said.

'In the losing your arm kind of way.' He smiled bitterly before leaning back in his armchair.

143

So, Rajesh Baqri had tried to help Angela Corrigan and then ended up without an arm. Adrian had to wonder if Reece Corrigan would have the balls to go after a police officer. He took an arm from Baqri, would he try to take something from Adrian?

'Did you try to help Angela?' Adrian said.

'I didn't want to get involved, but I used to ask her how she was doing, which was more than anyone else seemed to do. I guess I know why.'

'Did you know Simon Glover or Leon Quick?'

'Simon was one of Corrigan's shadows; he's always got one or two around him. They are probably the smart ones – keep your enemies closer and all that. What's happened to Simon?'

'What makes you think something has happened to Simon?' Imogen said.

'Well, aside from anything else, why would you be asking me about him?'

'We pulled Simon's body from the River Exe,' Imogen said.

'I saw that on the news. That was him?'

'It was. He was beaten. Did you ever see anything like that happen while you were there?'

'Obviously not to that level, but I did see a couple of beatings take place.'

'Beatings for what?' Imogen asked.

'Anything Corrigan felt like, shoddy work, being lippy – we were walking on eggshells a lot of the time,' Baqri said.

'Who administered the beatings?' Imogen said.

'The ones I saw? Simon did. He did whatever

Corrigan told him to do. Let me guess, he got involved with Angela.'

'That seems to be the case,' Adrian said.

'How about her? Is she all right?' he asked with a heavy sigh.

'How close were you with Angela?' Imogen said.

'Not close, but anyone with eyes could see what was going on in that relationship. Most people were too afraid to do anything. I took her to the hospital once and I lost my arm for it. There's something about Corrigan. It's hard to explain, but you kind of get the feeling he would do anything, that nothing is off limits. He is one sinister individual.'

'Why didn't anyone go to the police?' Imogen said.

'It was understood that bad things would happen if you did. They weren't empty threats – as you can see.'

'We spoke to Leon Quick and he seemed terrified. Do you know why?' Imogen said.

'Quick was a bit of a gobshite, but he wasn't in with Corrigan, not like Glover was. I don't know why he would be terrified, though. Most of these little accidents at work came without warning. Sorry. I really don't have much information. I wasn't even there that long, so I'm not sure how much I can help you.'

'We are trying to encourage Angela to make a state-ment telling us what happened the night Simon was attacked. We believe she has some information. Would you be willing to speak to her?' Imogen said.

'Life is hard enough with just one arm. I've been off Corrigan's radar for a while and I prefer it that way. I doubt Glover is the first person he killed. I just can't help you, I'm sorry.'

'Well, thank you for taking the time to talk to us,' Adrian said.

'I hope you get him.'

They stood and left the flat. Adrian turned to Imogen as they walked back to the car.

'How does Corrigan have that much power? How does he get away with it?'

'Some people just feel entitled to it. They take what they want and screw anyone who gets in their way. Like Baqri said, it's narcissism.'

'We need to put him away.'

'We do. We also need to be careful. I know you, Adrian. You think you're bulletproof, but you aren't.'

'We can't be afraid of people like that. They can't be allowed to get away with this stuff.'

'No one's saying that. We just need to make sure not to piss him off before we can put him away.'

Adrian thought about what Baqri had said. What if Reece Corrigan knew that Adrian had tried to help Angela? What would he do then? Adrian wasn't afraid, just curious. How far was Corrigan willing to go to protect what was his? Was he willing to hurt a police officer, or worse? At this point, Adrian had very little concern for his own safety; he just wanted to put Reece Corrigan away.

# Chapter Thirty-Five

'Where's Adrian?' Gary asked as he approached Imogen's desk later that day. He looked more panicked than usual.

'Last time I saw him he was coming to see you. What is it?'

'Adrian asked me to check in with dispatch about the call Angela Corrigan claims she made to the police.'

'You've got it?'

'I've got more than that. I showed it to Adrian.'

'And?'

'He flipped out.'

'Why? What's on the call?'

'It's not what's on the call that's the problem. A uniform went to check on the call and he was wearing a BWV for at least part of the call.'

Body worn videos were there both to protect the officers and to keep records of incidents that were likely to escalate. People generally behaved themselves when

147

they knew they were being filmed. Domestic violence was one of the situations that had a propensity to get out of control.

'Part of it? The first part, or the second part?'

'He turned it off after a brief chat. I get the impression from what I saw that some conversation occurred after the camera was switched off.'

'Which officer was it? One of ours?'

'PC Ben Jarvis.'

Imogen exhaled. Gary was right to be worried. Adrian already had a little history with Jarvis and this was hardly likely to build any bridges between them. Imogen was worried. Whenever she looked at Adrian at the moment, he had that look in his eye again. Dog with a bone. If he thought Jarvis had protected Corrigan in any way, he would kick off.

'You watched it?'

'Yep.'

'Was it all by the book?'

Gary screwed his face up and shrugged. 'Yes?'

The way the intonation in his voice went up several octaves indicated otherwise.

'Shit.'

Adrian was determined to get Corrigan put away and his determination concerned Imogen. Several days in a row now he had already left when she had woken and he wasn't sleeping at night. He was wired. She knew this was all going to go wrong. Adrian was a good police officer and his heart was always in the right place, but he struggled to enforce the law when it came up against his own personal code.

She had admired that about him at first, but then as time had gone on, she realised that it only led to more problems. From now on she had to rein him in, or he was going to do something stupid, maybe even get himself fired, or worse. She looked at the clock: it was lunchtime. If Adrian was looking for Jarvis, he probably went to the canteen. Time to do some damage control.

Imogen rushed to the canteen, with Gary following close behind. When she got there, she found Adrian and Jarvis standing unnaturally close to each other by one of the tables. Adrian was leaning in and saying something – it looked like a threat. She hurried over to them.

'Adrian, I need you to come take a look at something.'

'I'll be there in a minute,' he said, not taking his eyes off Jarvis.

'You need to keep your partner under control, Imogen,' PC Jarvis said, smiling at Imogen.

'Why didn't you bring Corrigan in when you went to that house call?' Adrian snarled.

'You saw the video; she said she made the call as a joke,' Jarvis replied.

'But she made the call. It's your duty to investigate.'

'She insisted she had done it to wind him up.'

'And you accepted that? I mean, I know you did; I saw it.'

'There really wasn't enough to bring him in on. She told me she was fine and so I left.'

'Why did you switch off the camera?'

'Because the call was over. I was leaving. What are you implying?'

'I'm implying that you're bent.'

'Me? That's a joke coming from you.' Jarvis laughed. 'How many rules have you broken? How about all the accusations that have been made against you for harassment or assault? And you think no one knows you're banging DS Grey here? We all see you for what you are. You're going off the deep end, mate.'

Before Imogen had a chance to react, Jarvis was on the ground. He touched his lip to check for blood. Imogen grabbed Adrian's arm; it was rigid with anger. She yanked him back and pulled him towards the door.

'For fuck's sake, Adrian.'

'I suppose I was wrong?' Adrian snapped.

'The man is a dick – doesn't mean you have to be one, too,' Imogen said.

'Is everyone insane? Am I in Upside-down Land, or something? Jarvis was sent to a domestic abuse call and he barely even questioned the accused. Does he not understand how these things work?'

'We are supposed to use our judgement on call-outs, his was wrong. Are you telling me you've never been wrong before?'

'Great. Did you hear what he said to me? And I'm the bad guy?'

'I didn't say that. You need to keep your head. I don't want to work this case alone and if you carry on this way then I will be,' Imogen hissed at him angrily.

Adrian shook his arm free and walked out of the canteen. Imogen went over to Jarvis, who was pretending to laugh it off in front of all the others in the canteen.

'What the fuck was that?' She got up close and spat the words at him.

'Miles came after me!' Jarvis said.

'Because you turned your video off. What was it you didn't want anyone to see? Did Corrigan pay you off?'

'Actually, no. I turned the video off because I wanted to have a candid word with the husband. I told him in no uncertain terms to leave his wife alone. She wouldn't report it, so what could I do? I had to walk away.'

'How did he take that?' Imogen said, not quite sure she believed this spontaneous chivalry on Jarvis's part; it certainly didn't line up with what she knew of him. She also wondered why he had left this out of his report.

'He told me he would fuck me up if he saw me again. He was very convincing,' Jarvis said, with a little more conviction than his last statement.

'Why didn't you just tell us that?' Imogen said, frustrated.

'Well, at least I figured out why you keep knocking me back.'

'I knock you back because I think you're an immature twat and I'm not interested in you, Ben. Thanks for proving me right.'

'You'd better go check on your boyfriend.'

'He's not the one bleeding,' Imogen said.

She walked away from Jarvis. She hadn't lied to him – even if she had been single, she wouldn't have gone out with him. Jarvis had asked Imogen out almost as soon as he started working at the station over a year ago. She said no to him, but that didn't seem to stop him from asking again. If you have to say no to someone three times and they ask you a fourth time, that's just unwelcome and off-putting.

He had that air of entitlement around him that some men have, as though they should get everything they want just because they want it. The universe doesn't work like that. When Imogen had first met Adrian, she assumed he was like that, but that wasn't him at all; it wasn't the women he slept with he didn't have any respect for, it was himself.

Still fuming from the things PC Jarvis said, Imogen went to find Adrian and reprimand him again for letting Jarvis anger him in that way. But the truth was, if he hadn't punched Jarvis, she probably would have.

# Chapter Thirty-Six

The car journey that afternoon was unusually quiet. Adrian stared intently at the road ahead as they made their way to the construction site that Corrigan was on. The traffic jam added to the tension in the car. Imogen had told Adrian what PC Jarvis had told her. That he had turned the camera off to intimidate Corrigan, and that Corrigan had doubled down and threatened him back. They were going to find out what Corrigan had to say about the incident. As it was a recorded police incident they could say it popped up as part of their investigation into Simon Glover and his contacts, hopefully minimising the risk to Angela Corrigan.

'Are we fighting?' Imogen said after twenty minutes of silence, arms folded.

'No. I've just got a headache,' he lied.

They weren't fighting, but he was annoyed. He didn't need to be babysat. He wasn't blowing this out of proportion. If Imogen had been the one who pulled Angela out of the river, then she might have been reacting in this way, too. Sometimes in the second before he woke, he saw Angela's bright blue eye swollen and surrounded in blood. He felt her hand on his ankle. That one moment would never leave him.

'You should follow my lead when we get there,' Imogen said.

'You don't trust me?'

'Corrigan's one of those people who finds people's buttons and pushes them. You've got more than a few buttons.'

'Thanks,' Adrian said.

'After what you did to Jarvis, I don't see how you can disagree with me.'

'I don't disagree. It would be nice if you had my back, though.'

'I do. Always. Please don't ever doubt that. This is me having your back. Who else is going to make sure you don't get yourself fired?'

'What's that supposed to mean?'

'It means you're a sensitive guy. That's one of the great things about you, but it's landed you in hot water more than once. If the DCI hears about what happened with Jarvis, you will get a serious bollocking. I'm not saying he didn't deserve it, either, but you can't just let people wind you up like that. You make it too easy for them. It's reckless and it's going to get you into shit with the DCI.

'Even bloody Jarvis had the sense to turn his camera off before threatening the guy. We just need to make sure we don't give Corrigan the rope to hang us with.'

Adrian thought about what she was saying and felt his perspective flip. She was right. If he carried on this way, then Corrigan would get off and they would be left dealing with career-altering disciplinary actions. Imogen was also right about Adrian having a lot of buttons to push. He did need to be smart about this, but could he? Probably not. He reached over and put his hand on Imogen's, squeezing hard. Imogen wasn't the enemy here.

'You're right. I'm sorry. I will get my shit together. I promise I will. Some things just get under your skin, you know?'

'I know.'

'I'll let you take the lead in this interview with Corrigan.'

'No. I'll see if I can get anything useful out of one of his employees or something. I'm now thinking maybe your seething hatred will keep Corrigan distracted. Divide and conquer and all that,' she said, smiling.

They pulled into the construction site and saw Corrigan standing with Chilton; he rolled his eyes when he saw them. Chilton was obviously one of Corrigan's confidants; maybe Chilton would be the path to breaking Corrigan.

Adrian got out of the car and walked over to the two men. Corrigan's smile broadened as they approached.

'Detective . . . Miles, wasn't it?' Reece said, not looking at Imogen once.

'Mr Corrigan,' Adrian replied.

'How can I help you?'

'We need to speak to you again about a couple of former employees of yours.'

'Come over to the office; it's a bit noisy out here.'

Imogen nodded to Adrian that he should go. Maybe he could distract Corrigan for long enough for Imogen to get something out of Chilton. He gave her the nod and then followed Reece into a Portakabin.

'Haven't we discussed this already? I told Ruby to send you over the personnel file. Beyond that, I don't know what else to tell you. I heard you have been asking around. I haven't seen those boys for a while.' Corrigan gestured for Adrian to sit in the chair opposite his desk.

'You were close with Glover.'

'Who told you that?'

'Quick did, just before he killed himself in front of us,' Adrian said, watching, waiting for Corrigan to react.

But he didn't; he was eerily calm for a man at the centre of a police investigation.

'That must have been quite upsetting. Did he tell you why he did it?'

'No. No, he didn't. I don't suppose you have any idea?' Adrian said.

'Sorry, no. I didn't know Leon that well.'

'But you knew Simon Glover.'

'I did. Nice guy. Really awful what happened to him. Do you know who did it?' Corrigan said, the tone of his voice suggesting he was playing some kind of game.

'What about the call your wife made to the police six weeks ago?'

'I don't know what you're talking about.'

'It was the one where you threatened a uniformed officer. Ringing any bells, now?'

'That was all a misunderstanding; my wife was just messing around. The matter is resolved.'

'Let's cut the shit, shall we? I don't believe a word that comes out of your mouth. I'm sure you have people around you who hang on everything you say, but they don't do it because they respect you. They do it because they are afraid of you. I have met plenty of men like you over the years and you're all the same,' Adrian said.

'I doubt you've met anyone like me.'

'That's what they all say. You think you're something special? You think you're untouchable? You're not. You'll get caught. You know why?'

'Why, Detective?' Corrigan smiled and leaned back in his chair, amused more than anything.

'Because you're complacent and you rely on other people to do your dirty work for you. Not only that, but you also don't understand that as soon as they all realise you're going down and they don't need to be afraid of you anymore, they'll talk. Once we find those people and get one of them to open up, it will be like dominoes. One by one, they will flip on you.'

'I don't know who you think I am, Detective Miles.'

'I think you're so insecure that you need to beat up your wife to feel like you matter, but you don't. You don't matter, Mr Corrigan.'

'Big words from a nobody. You should be careful how you speak to people, Detective Miles. I could contact your superior officer and tell him you're being unreasonable.'

'*Her*, and go ahead.'

The amused look had disappeared from Corrigan's face. His eyes had narrowed and he was studying Adrian, sizing him up. Adrian was well and truly in Corrigan's crosshairs now and in a way that's where he wanted to be. Much like when he was a kid, he now wanted to draw Corrigan's fire away from Angela. The same way he would anger his father to get his attention away from his mother.

Adrian stood. He was surprised by how familiar this feeling of satisfaction with himself was. It would probably seem strange to anyone who hadn't grown up the way Adrian had, but to him, this was a victory. Corrigan was gunning for him now and that was exactly the way Adrian wanted it.

# Chapter Thirty-Seven

Adrian was sitting in the incident room waiting for DCI Kapoor; she had asked him to meet her a few minutes before the briefing started. Getting in trouble came naturally to Adrian.

DCI Kapoor walked into the room and sat opposite Adrian.

'I'm sure you know what I am about to say to you, DS Miles.'

'Corrigan called you?'

'No, Corrigan's solicitor did. He said if you continue to harass his client then you will have to take the consequences.'

'So, investigating someone is considered harassment now, is it?'

'It's a fine line and it's not one I am sure you know how to walk.' She raised her eyebrow at him.

'Thanks.'

'Your instincts are rarely wrong, but that's not

enough. We have to follow the law. If we don't, the system breaks and then where would we be? That's a rhetorical question; you don't need to answer. You need to learn to colour inside the lines.'

'Corrigan is bad,' Adrian said. 'I pulled his wife's broken and bloodied body from the water; I watched his employee drive a knife into his own heart rather than speak out against him. What kind of man instils that kind of fear in people? Who else has he hurt? What other hideous things has he done?'

'Let's pull his life apart: legally, financially, any way we can. If he is doing something bad, we will find it. You are not a stupid man, Adrian. You must know that going at this all gung-ho isn't going to help. Every time you have done that before it's landed you in trouble. Learn from your mistakes.'

'I know. I'm sorry.'

'Don't make me regret trusting you,' Kapoor said.

Imogen, DI Walsh and Gary walked in. Gary linked his computer to the magic whiteboard display screen and started typing, pulling up reports too fast for anyone to read them. Imogen sat next to Adrian.

'I have some information,' Gary said.

'Don't keep us in suspense, Tunney,' DCI Kapoor said.

'Fiona Merton's DNA sample confirms that without doubt, the body recovered from the River Exe is in fact Simon Glover, so that's one question off the list. Forensics went through his flat and said that it was most likely the crime scene. They got no evidence from it, not even Glover's fingerprints, which is highly irregular. As you suggested, it's been cleaned, but the black light showed some trace blood in the creases of the laminate floor. Not enough to test, but enough to signify that it was there. After looking at Glover's financials we found that he removed all of his savings from the bank three days before we found him.'

'How much was that?' Adrian asked.

'Seventeen grand; he had been saving that since he was a teenager by the looks of it. Probably for a deposit on a place; his flat was rented.'

'Angela Corrigan said he was trying to help her. We didn't recover any money at the scene, so where do you think that might be?' DCI Kapoor said.

'Either whoever physically assaulted them took it, or Glover had it stashed somewhere,' DI Walsh said.

'Well, it wasn't in his flat. That place was cleaner than a hospital. Karen Bell said there was no trace DNA at all. Nothing. That's very difficult to achieve,' Gary said.

'Corrigan has swathes of employees and plenty of money to boot. We know he can get people to do what he wants. We also know that people are literally terrified of him. He has more than means – he also has plenty of opportunity. I think Glover's death was a message to anyone thinking about crossing him,' Adrian said.

'Or, specifically, anyone thinking about helping his wife,' Imogen said.

'Do you think you could speak to Angela Corrigan again, DS Miles and DS Grey? If you go when he is out, then a confrontation should be avoidable. He has already started to make some unpleasant noises about being investigated, so we need to tread carefully. I think if we keep pushing gently, we might be able to get her in to make a statement. We absolutely need to get her to cooperate. If we don't, then there is only one other way this ends and I don't think any of us want that. I've seen enough domestic assault cases that end with a dead wife to last a lifetime. Speak to her again before it gets to that; we have to keep trying. Gently is the key, though. She's scared and she doesn't trust us.'

'Thanks to PC Jarvis,' Adrian said.

'I looked at the BWV content and Jarvis did everything he was supposed to do,' DCI Kapoor said.

'And not a single thing more,' Adrian said. He wanted to tell the DCI that Jarvis had switched off the camera and dropped the matter, but you didn't win any points for grassing on your colleagues, especially without evidence.

'I also looked into Leon Quick,' Gary said. 'He had money saved up, too – more than Glover – and I spoke to his former landlady in Exeter, who said he was a model tenant. Always paid the rent on time, kept the place spotless, even did some odd jobs around the building for her. When he told her he was leaving, she offered him a reduction in rent to stay on. He told her his mother was gravely ill and he needed to be home with her.'

'Is his mother ill?' DCI Kapoor asked.

'Nope, she's fine. He lied. The landlady said he didn't even serve out his notice, but he paid until the end of the month of November. She said it was like he couldn't get away from the place fast enough. We know his motive for leaving wasn't financial, either, because he had some savings.'

'I cornered Jimmy Chilton for five minutes while DS Miles was speaking to Corrigan and I think he might be softening,' Imogen said. 'He didn't give me anything except the same old flannel, but there was something about his demeanour that was different. He confirmed Corrigan's alibi, so they are both covered. But I don't think we should cross him off as completely unhelpful just yet.'

'So, to summarise,' DCI Kapoor said. 'We have no idea why Simon Glover was killed, but we think it was because he helped Mrs Corrigan, who possibly may have been trying to escape her husband. Then we have Leon Quick, who, to all intents and purposes, took his own life to stop us from learning the truth about something that happened at that bloody construction company – except we have no idea of what it was or who was involved. Then, of course, we have Angela Corrigan herself, who is less than cooperative. Are you following me so far?'

They all nodded and a few murmured yeses lingered in the air.

'Our biggest problem is why. Saving Angela Corrigan is nice and all, but I just feel like there is more to it. Why do we think she went back to her husband?'

'She could be scared of him, or she might feel the lifestyle she's got used to isn't worth jeopardising,' Imogen said, raising her eyebrow.

'She genuinely seemed scared of him when we spoke

to her,' Adrian said, annoyed at what Imogen was implying.

'Unfortunately, your perception of the situation doesn't really matter, Detective Miles. We need evidence. We need sworn testimony. Hunches don't work in cases like this.'

'Yes, Ma'am,' Adrian said.

'Miles and Grey? Take another run at the wife, see if you can get her to open up about what's going on there. Tread carefully, please. DI Walsh, I would like you to coordinate with Tunney. Go through the construction company's financials and any public information that could be of use to the investigation. Feel free to delegate.'

'Thank you, Ma'am,' DI Walsh said.

'Let's get this bastard and let's make sure that once we have him, he is going nowhere. I have seen too many domestic abuse cases in my career where the victim goes back to the perpetrator, only to be found dead later down the line. Chop-chop.' DCI Kapoor clapped them into action.

Adrian got up and walked out, feeling a little personally attacked, as if everyone thought he couldn't hold his temper and be professional about this. Like he somehow needed a babysitter.

# Chapter Thirty-Eight

If there was one thing Imogen appreciated about Adrian, it was that he was an open book. She rarely had to try to guess what he was thinking; he didn't play games like that. He just came out and said what was on his mind.

His current brooding mood was frustrating for many reasons and she knew that this case was closer to the bone than most of the other ones they had been on. Whenever Adrian had talked about his past he would focus on his father's addiction and not the violence he witnessed as a result. It was only when cases like this came up, when there was male-on-female violence, that he ever really mentioned it. Not that he would need to, because it was written all over his face. He had no poker face; his emotions were always on display.

Today, however, she was getting the cold shoulder. He was annoyed with her about something – it was mild, but it was there. The fact that they were driving in silence was a clear indication that something was wrong.

'Have I upset you in some way?' Imogen said.

'What?' Adrian said.

'You just seem to be a little off with me.'

Imogen felt needy for even asking. This wasn't how they did things. They were upfront with each other, weren't they?

'Would you care if I was?' Adrian said, folding his arms.

'What the hell is that supposed to mean? Of course I would care.'

'It's nothing, anyway. My problem, I expect.'

'So, there is a problem?'

'It doesn't matter.'

'You think I'm going to drop it? You're wrong. Don't you know me at all? What is up with you?'

'Me?'

'I'm not the one with a cob on. Just tell me what the problem is,' Imogen persisted.

He wasn't going to get away with it this easy. She knew if she let it go then it would grow. They needed to talk about it right now.

'Just those snidey remarks you made about Angela Corrigan. I didn't like it.'

'Snidey remarks? What *are* you talking about?'

'Like how she's in it for the money and stuff like that.'

'It's our job to ask these questions. The woman hasn't made a complaint herself and we have to ask ourselves why. I am not passing judgement on her. I just wonder what her angle is, that's all.'

'Why does there have to be an angle? Maybe she's just scared.'

'Of course. Maybe she's not, though. We just have to keep an open mind and investigate the facts without speculating as to why or who is doing what and for what reason. It is literally our job to find enough evidence to take this to court, where someone else can make the big, complicated decisions on morality and intent.'

'It's funny how you are the only one asking those questions, though,' Adrian scoffed.

'Well, I like to think I am thorough.'

She smiled, but he wasn't paying attention, still annoyed. There was a heaviness in the air – something bad was going to happen. They were headed for a fight, she could tell.

# Chapter Thirty-Nine

Adrian hung back and let Imogen take the lead at the Corrigan house, to prove that she was wrong about what was going on with him. To prove that he could keep his cool, that he wasn't hell-bent on some kind of latent transferred revenge.

When they knocked on the door and Corrigan himself answered, despite his car being missing from the driveway, Adrian felt the rage rise in him almost instantly. Maybe he couldn't keep his cool, after all.

'Look, Detective, I don't want any trouble,' Corrigan said.

'Then cooperate with our enquiries, Mr Corrigan,' Imogen said.

'I've told you what you wanted to know. I don't have anything to do with those dead men. I gave you my alibi and I assume the people whose names my receptionist sent you corroborated my whereabouts. You might want to check someone else out for a change,' he said, turning to Adrian. 'I know your girlfriend has a hard-on for me, but I didn't do what I'm being accused of.'

Adrian ignored his pathetic attempt to rile him.

'Your sudden change in attitude isn't fooling anyone,' Imogen said. 'No point acting all affronted now.'

Angela's car pulled into the driveway – the brand-new white hybrid Lexus. Adrian noticed Reece shooting an annoyed look at his wife as she stepped out of the car. She was immaculate, as usual: crisp white silk blouse, a calf-length black pencil skirt and red patent kitten heels. Her hair was a more vibrant golden blonde than the last time they had seen it. Where she normally had her loose barrel curls hanging around her face, today they were pulled into a loose updo.

There was something else Adrian noticed as she stepped out of the car. Despite the weather being decidedly grey today, she was wearing sunglasses. He knew he should just walk away now. The anger that had yet to abate stoked inside of him again. He really didn't want to prove Imogen right about his inability to keep his emotions under control.

They had already been warned about Reece Corrigan. The fact that they had already questioned him and were likely to do so again had obviously not deterred him from hurting his wife. Adrian remembered the police visiting his own childhood home – a verbal warning and then nothing. He thought things had moved on since then. Obviously not.

Adrian clenched and unclenched his fist as Angela approached. He noticed Reece's jaw straining under the pressure as he tried to mask his annoyance at his wife.

She was carrying shopping bags from some of the pricier shops in town. Retail therapy. Maybe Imogen was right and this was just a price Angela was willing to pay – the smile on her face was a convincing mask. It's not impossible that the negative aspect was just a trade-off for this life of privilege. His mother put up with a lot more for a hell of a lot less.

'Mrs Corrigan,' Adrian said as she went to pass them.

'Can I just put these bags inside?' she said, clearly hoping that she would have been able to avoid this confrontation altogether.

'Of course,' Adrian said, moving forwards a little, edging Imogen out of the way, rigid with anger at Reece.

Who the hell did he think he was? Adrian's eyes were fixed on Reece's now. He could feel Imogen tap him on the back of the arm, trying to remind him where he was, who he was. It was too late for that.

It wasn't as though Adrian had never been called out on a domestic abuse call before, of course he had. There was something about Reece Corrigan, though – something so entitled. He had no intention of ever stopping. Adrian wondered if he even bothered pretending to be sorry afterwards.

Angela reappeared at the door. Smiling through gritted teeth.

'Detectives.'

'Would you take those glasses off for us, Mrs Corrigan,' Adrian said, never once breaking eye contact with Reece.

She slowly pulled the glasses off and Adrian looked over.

'It's not what you think. I was in the gym and—' Angela said unconvincingly.

'Save it, love,' Reece said, annoyed that she was trying to cover it up.

He would have been annoyed no matter what she had done. He didn't need a reason.

'If you feel as though you are in danger, we can take you with us now,' Imogen said.

'Danger? Don't be silly! This was an accident,' she said, trying to laugh it off.

Reece rolled his eyes, exasperated, annoyed that Angela was even there. Angela Corrigan was the only one invested in trying to keep up the pretence that he hadn't done this. She had the most to lose.

'Mrs Corrigan, if you make a formal complaint, we can arrest your husband,' Imogen said.

'No. I won't. This wasn't Reece. You need to leave us alone,' she implored.

Adrian pulled out a business card and handed it to Angela, who took it reluctantly. He could see that she was resolute and he had a decision to make. He could either lay Reece out now with a swift punch, or they could step away and come back when Angela was alone. He knew which one he would rather do, but in the long run that helped no one but Corrigan. They were powerless. There was nothing to do now but walk away.

'Call me if you need anything. Any issue at all,' Adrian smiled.

'Mr Corrigan.' Imogen nodded and tugged on Adrian's elbow.

Adrian stepped away from the house and walked

back to the car, getting in the passenger seat. The anger coursed through him with force.

Imogen started the car and they drove out of the street. He watched Reece slowly close the door as they pulled out of sight and turned the corner. Corrigan was waiting until they were totally gone before dealing with Angela.

'Pull the car over,' Adrian said.

'What is it now?' Imogen said.

'We wait ten minutes and then go back.'

'We'll get done for harassment at this rate, Adrian. We've already been warned,' Imogen said.

Adrian folded his arms and leaned back in the seat, waiting for the ten minutes to pass. That should be enough time. Corrigan wasn't a measured man. He was angry when they had left the house and so it was only a matter of time, a short amount of time, before he punished his wife, Angela.

Adrian could feel Imogen's eyes burning into him as he stared ahead. How could she ever understand this? Maybe she was right and he was taking it a bit too personally, but he didn't feel like he had a choice. He couldn't leave Angela to the mercy of her husband. An image of her tangled in the riverbank flashed in his memory.

'Is this about her?' Imogen asked.

'What?'

'We've been on cases like this before, domestic abuse cases, and I've never seen you so angry. What is it about Angela that has you so riled? Is it because she's young and pretty?' Imogen said.

'What are you saying? Do you think I fancy her? Are you actually jealous?' Adrian said incredulously.

'She's beautiful. I wouldn't blame you if you did,' Imogen said.

'Please, no. She needs our help, that's all. I don't know about you, but she's the first person I've pulled half dead out of the river. I'm genuinely offended that you would think that of me,' Adrian said.

'I just don't understand. You punched Constable Jarvis and now we are waiting here, why? So you can catch him in the act?'

'Whatever gets the job done. This won't stop; this kind of behaviour doesn't stop. *We* need to stop it. Angela will keep making excuses for him and he will keep getting away with it.'

'I've just never seen you like this. Does she remind you of your mum or something?'

'So first I fancy her, now she reminds me of my mum? Come on, Grey. Give me a little credit. Yes, she is young. She deserves a better life than this, don't you think? I don't really appreciate the implication that I have some ulterior motive here.'

He nodded at her to start the car. She did without question and pulled the car into a U-turn, heading back to the Corrigan house.

Adrian's rage was only magnified by Imogen's remarks. Not letting criminals like this go unpunished should be top of their list. There was a huge correlation with domestic abusers going on to commit other, more serious crimes. In America, many of the mass shootings were committed by men who had previously been brought in on domestic abuse charges. Something about the mentality of a person who would beat someone physically weaker than them on a regular basis was dangerous and not limited just to beating up their wives. As Simon Glover could attest.

'I don't want to argue. I know this must be hard for you, but you can't behave like this. Let's at least drive round the back so we can see if anything is going on inside.'

'Fine,' Adrian said, aware that every second they delayed was maybe a second Angela didn't have.

As they drove past the Corrigan house via the back road it looked empty. They must have been in the one of the rooms not visible from this aspect. Imogen let out a frustrated sigh.

'You don't have to be a part of it if you don't want. Drop me off here and I'll walk the rest of the way.'

'Don't be ridiculous!' She turned into the street where the Corrigans lived. 'Just don't do anything stupid.'

Imogen stopped the car and Adrian jumped out. He walked towards the door and put his ear to the glass panel to see if he could hear anything inside. There was some shouting, followed by the muffled pleading of Angela. He looked in through the lounge window, but he couldn't see anything. He had to make a decision.

'Call it in. I can hear a domestic disturbance and fear that there is an attack taking place inside the house,' he said to Imogen, who was approaching the house. 'I'm going in.'

'Be careful,' Imogen said.

Adrian picked a rock from the path and smashed the

window on the front door. He reached inside and flipped the latch to let himself in. He threw the rock back down and slowly walked into the house. The arguing was coming from the back. He heard something smash and rushed forwards.

Angela was on the floor, surrounded by smashed crockery, her hand covered in blood. If Adrian was going to guess, he would say she was thrown against the dresser. She was crying. Reece looked up, shocked to see Adrian in his kitchen. Before he had a chance to speak, Adrian swung hard at him, the flat of his fist connecting with Corrigan's jaw.

Reece was a big man and while the punch stunned him, it didn't take him out; nor did it stop him. He turned around and punched Adrian in the side. Adrian jumped back in time to lessen the impact, but he felt his ribs jar all the same.

They both swung at each other again. Imogen rushed in and helped Angela into a chair. Reece grabbed Adrian by the hair.

'Who the fuck do you think you are?' He smacked Adrian's face into the counter.

'I could say the same to you. Never mind assaulting your wife, assaulting a police officer? That's not going to look so good, is it?' Adrian said, running his hand across his nose, checking for blood.

'I'll have your job for this,' Reece hissed.

'We've got you, Corrigan, just remember that,' Adrian said, smiling through bloodied teeth.

If there was one way to upset a man like Corrigan, it was to belittle him in some way. Corrigan was tough, though; he didn't seem to rile easily. Unless you were married to him.

'We'll see. I've come up against bigger and badder men than you, Detective. You'll live to regret the day you ever met me. I'll see to that.'

The police sirens outside got louder and two officers burst in, wrestling Reece to the ground on his front. Adrian's chest was heaving; he wasn't done. He wanted to punch the man a couple more times. He looked over to Imogen, who wore a mixture of concern and anger.

'You won't be able to hold him,' Angela said through tears.

'The paramedic will be here in a moment to take care of your hand.'

As Imogen said it, the paramedics walked into the kitchen.

'What's your name, love?' the paramedic said to Angela.

Imogen smiled and let them take over from her. She walked towards Adrian.

'Are you OK?' Imogen asked Adrian, not so much concerned as annoyed.

'Yes,' Adrian said, coming out of the moment and realising that he had just done some real damage to their case and probably not helped Angela in the process. Whatever they saw, whatever happened, could be explained away. It wasn't enough.

'Outside!' Imogen said then stormed out.

Adrian followed her, aware that he was about to get a grilling. He deserved it.

Outside, Reece was being bundled into the back of

the police car after being read his rights. Imogen put her hands on her hips and stared at Adrian.

'Don't look at me like that,' he said.

'What the fuck were you thinking? You can't just smash your way into someone's house without cause.'

'We both knew what was happening in there.'

'Well, I hate to say it, but you were lucky you were right. Still, I can't see this sticking, can you? We know he's got a good lawyer. You're going to come out of this one looking like a twat.'

'So, we just let it happen?'

'We do our jobs. Did you even announce yourself as you walked in? He could argue that he thought you were an intruder and hit out at you.'

'He knows who I am,' Adrian said.

'His lawyer will get him out. You can't just steam in. That's why there are rules, so that these bastards can't get off on a technicality. Not to mention the weight you have given to any claims he might make of harassment, now.'

'I suppose you think Jarvis was right, too?'

'He followed procedure, that's what he is supposed to do. Of course, I don't think he was right, but he wasn't technically wrong, either.'

'Maybe he can stand by while this shit happens, but I can't.'

'Yeah, well if Angela's body is the next one to turn up then that's on you! You probably just got her killed.'

Imogen's words hit him like a fist, as they were supposed to. He could see the regret on her face instantly; she knew she had crossed a line. This conversation was over, all evening plans cancelled. He needed some time to cool off before he responded in kind; he had enough to say something equally damaging, but who would that help? Some time alone was what he needed.

'I'll catch a ride back after I've seen the medic,' he said flatly, his voice emotionless.

'Adrian. Come on, I didn't mean that.'

He walked away without looking back and made his way over to the paramedic, who was just finishing with Angela's hand. When he looked back, Imogen was pulling away from the scene, so he pulled out his phone and called the DCI.

'DS Miles?' Kapoor answered.

'I was in an altercation with Reece Corrigan; I'm going to get checked out by a paramedic and then I'll head home, if that's all right? I'm sure Imogen will fill you in on what happened. I'll complete a report in the morning.'

'Are you OK?'

'Yes, we caught him beating his wife and you can imagine the rest.'

'Is Imogen all right?'

'She's fine. I'm fine, too, but I took a couple of punches.'

'We'll see you bright and early tomorrow, then. I look forward to hearing your explanation for what happened today. It better be a good one.'

'Of course.'

She hung up the phone before he did. He couldn't face going back to the station and sitting opposite Imogen for the next hour. His nose had stopped bleeding, but he waited to see the paramedic anyway, in case anyone asked. After that he was going out. He needed some time alone.

This relationship with Imogen was intense because they saw each other all the time. Nothing had changed in the way they worked together; nothing had changed in the things they said to each other. The only difference was the fact that there was more to lose now, so throwaway comments had a little more weight. They were still learning how to have everything. Maybe it wasn't possible.

# Chapter Forty

I told those police detectives to leave it alone but
they just won't. I know it's not that simple, I know
they can't just walk away from a murder investigation,
but still. I wish they would go away and leave us
alone; they have no idea how hard they are making
things.

I am sitting in the car a few hundred metres from
my house. I can see the two detectives outside my
door talking to R. I look in the mirror and see the
remnants of a very obvious shiner. The make-up I put
on was pointless, as my eye is still swollen from earlier
today.

We had a fight this morning. I ruined a shirt he liked
and so he sent me to the shops to get another one, but
not before cuffing me first. He has a million shirts – he
certainly didn't need a new one. It was more about
making me feel awkward and having to lie about my
injury to shop assistants, almost daring anyone to do

*anything about it. As if anyone believes any of those lies, anyway. I search my handbag for my shades and put them on before starting the engine and going to the house.*

*When I get out of the car, I pick up the shopping bags and go straight into the house. Maybe they won't stop me to talk, but of course they do. I feel even worse about the situation as I watch Adrian Miles get angry. His partner steps in the way a little and somehow that holds him back. I can see this is personal for him. I guess he had a similar upbringing. He's not protecting me so much as someone else, someone from his past – a mother, probably. I know how that feels. Every day I am grateful for the fact that I haven't fallen pregnant, yet.*

*The officers ask me what happened and I lie but it's pointless – everyone knows the truth. I can tell R is annoyed at me for coming home at that moment, but it doesn't matter. He would have found something else to be annoyed at me about if it wasn't that. He just woke up in one of those moods today. Sometimes it's as simple as that.*

*I go to the kitchen and drink a couple of mouthfuls of gin before he gets here; I know what will happen when he does. I'll just wait here.*

*When he comes back in he starts to taunt me about the detectives, asks me if I have spoken to them about him. I tell him I haven't, why would I? He gets his phone out and shows me the video of Adrian rescuing me from the river and asks me if I told them about him.*

I explain that they would have come sooner if I had told them, they would have asked him directly about it. No answer is good enough. He asks me if anything happened between DS Adrian Miles and me and I say no, how could it? I was barely conscious when he found me. He knows the real answers to all of the questions he is asking. This isn't about me, this isn't about the detective, this is about R making me squirm.

I flash back to the night of the attack again as he is talking to me. This time it feels more complete, not just a snapshot. I remember him asking me if Simon and I had fucked. I remember telling him no and then I remember him pounding Simon every time I said no. There was nothing else to say, if I had said yes then he would have killed him on the spot. I shudder at the thought of remembering anything else from that night, knowing that for me to block it out it must be so much worse.

Back in the present, he tells me that I need to make the police go away. He grabs me by the shoulders and whispers. I feel his breath on me and I recoil. He throws me backwards until I collide with the dresser. Something cuts my hand. I feel the sharpness followed by the familiar feeling of blood leaving my body. I fall to the ground and look at my hand. I remember that night again, another fragment of information to build on. I'm in the back of a van, Simon is lying next to me and I can't wake him. It's dark and I am afraid.

I am pulled back into the present by shouting. DS Miles is swinging for R and a silent cheer erupts in my

# Chapter Forty-One

At her flat, Imogen tried to call Adrian. It had been a couple of hours since she drove off and left him licking his wounds at the Corrigan house. He wasn't answering his phone. She had gone back to work and filed her report alone. Telling the truth but putting Adrian in a more favourable light than maybe he deserved. She guessed he was probably sulking in a pub somewhere. Maybe she should just find him and apologise again, or maybe she just needed to give him some space.

In the meantime, she went home. She pulled her hair into a bun so tight it pinched at her temples, a punishment for letting her mouth run away with her, for falling into Adrian's trap. He had been spoiling for a fight; it was his preferred method of escapism.

Grabbing a pair of rubber gloves, she filled a bucket with hot water and bleach before making her way into the bathroom. He wouldn't still be angry about it in the morning, would he? They had fallen out before, of course, but never over something so personal; usually it was just disagreements at work, or what to eat for dinner. This felt more serious, somehow. Some things stick and no matter how many times you say sorry, you would be better off if you had never said them in the first place. Once they are out there, it's impossible to put them back in their box, back in your mind where they should have stayed.

Her modest flat felt neglected. Since they had fully embraced the idea that they were a couple, she spent more time at Adrian's house; it was bigger and he liked to be where his son could find him. Not that Tom knew about them yet.

As she scrubbed the tiles in the bathroom, she felt a rising panic that this was the end of them, that he would disappear and she would never see him again if he didn't call her this evening. Abandonment had always been in the background of any relationship Imogen had ever had. Residual anxiety from growing up without a father.

She thought about her ex-boyfriend, Dean, and how he had left her. How if she called him, he would answer. He always answered. Their relationship had been doomed from the start. He was fresh out of prison and she was a police officer when they first got together. The reality of the relationship set in and they accepted that neither one of them could change, so they broke up. The only way to stay apart was not to contact each other or the pull would be too much.

It's not that she wanted to be with him more than she wanted to be with Adrian; it's just that they had a connection that was hard to ignore. Dean and Adrian were so different and yet she'd loved them both. They both made her feel like a completely different person when she was with them. Adrian made her feel normal and quieted the storm inside her. He was a calming person, because he was so totally at ease with himself, which somehow transferred to her.

Then there was Dean, who was the complete opposite. He'd made her buzz with confusion, but there was something about his survival instinct that made her feel completely safe, as though he could protect her from anything. He could take the world on so she wouldn't have to. Those feelings Dean gave her were nice to begin with but exhausting after a while. She entirely preferred the feeling she had when she was with Adrian.

The overpowering smell of bleach forced her to pull away from the floor. She raised her arm and covered her mouth for a moment, breathless, her eyes stinging from the fumes. She should open the window.

Why was she even thinking about Dean? He hadn't contacted her and she knew he wouldn't unless she asked him to first. The only thing that had changed with their circumstances was that she had Adrian now and that was an added reason to keep Dean at a distance. She knew that Adrian had his insecurities about Dean and maybe he was right. But she did find her mind drifting to what could have been every now and again. Not that she wanted it, but every relationship she managed to get into was fraught with complications that were insurmountable without some kind of life change.

This wasn't about Dean, though; she wanted to speak to Adrian. The idea that she had upset him made her feel uneasy; she didn't want to be the source of his pain. Not to mention the fact that it was probable that right now he was on some kind of bender, where more than likely he was talking his way into a punch in the face. It was a habit of Adrian's that Imogen couldn't get her head around. A throwback to his teens, from what she could ascertain, more than likely to do with the fact that he had felt a sense of achievement when he managed to goad his father away from hurting his mother and hitting him instead.

She felt like such a bitch for not being able to understand the draw the Corrigan investigation had for him. Besides which, that wasn't her job. Her job was to make sure the bad guys went to prison.

Confident that she had scrubbed every inch and happy that she had suffered enough, she pulled her rubber gloves off, pulled her phone out of her pocket again and pressed the A icon on the screen. It rang and rang. *Answer the damn phone.*

# Chapter Forty-Two

In the pub, Adrian sat alone at the bar. A group of guys chanted at the TV as the football came to an end. The bar was rammed with men in blue shirts. Chelsea had won at home and so there was much celebrating from a load of men who had probably never set foot inside the London borough. He ordered another Jack and Coke before going back to observing the rabble.

He picked up his phone and looked at the screen: no messages from Imogen, just a couple of missed calls. He felt guilty for storming off, but not guilty enough to apologise. He didn't want to speak to her right now. He needed this time alone, but he had a knot in his stomach from earlier, a bad feeling. He hated arguing with Imogen and hated the fact that he had made her feel like she had done something wrong. They were both at fault here.

He knew he was feeling sorry for himself without

good reason. As usual, he was hardly blameless. Either way, he couldn't face that conversation tonight; it could wait until the morning.

He welcomed the feeling of light-headedness the drink gave him, but it wasn't enough – he wanted to be drunk, to stop thinking altogether.

He ordered two more drinks and looked at the clock. The bar was open until two in the morning. He had a good four hours drinking left; he could do some real damage in that time. He felt like people were looking at him, judging him for being alone. He wasn't sure exactly who he was rebelling against. Adrian had always struggled with being told what to do, even when it was himself doing the telling.

Over time, the pub emptied of football fans and filled with other revellers, either on their way to or from elsewhere. The music from the jukebox got louder and the corner nearest the toilets turned into an impromptu dance floor. It was a fairly central pub, so the clientele largely consisted of people passing through.

By midnight, Adrian had had enough. Tempted as he was to be the last person in the place, he had work in the morning and should probably sleep it off.

His phone buzzed again in his pocket, but he wouldn't answer it now; he was too drunk not to say what he was thinking and he knew he wouldn't be thinking it forever, so better to avoid saying it. For once, he was going to be sensible and wait until he had a chance to calm down before he did any permanent damage to their relationship. Imogen was too important to have this disagreement with. He had also lost count of how much he had drunk, but he was way past merry. After polishing off the dregs of what was left in his tumbler, Adrian left.

The streets were quiet, almost eerie. Considering how busy the pub had been, Adrian expected more people to be out, but owing to that pub's late licence, most of the other bars in this area were already closed and any other people had moved on to the nightclubs, none of which were situated in this part of town. He walked down the hill towards St Thomas. It was a brisk fifteen-minute walk to his house and he had done it a thousand times or more. After the few people he saw on the lower part of Fore Street, the road ahead emptied with barely even a passing car.

Even through his drunken haze, Adrian's instincts were sharp. Something was wrong; he wasn't alone. Walking faster, he crossed the roundabout with ease, as there wasn't even a car on the road. The silence was noticeable. Almost suffocating. There was an apocalyptic atmosphere, where anything could happen.

He kept his eyes ahead, looking for the St Thomas the Apostle church tower in the distance, which meant he was getting close to home. He approached the railway bridge on Cowick Street and heard the sound of a bottle being kicked somewhere behind him.

'Who's there?' Adrian said, pausing for a moment.

Silence.

The red brick railway passage in front of him was like the entrance to another world, so close and yet so far. The archway was pitch-black. He could feel

191

danger now. His skin prickled and his hairs stood on end.

Adrian picked up the pace and started to jog towards the railway arch. He could hear footsteps, running faster than him, but couldn't tell if they were in front or behind him. Had someone followed him from the pub? He hadn't noticed anyone watching him, but then again, he hadn't really been paying attention.

Wishing he wasn't so drunk, he kept moving forwards. The surge of adrenaline was sobering.

But there was still someone there with him; they were closer than before. The feeling inside that he had written off as paranoia earlier that evening was growing in intensity. He remembered an experiment he once read about that proved you could tell when someone was looking at you, an inbuilt instinct called a gaze detection system, largely to do with survival or attraction. Right now, Adrian knew that someone was looking at him. He was a target.

There was something wrong. The streetlights on the other side of the passage weren't working; it was darker on that side than it was on his. Someone must have smashed them. He wished he had the strength and stamina that Imogen had when it came to running. She was a machine. He kept meaning to do more, to try harder. He was fit, but running for a long time took a set of skills that Adrian didn't have. He would start tomorrow. Always tomorrow.

Sucking in a big gulp of air before entering the passage, which was barely fifty feet long, Adrian sped up and ran full pelt. If he could get to the streetlights, he would feel safer.

Before he knew it, he was out the other side of the passage. Just as his body untensed, he felt something swipe hard across the back of his head. A fist. He fell to the ground.

# Chapter Forty-Three

Imogen pounded on Adrian's door. There was no answer. She looked around and saw that his car was parked a little further up the road. It was gone midnight, but she couldn't sleep. She didn't want to be one of those girl-friends who couldn't spend a night away from her man, but at the same time, she didn't want to leave it the way it was.

She had scrubbed her kitchen and bathroom until they looked practically new again and then she had hopped in the shower. After drying her hair and jumping in bed, she accepted that she couldn't just go to sleep. She at least needed to try to speak to Adrian again. Her mother had always said that you should never go to sleep on an argument. It was strange which pieces of advice stuck.

He wasn't answering, so she decided paying him a visit was the only way. Wherever he was, it was just a walk away. She could take a punt and try a few pubs, find him and tell him again that she was sorry. She hated the way she was feeling. She felt like a bitch.

Usually that would come with some implied victory, but this was not deliberate – she didn't play games with Adrian; there were no points to be won by upsetting him. Why couldn't he stay in and binge-watch TV like everyone else did when they were pissed off?

She could probably get into Adrian's place through the back if she wanted to, but he wasn't at home and so there was no point. She looked at her phone again, but there had been no activity. *This is bullshit*. She was going to save herself the humiliation of ringing him again just to have her call ignored.

She didn't understand his need for conflict. She could go to a pub if she wanted, flirt with some guy and get into some kind of disagreement with his girlfriend who she could pretend she hadn't seen before, knowing full well that it was never about the flirting, more about the fight afterwards. There were worse ways to blow off steam, she supposed, but it wasn't something she could ever imagine herself doing to relieve stress. For Adrian, it seemed to be the only way.

She got back into her car after a few minutes of waiting for him to turn the corner and walk towards her with his cheesy smile, telling her he was happy to see her and all was forgiven. The same when she pulled out of his street – she just expected Adrian to be walking right there. He wasn't.

That familiar feeling of anger mixed with dread settled inside her. Anger that he was ignoring her, out somewhere getting drunk, mixed with the fear that the reason he wasn't in touch was because he was lying dead somewhere. *Try not to overreact.* Imogen drove back to her flat; she would deal with Adrian in the morning.

# Chapter Forty-Four

Dazed from the blow to the head, Adrian tried to get to his feet. It was so dark. There was a man there, but Adrian couldn't make his face out. As Adrian tried to pull himself up, the man kicked him, hard. He kicked Adrian again. A steel-toed boot crashed into Adrian's rib and he screamed out in pain.

'Shut up, pig,' the man hissed.

This wasn't random, Adrian realised. He knew Adrian was a police officer. Did Adrian recognise the voice? Had the man seen that little video clip of him rescuing Angela Corrigan online? Is that how he knew he was police?

The man grabbed Adrian by the collar and punched him in the face before spitting at him. Adrian felt warm, wet saliva on his face, mixed with his own blood from where his face had hit the pavement. He was dazed. His nose, taking the brunt of the impact and still sore from earlier where Corrigan had smashed it into the kitchen counter, was starting to swell.

Still holding Adrian's collar, the man pulled Adrian towards the foot of the concrete stairs that led up to the Exeter St Thomas station platform. Parked next to the bottom of the stairs was a white van with the side door open.

The man heaved Adrian inside before jumping in himself. There was another man in the driver's seat and small light overhead, which he turned off as he started the engine. The van was dark inside; all Adrian could see were shadows.

'You're both making a huge mistake.'

'I told you to shut up.' The man hit him again.

'What is it you want?' Adrian could taste blood in his mouth.

'I told you not to fucking speak.'

Adrian felt fabric go into his mouth to shut him up. He wasn't sure what it was, but it wasn't clean; it was dusty and tasted of chemicals and grease. Adrian went to pull the fabric from his mouth and the man punched him in the ribs, a sharp pain shooting through him as the bones fractured. Breathing was difficult. His nose had swollen and without his mouth, he had to really concentrate on not panicking and making things worse.

The man reached inside Adrian's pockets and pulled out the contents – money, phone, keys, ID, everything – making Adrian feel even more vulnerable than before. Was he going to kill him and dump his body somewhere?

The man flipped Adrian over, so his face was pushed into the cold, hard van floor, and his knee pressed into Adrian's back, making it even harder to get air into his lungs. As they drove past streetlights, the van lit up every couple of seconds. Adrian strained to see who had taken him, but his head was firmly pressed against the cold, dirty floor. Surely if they wanted him dead, they would have done it already.

Adrian's head was thumping. The man in the back was bigger and stronger than him; Adrian hadn't even managed to get a punch in at all. He really wished he hadn't had those last three drinks.

As the road smoothed out, the lights got less frequent. They were heading out of town.

The man took his knee off Adrian's back. The road beneath them became rougher and so Adrian assumed they had left the city completely. He could tell from the movements in the van that they were on less developed terrain, windier roads, maybe one of the smaller towns outside Exeter.

What did they want from him? The man in front just seemed to be the driver. It was the man in the back with Adrian who was in charge.

Without warning, the man yanked at Adrian's trousers until they were around his knees and then his ankles. What was going on? The dread deepened as the reality of the situation hit Adrian. *Oh God, no.*

The man climbed on top of Adrian so that his knees forced Adrian's legs apart. Adrian's confusion was beginning to clear. This wasn't a mugging. Adrian tried to scream, but the rag in his mouth muffled it to the point where it probably couldn't even be heard inside the van, let alone any further away. Adrian was completely paralysed. He couldn't even distinguish what he was feeling as fear; it felt so much bigger.

The sound of the engine was loud and Adrian couldn't hear anything beyond that. The man's head was directly above his, his hands on the ground either side. Adrian focused on the man's chunky wrists to commit them to memory – he was white, that's all Adrian could ascertain at this point. He knew what was coming next.

The crushing weight of the man on top of him did nothing to mask the pain as he forced himself inside. Adrian clutched onto the edge of the van floor near the door; there was a lip leading to a step. He could feel his knuckles going white as he held on. With each thrust he felt his body breaking, the wetness on his legs merely confirming that he could smell blood in the air.

'What the fuck are you doing back there?' the man in the driver's seat shouted.

'Just keep driving!' Adrian heard the man shout, his spit landing on Adrian's face. 'I need to teach this pig a lesson.'

Sober enough, Adrian lay lifeless as the man continued, thrusting so hard it was pushing Adrian's head into the back of the van's front seats. He couldn't fight back, couldn't do anything. Even though it hurt a lot, that was nothing compared with the humiliation Adrian was feeling right now. He wished he was dead; Adrian had never wished that before, not really. He could never have imagined feeling that way until this moment. Not existing would be great right about now.

The man climbed off and lit a cigarette when he was done. Adrian was frozen still. He was cold and he could feel liquid on his skin at the top of his thighs; he didn't know if it was blood or semen. For now, he had to concentrate on breathing. He pushed his tongue against the dry rag in his mouth until it was out. It was still dark and as long as Adrian didn't make a sound, the man wouldn't know the rag was gone.

Adrian sucked in the foul air as quietly as he could, still motionless and face down on the floor of the van. He heard a can open and the sound of the man drinking, the faintest smell of strong, cheap beer in the air. He wanted to leave, to get out and run, but he couldn't. He couldn't do anything; he was completely immobile. Out of all his police training, nothing could have prepared him for this.

After what felt like an eternity, the man pulled Adrian by his ankles backwards, so his head wasn't mashed into the front seats anymore.

'Ready to go again?'

'Please, don't.'

Adrian choked on the words. The man probably didn't hear him, not that it would have made a difference.

The man moved Adrian onto his side and reached between his legs. Adrian's throat was sore. He hadn't realised he was crying and trying to hold it back. He knew this wasn't his fault, he knew it. He had said the same things a million times to victims who had recounted their attacks to him. He had been sympathetic and understanding. He thought he *did* understand. But right now, in this moment, he knew he didn't have a clue.

He should fight back. He shouldn't be aroused physically and even though he knew it was a physiological response, he was still disgusted with himself because he was hard. He tried to think about anything that would stop him from climaxing, but he couldn't. He let out a cry as he finished.

'You think you're above it all, don't you? Well, you're not so clever now, are you?' the man said right into his ear.

Adrian didn't recognise his voice. How could Adrian have driven someone to this and have no idea who it was?

Adrian sobbed into floor of the van, the weight of the man on top of him restricting the amount of air he could take in. The man kept talking, but Adrian couldn't hear him anymore. He just focused on not being here. Whatever was happening inside this van, it wasn't happening to him. He lost all sense of time. He couldn't tell if he had lost consciousness or not, but time seemed to be jumping forwards, as though he were blacking out in between.

The van kept moving and the man only seemed to stop to smoke. They drove through a few small towns; Adrian could tell by the way the van slowed sometimes and the streetlights were different. They paused at traffic lights and he wanted to make a move, do anything.

Paralysed with pain and fear, he just lay there. He hated himself for not moving. It was a small consolation knowing that the man clearly had no plans to kill him; though he wasn't sure he wanted to live through this. Adrian knew from his years of experience working on the force that this was a life changer; there was no amount of counselling, no amount of therapy that would ever make him OK again. He would never be that same person he was a few hours ago – that Adrian was gone.

'Where are you taking me?' Adrian called, wondering what could possibly be next.

The man flipped him over. Adrian still couldn't see his face. Nothing about him was familiar and it should have been – this was obviously personal.

The man put his dirty fingers in Adrian's mouth as far as he could. Adrian gagged and threw up, his vomit spilling out from the sides of his mouth and down his cheeks onto the floor beneath him. He drew his knees up to try to shield himself as the occasional streetlight illuminated the inside of the van and he felt even more vulnerable than before.

The taste of vomit was sour and unpleasant. Adrian pushed as much from his mouth as he could, aware of the hand pushing on his neck. The regurgitated whisky and syrupy Coke had pooled under his head. He tried not to think about was happening inside the van. The man let go of Adrian's throat and sat back, allowing Adrian to curl into a ball.

The man then left Adrian alone and after a few minutes, the van stopped. The door opened and the man jumped out before pulling Adrian out until his half-naked body smacked against the cold, hard concrete. He lay there for a moment, wondering what was next. The engine started and the van door slid shut before they pulled away. Adrian was alone again.

Silence descended. Adrian pulled on his trousers and looked around; it took a few moments for his eyes to adjust to the light. He looked up and saw the familiar sight of his front door. The man had dropped him to his house. They knew where he lived. Just like they had known where to grab him from and how they had known he was a police officer.

Bumping into them hadn't been an accident. There was no way this was a random attack. His phone, keys and wallet were on the ground next to him. He grabbed them and got onto all fours before standing. He looked at the time on his phone: half past five in the morning. Stumbling over to the side of the road, he threw up into the drain before staggering towards the house. He negotiated the lock as quickly as his trembling hands would allow and almost fell inside, slamming the door behind him and curling into a ball again.

# Chapter Forty-Five

All Adrian wanted to do was climb into the shower and wash himself clean, inside and out. The police officer inside him knew he needed to preserve the evidence, but his overriding thought was that no one must ever know about this. He walked into each room and methodically put all the lights on; he couldn't stand this darkness, even though dawn was breaking.

Adrian went into the bathroom and shivered as he undressed, wanting to be rid of those clothes but not wanting to be naked at the same time. He put his clothes into a bin bag that he had brought upstairs with him. There was so much blood. He didn't know what he was going to do. In terms of reporting it, he couldn't. He wanted to erase himself completely. Telling someone would mean saying it out loud. Reporting it would mean talking about it over and over again. No. Aside from the shame and humiliation of having people know what had happened to him, he was a police officer. He was supposed to keep people safe. How would anyone feel safe with him again knowing that this could happen, that he could let this happen?

He cut his fingernails down and deposited them in a smaller plastic bag, stuffing that one into the black sack as well, preserving as much evidence as he could. Even if he didn't use it now, there was a possibility he might change his mind later on – people do. He knew there wouldn't be anything under his fingernails, though; he hadn't fought back. Not even a little. He had to hope that was enough. Without going to the hospital and being examined properly, this was as far as Adrian was prepared to go.

Climbing into the shower, he turned it on as hot as he could bear without flinching. His skin burned under the pulse of the concentrated heat. He sat in the bottom of the shower tray with his knees pulled to his chest, staring at the stream of filthy water as it ran into the drain – a dirty deep red. The soap dissolved as he rubbed it against himself until it was nothing but a paper-thin wisp in his hand.

The water ran clear. He didn't suppose he would ever feel clean again, but this would have to do. Used. Stripped of his identity, of everything that made Adrian who he was, reduced to nothing but a vessel for the man to abuse. He had become nothing but a body in that van. A piece of meat to be pushed around a plate and discarded when the man had had his fill. Was it that easy to erase someone so completely?

Shaking off the feelings of disgust with himself, he got out of the shower and patted himself with a towel, wincing as the rough fabric scraped against the parts of his body that were grazed and bruised. He pulled on a hooded sweatshirt and loose tracksuit bottoms before climbing into bed and pulling the covers around him. It was light outside, but he needed to be asleep if he could; he couldn't face being awake right now.

Adrian was alone when he woke. He reached across the bed but there was no one there. His head hurt and his mouth was dry. A sadness came over him, a sadness he couldn't quantify. The hard swelling in his lip and his aching body brought home the nightmare that he had endured. He gasped aloud in anguish, unable to keep the grief inside him.

He realised his phone was ringing. He picked it up and looked at it. Imogen. There was a smear of blood on the screen. He dropped the phone as if it were burning his skin. An hour late for work. He couldn't go in, not today. He wiped the screen with a pillowcase before throwing the pillow across the room. Then he dialled the DCI.

'DS Miles, we've been looking for you,' DCI Kapoor said.

'I have a temperature,' Adrian rasped, sounding rougher than he had imagined he would. He didn't need to fake it – he sounded pathetic without even trying. Just hearing his own voice set his teeth on edge. 'I feel rotten. I'm so sorry, but I can't come in today.'

'You do sound terrible. I'll let Imogen and Matt know you won't be in.'

'Thank you,' he said, hanging up before he began to cry. He could feel it coming.

What was he doing? He should report this, but the thought of it made him feel bilious. His phone rang again: it was Imogen. He couldn't face talking to her right now. He was completely lost inside himself. Nothing existed outside his own mind. He couldn't think about his responsibility to report what had happened.

The moment he had realised what the man was about to do to him replayed over and over in his mind, as though if he could erase that one moment then none of it would have happened. He was in that van for over five hours, but he didn't remember it. He remembered bits, but there was a lot that was unclear. Was it because he had been drunk? He was drunk at the start, but his adrenaline was coursing so quickly he sobered fast. He couldn't stop himself from thinking about it; there was nothing else. He closed his eyes, praying that sleep would take him again.

# Chapter Forty-Six

Imogen was staring at her screen when the coffee cup appeared next to her. She looked up, hoping to see Adrian staring back at her, but it was DI Matt Walsh.

'Sorry to disappoint you,' Walsh said.

'What?'

'Still no call from DS Miles?'

'DCI said he called in sick, so I guess I'll see him when he gets back,' Imogen said, unsure whether Walsh was hinting he knew something was going on between Adrian and her. Her tension since yesterday certainly could be construed as a dead giveaway.

'What are you working on?' Walsh asked.

'Just looking up any mentions of Corrigan Construction online.'

'Wouldn't it be quicker for Gary to do that?'

'Probably, but I need him to break down the financials and so I thought I would get on with this,' she said, trying not to snap.

Walsh wasn't the one she was annoyed with. She wasn't even sure it was Adrian she was annoyed with. Why didn't she keep her mouth shut?

'Well, I hate to be the bearer of bad tidings, but Corrigan's out already. He said Adrian didn't identify himself as a police officer and he thought he was an intruder; his wife has backed him up.'

'What is wrong with that woman?' Imogen asked.

'She's scared, that's all. She sees him getting away with it time and again. It's self-preservation. She doesn't trust that we can stop him and so far, we haven't proven otherwise,' Walsh said.

'Sounds like you speak from experience.'

'Not personal experience, thankfully, but I have had a few cases like this. We just have to remember that she's the victim in this, even though she isn't cooperating. Luckily for us, it looks like Corrigan's behaviour has affected more than just his wife. It's only a matter of time before we find someone willing to speak out against him.'

'Well, let's hope we find them before he kills his wife.'

'Or before DS Miles kills him.'

'Adrian wouldn't,' Imogen said. 'I get the feeling you have Adrian all wrong. He's not the bad guy here, either.'

'He seems to be an unpredictable variable. I read the report you filed yesterday about what happened at that house and knowing how loyal you are to DS Miles, I can only imagine the reality was a more extreme version of your truth. I have asked the DCI to take him off the case.'

'Oh,' Imogen said, unable to think of a more appropriate reaction.

After the way Adrian had behaved at the Corrigan house, she could hardly defend him.

'You're a good cop, Grey. I would hate to think of you letting DS Miles hold you back.'

'Adrian and I work well as a team; our track record proves that.'

'I get the feeling you are the driving force behind most of that success.'

'Well, you would be wrong. DS Miles' determination is a huge factor. I'm not comfortable talking this way about him without him here to defend himself. I also don't really appreciate your suggestion that I falsified my report in order to paint DS Miles in a more favourable light.'

'There's nothing to defend; these are observations. Not attacks. All I am saying is don't let your loyalty ruin your career. He's attacked both an officer at this station and a civilian now. We have to be held to higher standards than that.'

'I think you mean suspect, not civilian.'

'Does that make it OK?'

'This conversation is over. Unless there is anything else?' she snapped.

This time, it was most definitely Walsh she was annoyed with.

'Let's move on. Have you found anything?'

'The usual, really: announcements for construction bids they won and things like that. A picture of Corrigan with a bloke called Gerry Thompson from a couple of years ago; apparently, he was his right-hand man, but I don't remember seeing him on any of the staff lists.'

'Maybe we should give him a visit.'

'I'll get his address,' she said.

She hated it when other people pointed out her flaws to her, especially if they were right. She wanted to call Adrian and tell him about the conversation she had just had with DI Walsh, but she didn't much feel like calling just to have her call rejected again.

# Chapter Forty-Seven

Gerry Thompson didn't live like a man who had until recent years been working for the top construction company in the area. His home was a run-down studio flat just behind Paris Street. He opened the door and limped back to the sofa, flopping down and muting the TV. They followed him inside. The smell of overripe rubbish hung in the air; Imogen wondered how he slept in here. The curtains were drawn and swirls of dust circled the air. Her stomach turned. *Let's get this over with*.

'Mr Thompson, you used to work for Corrigan Construction, correct?' DI Walsh said.

'How did I know this was going to be about that?'

'Have you been expecting us?' Imogen asked.

Thompson was the second person to make a remark like that.

'I guess. Eventually.'

'What did you think we would need to speak to you about?' Imogen said.

'I am guessing I am not your first port of call for whatever you are here for. Reece upsets a lot of people. It's what he does. So really I don't know what specific thing this is about.'

'Do you know his wife, Angela?' DI Walsh said.

'Lovely girl. She's still there, then?' Gerry Thompson looked at the ground, shaking his head as he spoke.

'You knew about the domestic violence?' Imogen said.

'That's one of the reasons why I don't work there anymore. I wasn't comfortable with it and challenged him one too many times.'

'The limp?' Imogen said.

'You noticed? An accident onsite, apparently. I am still not sure,' Gerry scoffed.

Reece Corrigan was certainly consistent.

'What do you mean?' DI Walsh said.

'Only the people Reece wanted out of the way seemed to have these career-ending accidents.'

'Do you know of anyone else who had an accident at work?' Imogen asked.

'I hear rumours mostly, but there is a ring of truth to them. A few guys quit without working out their notice while I was there. I got the distinct feeling they were running away. God only knows what he did to them. I only stuck it out as long as I did because I needed the money. If you have met him, you know he gives off that scent of *Eau de Nutcase*.'

'Did you go to the police about it?' DI Walsh said.

'I never had any proof; just a hunch, really. Reece doesn't like being challenged on anything. If this was

214

retribution, I got off lightly. There's a darkness about him. I don't even know how to describe it, but you just know not to fuck with him. His threats aren't idle.'

'Did you ever witness anything first hand? Would you be willing to testify?' DI Walsh said.

'I was his right-hand man on paper, but really I wasn't someone he came to when he needed something. I don't know if he is still there or what, but a bloke called Jimmy Chilton is who you need to speak to. He knew the ins and outs of what Reece was up to. I think he probably arranged for my little accident.'

'Did you know Simon Glover or Leon Quick?' Imogen asked.

'No, sorry. What's happened to them? It was a long time ago, though I try to remember as little as possible. Everything gets skewed when you are working there. It's almost a hostage situation, or a cult, like you can't leave unless he says so. I just want to forget about all of it. It changed me and I lost my family because of it. My wife, my kids, they didn't recognise me anymore. Now they are gone. I can't work in construction anymore because of my leg.'

'Did Corrigan openly threaten you, then?' Imogen said.

'He openly threatens everyone. If you're smart, you listen the first time.'

'So, why would you stay there? Just money?' Imogen said.

'I wasn't exactly swimming with career opportunities. He gives chances to people with a lot to lose and then that's it, you're on the hook.'

'Lots to lose, how?' Imogen said.

'In my case it was debt. I took out a loan with some dodgy outfit at three thousand per cent interest and he paid it off for me. Took payments out of my wages. Took me years to pay it off. At first I felt indebted to him, but then I realised it was just a way of keeping me loyal no matter what he did. Which I couldn't do in the end.'

'Like, what did he do?' Walsh asked.

'He would blackball people who didn't do what he wanted. He cut corners on jobs, sometimes he didn't pay people, sometimes he got people hurt. I don't know, really; it was a long time ago.'

'And you worked there how long?' Walsh asked.

'Just over five years. He must have got wind that I wanted to leave and then this happened. My disability benefit is barely enough to keep me in fish fingers, let alone all the alcohol I want to consume. I just wish I had left a long time before I got fired.'

'I thought you left because of the accident?' Imogen said.

'This is how Corrigan fires people. Makes sure you can never work in construction again.'

'What happened? Was he always like that?' Imogen said.

'Yes and no. His behaviour got worse over time, but there was no definite moment when I noticed a change; it crept up on us. It's not like he ever seemed completely "right", if you know what I mean. He just got more brazen with his aggression. He wanted us to be scared of him.'

'What about his wife? Did she come on site often? Did you ever witness any aggression towards her?' Imogen asked.

'Not very often, no, but I saw the aftermath more than a couple of times. He didn't even bother trying to hide it. He didn't like it if any of us even spoke to her.'

Imogen looked around the room. Thompson was hardly living the high life. While she had mostly acclimatised to the smell of rubbish in the flat, she could see that Thompson didn't have a whole lot going for him at the moment.

'Do you know anything we can say that might get Angela Corrigan to speak out against her husband?' DI Walsh asked.

'If she's stayed there that long then no. My guess is there is only one way out of that relationship for her.'

Walsh handed him his card.

'If you think of anything else, if you remember anything specific, then give me a ring.'

Gerry Thompson stood again and walked towards the door, opening it to let them leave.

Imogen wondered how honest he had actually been. She noticed that same apprehension and fear that Leon Quick had had. What on earth had Corrigan done to make these men so afraid of him?

She still didn't understand Matt Walsh and wished Adrian was here. There was very little chit-chat with Matt and so she realised she didn't know anything about his life. They had worked together for a few months now and she didn't know if he was married or if he had children. He was completely closed, all business and nothing else, and it made it hard for her to trust him. The only real conversations they had had together were about Adrian's behaviour on both this and previous cases. She had to be the adult and get to know him better if she was going to end up being partnered with him. At the moment, the thought of that filled her with dread.

# Chapter Forty-Eight

It was early evening and the sun had already started to fade when Adrian woke again. The street outside was washed with grey light. He didn't feel rested. His sleep had been plagued with voices and with the ever-present pain in his body. In his dreams, he could feel himself clinging onto sleep, trying to stay inside the dream.

He was thirsty again when he finally opened his eyes. He got up slowly, his bones creaking into action, trying to ignore the places where it hurt most. His body jarred as he walked down the stairs. With every breath, his lungs pressed against his sore ribs, a sharp pain shooting through him.

He walked past a mirror but was too afraid to look, as though it would be written on his face, what he had been part of. Inside the fridge the smell of leftover Indian made his stomach turn again. He looked at the beer, but he didn't want alcohol. As much as he wanted to be drunk, he also wanted to be sober, to keep his wits about him. He pulled out a carton of juice and opened it, his lip stinging as the citric acid infiltrated his cuts.

The doorbell rang and Adrian felt his whole body tense. Was it them? Were they back? They knew where he lived, he knew that much. Struggling to breathe, he grabbed a knife from the block on the kitchen worktop and held it out in front of him, unsure of who he was planning to use it on if anyone burst through the door. He half thought he might just cut his own throat if it was them.

The bell rang again, followed by hard thumping. Adrian's heart beat faster. He backed against the wall with the knife pointed at the front door as the banging continued, the handle slipping around as his palms got sweatier.

'Adrian,' Imogen called. 'I know you're in there; I can see the lights on!'

He took a deep breath at the sound of her voice, wanting nothing more than to hold her right now, but he was still frozen in place, his body taking time to catch up to the fact that his attackers weren't back.

She banged on the door again.

'Coming,' he said before he had time to think.

His primary concern right now was making sure she didn't get suspicious. If he didn't open the door there would be questions he didn't want to answer. He put the knife on the counter and walked to the front door, wiping his wet cheeks before touching the handle. He pushed past every feeling inside that wanted to keep the door closed and stay locked in here for ever.

He opened the door.

Imogen took one look at him and a flash of annoyance passed across her face.

'One of those nights, was it?' she asked as she took in his appearance. 'You could have answered your phone. I've been worried sick.'

She had obviously assumed that he had got into a fight on purpose; it wouldn't be the first time. If anything, it was a perfect cover for him. Having bruises or cuts on his face was nothing new. No one would ask many questions.

'Sorry, I don't feel well.'

He held onto the door, partly to hold his broken body upright, partly blocking her passage into the house. He didn't want company.

Imogen reached forwards to place her hand on his forehead and he involuntarily flinched backwards. She ignored him and continued.

'You are a bit warm. You don't look right.'

'I'm just going to sleep it off. I'll be fine.'

He tried to say the things that would make her go away.

'Are you still annoyed? Is that what this is? I said I was sorry,' Imogen said.

'No, I'm not annoyed at all. I just feel terrible,' Adrian said.

He desperately wanted her to leave, but he knew if he said that then she would push her way in. He was surprised she hadn't already. At the same time, he didn't want to be alone, either. He just wanted to be asleep, unconscious, dead.

'Let me in; I'll make you some soup,' Imogen said.

He didn't want a confrontation and so he let her through. He didn't know his own mind anymore. He felt weak.

Imogen walked past him into the kitchen. By the time Adrian had followed her inside, she had a tin of soup out and was emptying it into a bowl.

'I'm going to go back to bed,' Adrian said, looking at the dining chair, not wanting to sit on it, knowing that he couldn't.

'I'll bring your soup up when it's done.'

Out of her sight, Adrian allowed himself to feel the pain. He winced as he walked up the stairs. He blurted out a sob, unsure where it had come from and hoping that Imogen hadn't heard it. He walked over to the bed and noticed there was blood streaking his sheets. Imogen would be up any moment.

He quickly pulled the bedding off and rolled it into a ball, stuffing it in the bottom of the wardrobe. He grabbed a clean set from the cupboard and redressed the bed, covering the large red rose-shaped stain on his mattress with a towel before putting the sheet on. He would have to replace it. He couldn't risk Imogen seeing it.

His body begged to be lying down again, but he was desperate not to be discovered. His eyes were streaming and he didn't know how to stop them. He changed his tracksuit bottoms as well and climbed in bed just moments before he heard Imogen on the stairs. Wiping his eyes, he turned onto his side – lying on his back hurt too much and he didn't want to get more blood on the sheets.

'Thank you,' he said as Imogen entered the room and put the soup by the bed.

'You really look terrible, Miley. Have you been to see a doctor?'

She leaned over and put her hand on his cheek again. He braced himself as her hand touched him. He didn't want any hands on him at all. *Be normal.*

'I'll be OK. I just need to sleep it off.'

He resisted the urge to push her hand away and just screamed on the inside.

'Well, I'm staying here to look after you. I don't care if you're annoyed at me.'

'I don't want to give you what I have got. Maybe you should sleep in the other room.'

'Nonsense. I never get sick. I'll be downstairs. Call if you need me. Maybe a hot shower will make you feel better.'

'Good idea.'

He smiled and she removed her hand. He could breathe again.

He waited for her to leave the room and then went into the bathroom. The black sack with his soiled things inside was still on the floor. He pulled his clothes off and stood in front of the mirror. Pale and bruised, the tears started to form in his eyes and dripped down without him even feeling as though he was crying. This was just who he was now. Pathetic.

He turned around and looked back in the mirror, checking his body. There were several bruises on his back. He daren't look lower, but then he took a deep breath before casting his eyes down and then looking away immediately. He saw the dried blood at the top of his thighs and gagged. He managed to open the toilet just in time to throw up again. He clutched at his rib as he retched until his stomach was dry.

'You all right in there?' Imogen knocked on the door.

'I'm fine,' he said, panting, trying not to sound as fucked up as he felt.

He quickly turned the shower on again and got in, as though maybe this time he could wash the injuries away. Sobbing into the water, desperate to stop crying but finding it harder and harder to control, he gently rubbed shower cream between his legs, front and back. Even his own hands on his skin were making him feel worse.

Composing himself and getting dressed again, he took deep breaths until he felt he could pass for human again. He picked up the black sack and opened the bathroom door. Imogen was standing there.

'You're not right, Adrian. What have you taken for it?'

'Nothing, I'll be fine.'

He walked back into the bedroom and kicked the black bag under the bed before Imogen mentioned it.

'Shall I get you some painkillers?'

He didn't know why he hadn't thought of that; maybe because the pain was incidental. It wasn't the worst part of what had happened, it was the side effect. He could handle the physical pain – it hurt, of course – but it wasn't what was upsetting him. The main source of his agony was inside and untouchable.

'Yes, please. They are in the high cupboard next to the fridge.'

He felt he should be hungry, but somehow that was the last thing on his mind. The emptiness inside him was not a priority.

He climbed back in bed, careful to lie on his side propped up on the pillows to relieve the pain in his ribs, terrified of soiling the sheets again. Knowing full well if he told Imogen she would understand and that it might even relieve some of this internal pressure, the thought of saying it out loud made him gag. The idea of her thinking about him in that situation was not something he could entertain. He wasn't sure if he could say it, wasn't sure if his mouth would work enough for the words to come out.

Imogen reappeared with the painkillers. He leaned up on his elbow and took two, knowing that it would make no difference, not really. He lay back again and closed his eyes.

Imogen stood in the doorway for a few moments just looking at him. He could feel her wanting to say something but deciding against it. Eventually, she left the room and Adrian attempted to sleep again.

Sleeping was strange. There was an anxiety within him that didn't switch off, a constant reminder that he was in danger. There was still pain but it was a little less intrusive than it had been before.

He drifted in and out of sleep, but not enough to open his eyes. Just enough to be aware and remember what had happened. Occasionally, the impulse to scream took over, but he suppressed it, he suppressed everything. He felt as though he were climbing into the smallest box, all his armour now removed, destroyed. He had to hide in the box to stay safe. They wouldn't find him there.

He could hear sobbing. The familiar pain in his throat returned and then he felt hands on his shoulders.

'Adrian! Wake up!'

This time he did push her hands away, as he woke with a start. He was breathless and his face was wet. He had been crying, maybe talking in his sleep.

Imogen was lying with him. The room was dark and he wanted to cry out, but instead he turned in the bed, putting his bedside light on, the extreme movement causing him to wince yet again. He took several slow, deep breaths as he moved, unsure why that eased the pain in any way. He looked over to Imogen, who looked as though she had seen a ghost – a concerned and surprised face.

'Bad dream, that's all.'

She reached across to put her hand on his face again to check if he had a temperature, but he got out of the bed before she could touch him.

'You were crying in your sleep. Are you sure you're OK? Let me see if you're warm.'

'I said I'm fine. Will you stop fucking harassing me!' Adrian snapped before leaving the room.

In the bathroom, he ran the cold water and splashed it on his face. His cheeks and nose were wet where the tears had fallen. He felt so broken. No control. It was as though he had given it away by not fighting back. Why didn't he fight back? Why didn't he fight to the death? Adrian wasn't sure he could do this anymore. *What alternative is there?*

There was a gentle tap on the bathroom door.

'Adrian?'

As the towel enveloped his face, he had the urge to scream into it, but instead he just dried himself off and opened the door. Imogen was standing with her arms folded, hugging herself for security. Her face was full of concern.

'I'm sorry. I didn't mean to snap. I feel like shit,' he said. 'I don't think I'm great company right now.'

'I'm worried about you. What was your dream about?'

'I can't even remember,' Adrian lied.

'You were really sobbing. It was awful. I kept trying to wake you and you were freaking out.'

'It's just this bug and this case. I think you were right and it's getting to me. I need more rest, that's all. I might go and lie on the sofa for a while.'

Adrian walked past her and down the stairs. He grabbed a cushion and clutched it to him as he lay down again, propped up on the arm of the sofa. He picked up the remote and put the TV on – silence and darkness were not things he wanted to deal with right now.

The sound of the bed creaking upstairs as Imogen climbed in alone relaxed him a little. At least he didn't have to pretend to be all right for a while. He found it impossible to pretend he was all right, even though no part of him wanted her to know what had happened.

He watched TV until the sun rose. But he couldn't keep his mind on anything. His thoughts kept returning to that van, to specific moments in there. The overwhelming smell of his own blood as it pooled underneath him. The sensation as the man forced himself inside him over and over again. He could still feel the sting in his skin where it had split and ripped. The taste of the man's grubby fingers in his mouth, pushing against the back of his throat. Nothing existed outside those moments for Adrian. Everything was gone. There was nothing else to think about, nothing else to remember. It had built a wall around him and trapped him inside.

# Chapter Forty-Nine

Imogen thrummed her fingers against the steering wheel as Adrian's phone went straight to answerphone again. When she left Adrian's house that morning, he was sleeping on the sofa. She felt bad leaving him there alone; he really didn't seem right. He had told her that he wasn't still annoyed with her, but she didn't believe him, as a few moments later he said he would prefer to spend the night alone. There was something very cold and unfamiliar about his behaviour. But maybe it really was just a bug and she was overreacting.

It occurred to her that she took for granted that Adrian would always be the one who was OK, even when he wasn't. He usually put on a brave face for others, but this time it really didn't feel like he was doing that. Was it selfish of her to want him just to be Adrian again?

As hard as it had been for Imogen growing up the way she did, with a bipolar single mother and no idea who her father was, it was no comparison to the pain Adrian obviously still carried with him after living with a violent addict as a father. She reminded herself to keep her mouth shut on things she knew nothing about in future.

DI Matt Walsh was waiting at her desk when she arrived at the station.

'Problem?' she said, unaccustomed to seeing him here like this and hoping this wasn't something she would have to get used to on a daily basis.

'The DCI wants us to go and see Reece Corrigan again. She thinks we might get different results. We called the Corrigan Construction HQ and they said he is on site. I've got the address.'

'Different results? Why, because Adrian isn't here? I am sure Corrigan will suddenly become incredibly cooperative for no apparent reason,' Imogen said, resisting the urge to roll her eyes, hoping her tone was enough to convey how stupid she thought this idea was.

'We can ask him about Thompson and maybe we can get a minute or two with his new bestie, Jimmy Chilton. Do you have a problem with this course of action?' Walsh said.

'I just do what I am told.' She held her hands up as if to surrender. 'I am sure the DCI has her reasons for sending us back there. Let me guess, you have to smooth things over with Corrigan because he has put in a complaint against Adrian or something.'

'Not that I am aware of. He is still a suspect and your last visit didn't exactly produce any results. Did it?'

'You had to be there. It certainly cemented things in my mind.'

'Well, this time I will be.'

At the construction site there was a tense silence, as though everyone had their heads down and was getting on with the job. Imogen had visited construction sites before and there was always a jokey comment or two being thrown around. But these men didn't even look at Imogen or Walsh as they walked towards the three men huddled in the corner.

Reece Corrigan spotted them as they approached. At first, he looked annoyed. Then she was sure she could see a smile on his face as he glanced at Walsh. He obviously assumed that Adrian had been told to stay away.

As Adrian had predicted, Corrigan was back at work before his wife's bruise had even healed. She thought the law would protect Angela. She also thought Adrian was overstating because of his own experience in childhood. Besides, the law had moved on in the last thirty years when it came to domestic abuse. Maybe it hadn't moved on as much as it should have, though. She was pissed off that Corrigan had barely even been reprimanded and she could tell from the look on his face that he thought he was untouchable.

'Detective Grey. It's good to see you again.'

'Save it.'

'Hello, Mr Corrigan. I'm DI Walsh,' Matt interrupted before Imogen could say anything else.

'Where's the other one?' Corrigan said, smirking.

'We spoke to your old friend Gerry Thompson the other day,' Imogen said.

She knew it was probably not the best idea to show their hand immediately, but she wanted to wipe that stupid look off his face. It worked.

'He got fired for drinking on the job. Very unprofessional. He was a danger to himself and to everyone else, so he had to go.'

'If you say so. A lot of your former employees turn to drink, do they?' Imogen said, folding her arms and putting on her best 'you're full of shit and we know it' face.

'Well, if you met him you will know what I mean. Does he still live in that rat-infested shithole in town? Where do you think all his money went? He was everyone's best mate at the pub. Life and soul of the party until he stopped buying everyone rounds. Now, he's Billy No-Mates and no one gives a shit about him. I wouldn't be surprised if when he eventually does drink himself to death it will only be the smell of his rotting body that would even alert anyone.'

'Thought about this a lot, have you?' Imogen said. 'That's *completely* normal.'

'My point is, he's not a particularly credible individual. My lawyers could discredit him within ten minutes. Whatever he has got to say, he's full of shit.'

'The problem we are finding, Mr Corrigan, is that no one has much of anything to say. They all say pretty much the same thing. It's all very interesting but a bit too vague for any kind of prosecution. It's almost as if they are scared of you. That alone is very interesting to me,' Walsh said.

'Don't worry, though. We will find someone who

doesn't have a problem detailing all the shady shit you do,' Imogen said.

'Did you just come here to try and intimidate me? Because it didn't work when your girlfriend tried it, so I don't know why you think it would when you do.'

'How long do you think before we find that one person?' Imogen said.

'I wouldn't hold my breath, put it that way.'

Corrigan smiled with an extreme confidence that put Adrian's concerns and behaviour in perspective for her. She really wanted to knock this guy's teeth out.

'Where's Jimmy Chilton today?' Imogen said.

'He's got the day off. By all means feel free to go and speak to him, though. I am sure he will tell you exactly what I have told you about that waste of space Thompson.'

'Don't leave town, Mr Corrigan,' Walsh said.

'Tell your other friend I hope he feels better soon,' Corrigan said to Imogen.

She walked away before she did anything she regretted. The sheer arrogance of the man was completely staggering. He knew they had nothing. He had all the power. Not for long, if Imogen had anything to do with it.

# Chapter Fifty

When Imogen arrived at Jimmy Chilton's house with Walsh, they had to ring the doorbell several times before there was a response. His car was parked alongside the house, in front of the garage. He looked behind them, past the front gate and at the road, checking for something or someone before ushering them inside.

Without even asking, Imogen could tell he lived alone. It was a clean and tidy place but there was something missing. Just like in her house, she supposed. You could tell when a person only had themselves to look after. He had a photo of himself with a couple of teenagers on his wall, grown-up children, no pictures of a wife anywhere. It was an old photo – she could tell by the plumpness in his face that had all but disappeared now.

'What is it you want?' he asked.

'I don't know what kind of man you are, Mr Chilton, what kind of person,' DI Walsh began. 'We believe your boss was involved in the murder of Simon

Glover. Whether or not he did it himself is another question, but so far we have found plenty of people who have told us he is no good but no one willing to elaborate.'

'I don't know what you're talking about.'

'So, you're happy with the way he does things? Or are you just scared of having an accident at work if you speak up against him?' Imogen pushed.

'He's a tough boss but no, I'm not scared of him,' Chilton said unconvincingly.

'What are your thoughts on Angela Corrigan?' Walsh said.

'Nice woman, no real thoughts beyond that,' he said, avoiding eye contact.

'You've never seen her with a black eye? Or worse? I don't believe that for a second; I only met her a few weeks ago and I've seen it more than once. Is that kind of thing OK with you?' Imogen said.

'Look, I don't know about that. Angela doesn't come to the site very often and I don't poke my nose where it doesn't belong.'

'How long have you known Reece Corrigan?' Walsh said.

'About nine years. I got a job with him not long after the company moved down here.'

'Moved down from where?' Imogen asked.

'Shropshire, around ten years ago.'

'That's a long way to move. Do you know why?' Imogen said, watching his face for any sign of reaction.

'Sorry, no.' Chilton said.

She believed him.

'I bet you've seen some things over the years,' Imogen said.

'I can't help you.'

'It's not us you would be helping. We could walk away; we don't have enough evidence to prosecute. You could all go back to whatever is going on at that construction site, in that world you all live in. Until the next person dies . . . might even be you,' Imogen said.

'There's nothing to tell.' Jimmy squirmed.

'How does a man like him get so powerful?' Imogen said.

'I don't know what you want from me.'

'I was talking to Leon Quick when he killed himself. Picked up a knife off his kitchen counter and stabbed himself in front of me because of something that happened while he was working for Corrigan Construction. Why would anyone do that to themselves without good reason? Considering how close Corrigan usually keeps you, I am going to bet you know a lot about the kind of things he does to people who cross him. How about I just tell him that you've decided to talk to us? I could go back there now and say you were giving us a statement,' Imogen said.

She stared straight at Chilton, who was visibly sweating. She made a move for the front door.

'Wait!' Chilton said.

'What is it?' Imogen said.

'Don't. I don't know anything. I've got nothing to do with any of it,' Chilton said desperately.

'If you don't know anything then what exactly is it that you have nothing to do with?' Imogen said, staring at him, making it almost impossible for him to look away.

'I was away when Quick left. He didn't get fired, though, that's all I can tell you. Corrigan made me put that in his and Glover's file. I made up all the stuff about them being shit workers, too. They weren't. Glover did something that pissed Corrigan off. I swear, I don't know what it was. I would wager it was something to do with Angela, though. She is a real trigger for his temper.'

'So we've seen,' Walsh said.

'What about Leon Quick?' Imogen said.

'I really don't know any specifics. But he left suddenly. I overheard Reece on the phone talking to someone about teaching him a lesson, though. I think all he did was make a couple of jokes that Reece didn't approve of. If it was something else, then I didn't hear about it. As for what lesson he taught him, I have no idea what it was.'

'And you have no idea why Quick killed himself?' Walsh said.

'He used to make a lot of jokes around the site; one of those people who always goes for the gag, if you know what I mean. He said a couple of things about Angela that got back to Reece. I genuinely don't know what happened, but Quick took a week off work. He only came back for a few days before leaving and moving back in with his parents.'

'How was he when he came back?' Imogen said.

'He wasn't cracking jokes anymore, that's all I know. After he left I assumed it was something to do with

Reece. I saw Angela around that week, too. She had her arm in a sling,' Jimmy said apologetically, looking down at his feet.

'I'd like you to come in and make a statement about Glover and Quick,' Walsh said.

'I won't. If Reece finds out about this . . .'

'So, we tell him you told us anyway. What do you think will happen to you then?' Imogen said.

In many ways, Chilton was on the brink of telling them everything they wanted to know. He clearly wasn't as strong as Angela, or as conflicted. Imogen just had to find the right button to push. In this short time of questioning she had already cracked him a little.

'Come on, that's not fair.'

'Life's not fair, Mr Chilton. That's why we have to stop people like Corrigan from getting away with it. He's literally ruining other people's lives. How long before he turns on you?' Walsh said.

'I swear to God, I don't know anything about what happened to Glover or Quick. I've told you everything. I had nothing to do with that. I only deal with stuff to do with work. I don't get involved in any of Corrigan's extra-curricular activities.'

'But you must know something. Was he always like this? Has he been like this since you started?' Imogen said.

'He doesn't like being told he can't have something and the only people who say no to him get hurt. I think maybe he's come to think that he is untouchable and to be honest with you, it certainly seems that way.'

'What if that was your daughter? Don't you think

Angela's father wanted more for her than this?' Imogen pointed to the picture on his wall.

'We will still need a statement from you,' Walsh said.

'If he finds out then I'll lose my job. He is really big on loyalty. He can make it so no one else will hire me again.'

'By orchestrating an accident so you lose a limb?' Imogen said.

'I don't know anything about those accidents, I swear. He doesn't come to me about things like that.'

'Who does know about those accidents? Who might Corrigan confide in aside from you?' Imogen asked.

'I don't know.'

'That's not good enough.' Imogen moved towards the door again.

'I can find out!'

'How?' Walsh said.

'I spend most of my days in the Portakabin on the main site going through admin and making calls, but I could ask around. See who he's been talking to.'

'How do we know we can trust you?' Walsh asked.

Chilton hesitated for a moment before glancing at the picture of his daughter again.

'She deserves better than him, you're right. It might take a while; I don't want him to get suspicious.'

'OK, we'll give you some time to get the information and then you need to tell us everything you know,' Walsh said.

'I will. I'll try.'

'I wouldn't tell anyone about this arrangement, if I were you. Not even Angela. You could get hurt and we need you to help us build a case against him.'

'I'm not stupid. Please, you had better go.'

'Don't leave town,' Walsh said.

They left the house and walked back to the car. Imogen looked back over to Chilton's house and saw the curtain moving. He was watching them, waiting for them to leave. Had he really decided to help them out or was it all just an act to get them off his case? Was he going to run straight to Corrigan and tell to protect himself? Or was he going to do what they asked? Only time would tell.

# Chapter Fifty-One

Adrian hadn't been into work since the attack two days ago. He couldn't put off going back for much longer, not without a medical note, but he wasn't sure how to get one, or even if he wanted to. He was going crazy at home, waiting for those men to come and get him again. He knew Imogen was worried about him and he didn't know how to stop it. The only way he knew was to start acting normally again. The only problem was he couldn't remember how to do that.

After Imogen left for work, he got up and showered before walking to the hospital. Going outside was hard, but staying at home was no better. They knew where he lived and they had got to him before, so they could get to him again if they wanted to. Where he was wouldn't matter, so he opted not to be housebound.

He walked into accident and emergency and showed his warrant card to the woman on reception.

'I need to speak to Dr Hadley. Is she in today?' Adrian said.

He felt stupid for coming here, bad for involving her in this, but he knew he couldn't just go to someone random; he couldn't trust them to be discreet. The one thing he knew about Dr Hadley above everything else was that she respected a patient's privacy and would never violate that. He also trusted that she would be sympathetic; he had seen her with other victims in the past. He needed to speak to someone who understood this sort of thing, someone who would react appropriately. He wasn't sure how he would take any kind of judgement at this point; he needed kindness and empathy.

'I'll see if I can get hold of her for you. Take a seat,' the receptionist said.

Adrian stood by the counter and waited for the doors to the ward to open. He looked at the seats, but he wasn't there yet – standing was easier. He crossed his arms, even though it hurt his ribs. Since the attack he found himself looking at people with suspicion. The fact that he knew so little about his attacker made everyone a suspect. He listened out for that voice, looked for the face he had not seen, knowing he wouldn't know the man if he met him.

He clenched his jaw and fists to stop himself from crying again. His tears seemed to come in waves when he least expected them and his control over it was tenuous. He concentrated on his breathing, trying not to breath too deeply as it aggravated his damaged rib.

'DS Miles. Has there been a development in the case?

I heard you found that young lady, is she doing OK?'
Dr Hadley asked as she appeared at the double doors.

'We are still investigating. I was wondering if I could speak to you in private,' Adrian said.

He had gone over this in his mind. He had to get some kind of treatment; he was in too much pain to go back to work as he was.

'Is this about the case? I can't break doctor–patient confidentiality, if that's what you want. I already told DS Grey everything I could and even that felt unethical.'

'No, a personal matter, actually.' He didn't know how to describe what it was.

'Oh, OK.' She seemed surprised. 'Come with me.'

She led him through the ward out into a small corridor. There was a door with her name on it and they went inside – it was a small office with no window. She had some toys in the corner of the room and a trolley pushed against the back wall. There was a book-case stacked with medical magazines and serious-looking books. Her walls were a bright, cheery sky blue, covered in framed certificates and accolades.

'What can I help you with, DS Miles?'

'Adrian, please.'

She sat in her chair and nodded to another one for guests. Adrian shook his head and took a deep breath. He paced the room a little, trying to work off the anxiety enough to speak.

'I need to see a doctor, but I need it to stay off my medical records.'

'You should see your own GP. But it would be up to their discretion. I will say, however, keeping information from your medical files will only harm you. Future doctors will need a full and correct history in order to be able to treat you properly,' Dr Hadley recounted with a sigh.

This was clearly a speech she had delivered before.

'Either I see a doctor off the record, or I don't see a doctor at all.'

'I'm afraid I can't help you, Adrian. It's extremely unethical. If you've been abusing drugs, self-harming or anything illegal, then it really needs to be on the record. For my sake as well as yours.'

'It's not that,' he said.

'I would strongly advise against urging a doctor to do this for you. Why did you pick me and not your own doctor, out of interest? Because we went for dinner once?'

'Because you're nice, and fair. You seem trustworthy. I've seen the way you deal with your patients. I need to speak to someone I can trust to be discreet. Knowing how hard it is to get any pertinent information about patients from you, I know you can be trusted. I don't want to go to someone I don't know with this. It's too important,' he said.

He could feel his eyes brimming again.

Dr Hadley stood and folded her arms, taking Adrian's statement as flattery and rolling her eyes.

'Let's have a hypothetical conversation, then.'

Adrian took a deep breath before speaking.

'Hypothetically, I have some injuries that I need a doctor to look at. I may also, hypothetically, need a prescription for pain relief. I need to take some time off work because of the pain, but I want to get back to work as soon as possible and I need to know that I physically can. I don't want my DCI or my colleagues to know about this. I promise I haven't broken the law in any way, but I am in a somewhat impossible situation.'

After some deliberation, the doctor finally spoke again.

'All right. I will look at your injuries. I can see you've been in the wars.'

Adrian took his jacket off and slowly pulled his sweatshirt over his head, exposing his bruises. Dr Hadley put her latex gloves on and started to press against the Seville orange-sized bruise on his ribs. He flinched at her touch.

'Is it broken?' he asked.

'A tiny fracture, I suspect. As long as you have been resting then it shouldn't be a problem; a couple of weeks and it could be back to normal. The bruise on your back will heal in less time; nothing there is damaged. Why don't you want these on your record?'

He picked up his oversized sweatshirt and she helped him to put it back on.

'Is your door locked?' he asked as he kicked off his shoes. He walked over to the trolley and started to unbutton his jeans.

'Could you turn around, please?'

He had no choice.

Dr Hadley locked the door and waited as he climbed up on the bed facing away from her. Every movement caused him pain, his eyes wet with those unexpected tears. He wasn't sure if it was the constant pain or deep-rooted humiliation that was causing them.

'OK,' Adrian said.

'What happened to you, DS Miles?' she asked as she approached, pulling the sweatshirt up and exposing his injuries.

'What does it look like?' Adrian said.

'Jesus! When did this happen?'

'A couple of nights ago.'

'This was non-consensual?'

'I did not consent, no.'

'And you've not seen a doctor until now? Why did you wait?'

'I thought I could get better on my own.'

'Do you mind if I examine you?'

'That's why I am here. Sorry to spring my pasty backside on you like this,' he tried to joke.

'I'm going to have to touch you to do a proper examination. I'll use lubricant and I'll be as fast and gentle as I can, is that OK with you?'

'Yes. I need to get back to work and at the moment, I can't even sit down. Is there anything you can do about that?'

'Have you spoken to anyone about this?' she asked quietly.

'Just you. I haven't told anyone else and I don't want anyone to know. This could destroy my career if anyone finds out.'

'You didn't report it?' Dr Hadley said.

'No. The thought of anyone else knowing is making

me suicidal. I can get through this, but I need to do it my way,' Adrian said, appreciating his own hypocrisy. He had always implored victims to come forward and speak out and yet here he was unwilling to do the same.

She placed her hand on his hip to warn him that she was starting her examination. Adrian couldn't talk anymore. He was concentrating on staying still, terrified of the pain that he knew was coming. She was gentle, but it made no difference. The crying started again and he hated himself for it. He wanted to throw up again; he wanted to run away.

'We are still within a window where a swab might provide results if it only happened a couple of nights ago.'

'Would you be able to keep my name off the test? Could you get it analysed anonymously?' Adrian asked.

He wanted to know who had done this to him, but he still didn't want anyone to know what had happened.

'I could process as a John Doe. All you would be is a serial number. I can process the kit through the crisis centre.'

'You would do that?'

'I would.'

'OK, then do it,' Adrian said.

He didn't have to use the evidence right away. There might not even be any, but if there was, he instinctively wanted to preserve it. So many victims of sexual assault change their mind about prosecuting after allowing themselves time to heal. He would hate to think he destroyed any evidence and any chance of catching the people who did this to him. Even if he couldn't face going after them this week or even this month, it could happen and if it did, he wanted to have as much information as possible.

She opened a drawer in her desk and he heard the rustling of a plastic bag before feeling her hand on his hip again. The swab didn't hurt, even though he had braced himself for pain.

'You can get up now,' Dr Hadley said when she was done.

Adrian got up and put his trousers back on, every breath a struggle.

'What's the verdict?'

'I'll prescribe you some lidocaine ointment. Things should ease up after a couple of days. Although you have sustained a lot of injuries there, none of them are going to require anything more than time to heal. The lidocaine should help, but for the most part you just need to be careful for a while.

'The fissures in your anus are mostly superficial, even if there are a lot of them. I don't want you to take this the wrong way, but you got lucky. Those injuries are as close as it gets to serious without being anything other than painful and inconvenient. A little more force and you could have needed emergency surgery.'

'So, I just keep using the ointment?' he said, blocking out the rest of her words, still struggling to believe he was even in this situation.

'Yes, they should be completely healed in around four weeks, but you should regain full mobility a lot sooner. I'll also prescribe you some proper painkillers.'

'You'll keep this between us?' he asked.

'I've put something innocuous in the file to explain the treatments I'm prescribing. The medication really needs to be documented on your records, in case you have an adverse reaction or need to take any other medication that may not be compatible with it. It's for your safety.'

'Thank you.'

'I'll get that sample processed as soon as I can. It could take a while,' she said. 'How are you feeling?'

'Don't!' Adrian's eyes filled again. 'I don't even know.'

'You should speak to someone, Adrian. You've been through a serious trauma. If you can't face seeing a counsellor, then maybe a friend. If you are religious, then you could go and speak to someone at the church. Have you experienced any symptoms of PTSD?'

'I don't know what I'm experiencing. I can't think straight.' He wiped his face with his sleeve.

She handed him a box of tissues from her desk.

'Difficulty sleeping? Nightmares? Are you more irritable than normal? Are you emotionally numb to situations or people? Are you avoiding things so you don't get upset? Are you more aware of your surroundings? Are you afraid?'

'All of that, yes.'

'Do you find yourself reliving the attack, or reminded of it constantly? Are you blaming yourself? Are you struggling to remember details of the attack? Are you full of negativity towards yourself and others? Is your concentration off?'

'Yes,' he said. 'What do I do? What's the treatment for that?'

She searched on her desk and found a business card then handed it to him. She sat down and logged into her computer. Then she found his records and typed up a few notes before writing him a prescription. The printer came to life.

'Well, there is no pill for it. It's possible that it will go away on its own; sometimes it does. What I think we should do for now is keep an eye on you. We call it watchful waiting. After a month, if it's still as persistent as it is now, then we can move forwards with treatment.'

'What if it doesn't go away?'

'Then you will need a mixture of medication and psychotherapy. I'm not going to lie to you, Adrian. You've got a long road ahead of you. It's really important that you try to trust the people around you to help you through it. Don't push people away; it will only make it worse.'

'I don't feel like I have any control over what I do at the moment. My actions and reactions are beyond me . . . if that makes any sense.'

'Do you know who your attacker was?'

'I have no idea.' He shook his head.

Dr Hadley hesitated. 'I'd like you to consider having an HIV test.'

'What? No.'

Adrian hadn't even thought of that. Another thing to add to the ever-increasing mound of shit his life was becoming.

'If you are concerned about anonymity then you can go to the GUM clinic on Sidwell Street and get tested there. It's a walk-in clinic, so you could go straight from here.'

'I don't want an HIV test on my medical record.'

'If you go to the GUM clinic then the test is completely confidential. Even if it comes back positive then you need to sign a consent form for the information to be released to any other medical bodies, including your GP. The information would stay completely within that specific clinic and wouldn't be shared with anyone.'

'I can't get my head round this,' Adrian said.

'Did the attack happen less than seventy-two hours ago?'

'Yes.'

'Then I will give you some PEP, post-exposure prophylaxis.' She unlocked the steel locker in her room and took out two separate bottles of pills. 'Here you go. One of each a day for the next thirty days. When you finish the course, we can run the HIV test again if you want to. Call me if you need me to arrange an appointment.

'There is another self-test you can do yourself, at home, anonymously, if you need even more reassurance. It's not worth taking a risk with this, Adrian. Just get the test done. I work at the GUM clinic once a week; if you want, I can call with the test results once they come through. I know how stressful this must be for you.'

Adrian let out an incredulous laugh at her remark but then instantly felt guilty – she was trying to help him.

'You don't mind doing that for me? I would really appreciate that, thank you.'

'Come and see me next week. I'll check your injuries

again; make sure you are healing properly. You can expect some bleeding after bowel movements. Rather than wiping, maybe have a shower whenever you can or use wet wipes. Eat fibrous food to try to keep your stools loose. You need to give yourself time to heal. I'll write you a sick note for work. We'll start with two weeks off, then we can see how you are then.'

'Thank you, Dr Hadley.'

'Adrian, call me at any time if you're feeling suicidal. I'm usually in the hospital, but if I can't take your call, I will ring you right back as soon as I can.'

'Thank you, Dr Hadley,' he said, his voice cracking and the tears springing again.

What the hell was going on? How was he even having this conversation? *Whose life is this?*

'Zoe, please. I'm glad you trusted me with this. You did the right thing coming to me. It's important you don't go through this alone.'

She handed him the slip of paper for the pathology lab before taking his other hand in hers. For the first time since it had happened, he didn't flinch at someone's touch. He felt safe here.

He took as deep a breath as he could before unlocking her office, his sanctuary, and venturing out into the unknown again.

# Chapter Fifty-Two

Imogen and DI Walsh drove mostly in silence. She missed the banter she had with Adrian. Walsh didn't really speak much when it wasn't work-related. She didn't even know if he owned a TV; he was a very strange and secretive man.

The fact that, so far, they had not found a single person who would come forward and speak against Reece Corrigan was exasperating. Nor had they found any incriminating evidence against either him or his company. No one had anything good to say about him, but no one claimed to have anything but rumours or suspicions, either. What hold did he have over those people? How could any one man have so much power? There was only one person left to appeal to: Angela Corrigan. They knew where Reece was and so, with any luck, she would be at home alone. Maybe Imogen could get her to talk.

When they pulled into the driveway of the Corrigan house, the white Lexus was parked outside.

Imogen turned to Walsh. 'I'd like to speak to her alone, if that's OK? As a woman, maybe I can appeal to her in the way a man can't.'

'You want me to wait in the car?'

'If you don't mind.'

'Would you ask DS Miles to wait in the car, out of interest?' Walsh asked.

'This really isn't personal and it isn't about you. I think I have a better shot of talking to this woman alone and getting somewhere. That's all. For what it's worth, I actually think DS Miles would be asking me to wait in the car. And I would do it, because I trust his judgement as a police officer. I don't have a problem with you, Matt. I hope I haven't given you that impression.'

'OK, DS Grey. I will take your word for it.'

Imogen got out of the car; she couldn't be bothered to talk it through with Walsh anymore. The fact was, she didn't think bombarding Angela with questions from all sides would work. If she was honest, she was actually doing this because she thought it was what Adrian might do. Whatever she thought of Angela, she was a victim. It wasn't as though Imogen didn't see her that way, but she just couldn't understand why she would stay with a man who treated her so appallingly.

There again, Imogen also had to admit that you never know how you would react to a situation until you are in it. She couldn't know for sure she wouldn't do exactly the same thing. The people they had interviewed about Reece Corrigan were terrified of him. Imogen reminded herself that Angela had tried to get away and almost died because of it. Of course she was too scared to try again.

Imogen knocked on the door.

'Detective.'

Angela answered the door and looked around the front of the house to check for anyone else. She spotted the car and saw DI Walsh in there. Angela took a step back to allow Imogen to come inside. After closing the door, Angela walked into the dining room and sat at the table, letting out a big sigh.

'I hope you don't mind me stopping by,' Imogen started. 'We just spoke to your husband at work and so we knew you would be alone.'

'Well, he could be back quite soon, so just ask what you want to ask and I'll consider whether I can answer or not.'

'Why did you leave the hospital? Why did you come back here?' Imogen asked.

'As soon as I knew about the video of DS Miles rescuing me being on the internet, I knew I had to get back here. I just panicked, I guess.'

'Do you remember what happened to you and Simon yet?'

'I really don't. I swear. I feel like it's there, but I just can't quite get to it, like it's on the tip of my tongue. It's very frustrating. Maybe my mind doesn't want to remember.' Angela shifted uncomfortably.

'Why didn't your husband report you missing?'

'You would have to ask him that. Why haven't you told him that you spoke to me at the hospital?'

'We need to know that you are safe. After what the doctor suggested you had been through, we thought it best not to exacerbate the situation between you and your husband. Unfortunately, we can't help you unless you help us.'

'He knows anyway; he saw the video of DS Miles pulling me out of the river. He saw it before I even got back.'

'He didn't mention that to us.'

'He likes to play games. I expect he is waiting for you to ask him about it.'

'Simon Glover. Were you and he really just friends?'

'Yes, we were. I'm not stupid enough to cheat on Reece. Reece made it clear years ago what would happen to any man I cheated on him with. Simon was a good friend to me. I should never have asked him for help.'

'Would you testify about what happened to you and Simon?'

'I really don't remember that night, that wasn't an act. When I woke up in the hospital, I didn't know how I got there.'

'You're lucky Adrian found you in time.'

'Am I? Doesn't feel like it.'

'We can help you leave if you want to leave. Even better, if you can testify against the man, then we can get him put away for a very long time. We can put in a request to get you a new identity and somewhere safe to live as well, if that's what you need.'

'I don't believe you. I don't believe he can be stopped that way. Where's Adrian, anyway?' Angela asked. 'Why isn't he here? Did Reece do something to him? I told you both to get away while you still could.'

'Adrian's got the flu, that's all; nothing to do with your husband. Is there anything you can tell me about

Reece that would help us get him? Something we can corroborate independently, so you don't have to testify?'

'You think I know anything? I don't. He doesn't tell me shit. Let me ask you something, Detective.'

'What?'

'Have you ever been terrified of a person? Not just in a bad situation. But scared all the time, from the moment you wake until the moment you finally fall asleep at night?'

'No.'

'Then how can you tell me what to do? Even here, now, I can feel him breathing down my neck. I hear him telling me what's going to happen if I do anything that upsets him. I may not remember the attack, but I remember waking in that hospital bed. I remember looking in the mirror and the nurse telling me I was lucky to be alive. I don't feel very lucky, DS Grey.'

'I understand, no one should have to endure what your husband has put you through. You deserve better than that.'

'Are you sure about that? You don't even know me. I have eyes – I see the way you purse your lips together every time I refuse to speak against Reece. I hope you never know how it feels to be living under a shadow like this.'

'You don't have to live like this for ever, not if you testify. What's your alternative? What about your parents? Do you have any family you can go to?'

'Reece is the only family I have left. Everyone else is dead or gone,' Angela said as she swiped her sleeve across her face to catch a tear.

'Can you give me a name at least? Someone else we can talk to about him? Has anyone ever tried to help you before?'

Angela stood and walked to the window. She hugged her arms and Imogen could tell she was considering whether or not to say what she had on her mind.

'There is one man who tried to help me before.'

'What's his name?'

'Clive Osborne. He worked for the company for years and I confided in him; he offered to get me out of there.'

'Where is "there"?'

'Our old place, back in Oswestry, Shropshire. Reece must have got to him, because after I arranged to meet him, I never saw him again.'

'What happened? Why didn't he turn up?'

'He just never showed up on the night we arranged to go.'

'Where is he?'

'I don't know.'

'Do you think he is dead?' Imogen asked.

'I didn't until what happened with Simon. I just assumed Clive got warned off and thought better of helping me. Reece can be very persuasive when he needs to be. I think Simon's death really drove home to me that I am never getting out of here. That Clive is probably dead, as well.'

'How long have you been together?'

'For ever and a day. A lifetime, a life sentence,' Angela said and wiped an invisible tear from her cheek. 'I'm sorry I can't tell you what you need to hear. You had better get going before he gets back.'

Imogen didn't feel right leaving Angela here. Each time she left felt more wrong than the last, as though some invisible clock on Angela's life were running down. She couldn't force her to leave, though. Who would that help?

'Stay safe, Angela.'

'Thank you. You, too,' Angela said.

Imogen stood up from the table with a little more understanding of what Angela was dealing with. She could see the hopelessness in her eyes. Angela was little more than a possession for Reece and he would not relinquish her without a fight. Imogen felt completely impotent at the situation.

Imogen walked out of the house and back to the car. She had to go back and write up both of the pointless interviews she had conducted today. It felt wrong to walk away. Thank God, at least, they didn't have any children.

# Chapter Fifty-Three

I knew this would happen. I wish I had just died in that river, then no matter what happened to R, I wouldn't have to deal with this guilt. I don't feel bad for him; I feel bad for anyone who tries to help me. I'm not worth all this trouble. Simon is gone now because of me. I still see the images of him in my head. Are they real, or am I creating them to fill in the blanks?

He's bloody, he reaches out to me, then he stops moving. I remember him staring at me, eyes fixed, one pupil blown and his face barely recognisable. I did that to him. My selfishness. R told me there was no way out. I should have listened to him. Am I this weak that I can't just leave on my own and disappear?

Maybe I can sell my belongings and put some cash together to start a new life. I don't have access to the jewellery in our safe; only R has the combination for that. I know he doesn't trust me with anything of value, but I know even my shoes could fetch a couple of hundred pounds each if I sold them. I don't have a bank account, though, so unless I get paid in cash, I don't see how I can do this. I can't sell anything on the internet. All my documentation is in the safe with the other things that might help me to get away. He has thought this through. I am nothing but a pet.

I need to stop this madness – hope has only ever got me in trouble before.

I hear a car on the gravel outside and look to see the police pull into the driveway. It's DS Grey and another officer who I haven't seen before.

Where is Adrian Miles? My mind immediately thinks the worst, but on closer examination of DS Grey's face, she doesn't look grief-stricken, so maybe there's a good reason for him not being here. Still, I have that sinking feeling. What if R has done something to DS Miles?

I feel sick at the thought of someone else getting hurt because of me. If only I could make R happy, make it so he doesn't want to hit me anymore, then maybe we could be happy. I could accept my place here and no one would feel sorry enough for me to get involved. Part of me wonders if some of the reason R does the things he does is so that people will interfere, like he is looking for a reason to hurt people. It wouldn't surprise me. I am exhausted trying to think of ways to fix this. I can't.

Maybe I need to tell the police more. This will go on and on until R finally tries to kill me again.

I remember. What do I remember? I remember R telling me that I had gone too far this time and that he was going to kill Simon and make me watch. I can't

261

believe that he would let me go after that, but I just can't remember how I ended up in the river.

DS Grey is different without her partner around. She seems softer, somehow. I wonder how much of her energy goes towards managing DS Miles when he is around. I notice women doing it a lot with their partners, trying to instigate damage control for some imaginary scenario that hasn't even happened yet. I do it with R, so maybe that's why I recognise it in her.

Even though I didn't get educated past my GCSEs, I am not stupid. I might look stupid, and I know people constantly underestimate me and think of me as some gold-digging airhead who is just in it for the money. But they have no idea how wrong they are. I couldn't give a shit about R's money.

When I talk with the detective, I realise she has absolutely no concept of what it is she is asking me to do. But then I think about Simon and how much he wanted to help me, too. He would tell me to be brave and speak to DS Grey. R told me brave was just another word for stupid.

I genuinely don't recall anything useful about the night Simon died, but I remember another man who tried to help me once. Clive Osborne worked for R and he saw me with some bruises that were difficult to explain away. He promised I wouldn't have to spend another day in that house. He left to get the things we needed to get away, but he never came back. Maybe the truth was too much for him. I always figured he got scared, but now I think I was being naive.

Back then, I didn't know the depths of R's evil. I still

*had a rose-tinted view of him, as if somehow if I loved him enough that would change him, but it never did. All it did was change me into a person I can barely stand to look at.*

*I am all but erased – changing a little each day to accommodate his demands but never being quite good enough. I wonder if anything will ever be good enough for R. He tells me often enough that there is no one else for him but me. Those words are like a noose around my neck. He likes to make sure I know he can take my life from me whenever he wants to. I wonder how he will react when he finds out that I have told the police about Clive. Maybe he will be so angry that he finally finishes me and I can finally get out of this hell.*

# Chapter Fifty-Four

Imogen finished up the paperwork ready for the team progress meeting in the morning and looked at the clock: it was time to go home. She wanted to check on Adrian again. It was unusual for him to take any time off. Whatever this illness was it was really taking its toll on him. When she went to his house to spend time with him he was either asleep or glued to the television. He wasn't himself at all. She wasn't sure the medicine the doctor had given him was making any difference. It occurred to her that she had never really seen him sick before. He wasn't a good patient. She had also never known Adrian to be this irritable with her; he just wasn't like that.

DCI Kapoor walked over to her desk.

'You going to see Adrian?' the DCI asked.

'Yes. I don't think he eats when I don't feed him,' Imogen smiled, half joking.

'Well, give him our regards. The place feels strange without him. Are you and DI Walsh getting on?' Kapoor asked, then, without waiting for an answer, added, 'I know you and Adrian have a very tight working relationship. It can be difficult to get used to other people's habits.'

'We are working together fine; did he say otherwise?' Imogen said, aware that this was leading somewhere.

'Good. I wanted to talk to you about that. We're getting a new DS soon. I think you and DS Miles might benefit from switching things up a bit.'

'With all due respect, I wouldn't be happy with that. Adrian and I work well together, we trust each other and we get good results,' Imogen said.

Was the DCI hinting that she knew they were in a relationship together? Their argument had caused a scene in the station and was something Imogen would rather forget, both personally and professionally.

'I'm just concerned that sometimes it's harder to be completely objective when you are too close,' DCI Kapoor said.

'No. Not us. I assure you, there won't be a problem.' Imogen folded her arms.

'Let's just see how you get on working with Matt. We can leave this discussion open for now. I was just sounding you out.' DCI Kapoor smiled. 'This fight that led to Adrian's irrational and unprofessional behaviour, not to mention his subsequent injury, is a cause for concern.'

'If you order us to do it then we will, but I think you would be making a huge mistake.' Imogen tried not to sound too annoyed.

'Prove me wrong, then. When Adrian gets back, I'll be watching both of you to make sure.'

'That's fine.'

'I'll see you tomorrow.'

Imogen grabbed her things and left the station. She took a few deep breaths before starting the car to go and see Adrian. He was hard work at the moment. Resistant to everything. She was sure he was still upset over what she had said. Maybe the DCI was right and they needed a break from each other when he got back to work. There was so much at stake now; it would be hard to choose which aspect of their relationship she would find it hardest to be without. He was her partner, her lover and her best friend – so much to go wrong, so much to lose.

She parked the car and rang the doorbell. Adrian answered the door and smiled when he saw her. He was looking better. He walked back into the lounge and lay on the sofa. Imogen could smell food.

'Did you cook?' she said, surprised.

'Yeah; nothing special, though. Just a prawn curry. Thought you might be hungry.'

'You mean you didn't want my cooking again?'

'Pot Noodles are not classed as cooking. Besides, I thought it was only fair. You've been an excellent nurse.'

Imogen sighed and walked into the kitchen. It was clean and the food was cooked and ready on the stove. She had been really concerned about Adrian, more than she had let on even to herself. He just hadn't been himself. The relief she felt was noticeable. Adrian seemed almost happy to see her.

She was starving and the food smelled so good. She made up two bowls and took them into the lounge.

She put Adrian's on the dining table and sat down. He was engrossed in the TV. She was a little bothered by his lack of interest in what she was doing. These days, he never asked how work was, never asked about the case or how she was. At least he had cooked, though.

'The DCI wants us to work with other people. She doesn't think it's a good idea for us to partner anymore,' Imogen said.

'What do you think?' Adrian looked up at her affectionately, a little surprised at the revelation.

It occurred to her in that moment that he hadn't looked at her affectionately since they'd had their argument at the Corrigan house. He had been so distant. She knew he was ill, but she couldn't help thinking he was still upset with her. She felt a lump in her throat. She wasn't sure why that made her emotional; maybe because he had always looked at her with care and affection and she hadn't noticed until it wasn't there anymore.

'I think she's wrong,' Imogen said. 'I think the argument we had was nothing to do with us. We would have fallen out about it regardless of our relationship.'

She didn't want to say that she thought he was wrong again for storming in and attacking Corrigan. She knew she was wrong for what she said, but it didn't make him right. They seemed to have moved past it and she wasn't about to stoke that fire again.

'Then we'll tell her that.'

'Aren't you going to eat?' Imogen asked.

She watched as Adrian laboured to get off the sofa, clutching his side as he moved, anguish on his face. His face was puffy again, as though he had been crying.

Her mother had suffered with depression many times, when she wasn't going through one of her manic episodes, and so she recognised it in Adrian. No amount of telling him to cheer up would fix it and she daren't suggest antidepressants to him, but she knew what he would say if she ever suggested it to him.

She wished there was something she could do, but she had seen that bruise on his rib – time was the only thing that could help. He shuffled over to the table with a cushion and put it on the seat, lowering himself onto it slowly. His eyes watering again.

'Are you feeling any better? Are your pain meds working?'

'The doc said my rib was going to hurt for a few weeks. When I get back to work, I'll have to do desk work for a while. As long as I stay rested it should be fine.'

'I want you to promise me you won't do that again,' Imogen said.

'Do what again?'

'Get yourself into a fight. I know this case has been difficult for you, but going out and pissing people off after work until they punch you is not the answer. You were already hurt. What if someone pulls a knife on you next time? I've been so worried about you.'

Imogen didn't want to push too hard, didn't want to ask what the hell he was thinking. They only had a minor disagreement. He was so impulsive and hotheaded sometimes. She didn't really understand why he would want to be in pain. Surely this wasn't worth it. Surely this wasn't what he wanted.

'I just got unlucky getting sick at the same time. I'll be fine. You don't need to worry about me,' Adrian said gravely; her words had obviously hit home.

'You look so pale and you've lost weight. I just want you to look after yourself.'

'I will. I won't do it again. I learned my lesson.' He smiled a tentative smile and took a mouthful of food.

She reached across the table and touched the tips of his fingers. She wasn't sure, but she thought he twitched at her touch, as though it were unwelcome. What she had said back at the Corrigan house had obviously crossed a line; she just hoped they could get back from it.

# Chapter Fifty-Five

Imogen watched Gary tapping away at the computer, pulling up various documents and sending them to the printer.

'How's Adrian?' Gary said.

'He seems to be improving. He's lost some weight, though; this bug really has a hold of him.'

'What's the doctor given him?'

'I don't know. Antibiotics, I assume,' Imogen responded. 'What are we looking at?'

'I'm just looking at all the construction jobs that have taken place over the last few years since Corrigan Construction moved into town.'

Imogen remembered what Angela had said about moving from Shropshire.

'How long ago was it again?' she asked.

'Around ten years now. Which is not that long in business terms; he grew that company very fast.'

'Do you think we can get him on dodgy books or something?'

'Nothing obviously illegal as yet. We've tried reaching out to his competitors in the area, see if he has been strong-arming them into letting him win bids on big contracts. He seems to get more than his fair share and I find it hard to believe that's completely above board. Same story, though. No one has anything to say about him on the record. I mean, why aren't they kicking off about it?'

'Why wouldn't it be legal to win bids?'

'It was a huge deal a few years ago. Then the law was changed to ensure the bigger companies weren't fucking over the smaller ones, which they were by ensuring that they always won the biggest construction bid, basically putting lots of smaller companies out of business. You aren't allowed to create barriers to prevent other companies from entering a market; it's possible that's what was happening here. Again, nothing on paper that is untoward, but you don't know what he is saying to these people in person.'

'He's probably not taking them out to dinner. He knows how to make people do what he wants, which means there won't be a paper trail,' Imogen said. 'Can you find out more about Angela Corrigan when you have done that? Where she is from, if she still has any family that maybe we could connect her with. Do it when you finish that. Let me know if you need me to speak to anyone. Although so far no one wants to say anything specific against this guy; he is like a Sith Lord or something.'

'Oh no, has Adrian been making you watch *Star Wars?*'

'Last month he made me watch the first three movies.'

'The first three?'

'You know, the first three to come out, not the first three in the series.'

'Oh, good. I was about to go mad and text him some strong words,' Gary joked. 'Do you think he would be up to a visitor yet?'

'I don't know. He's really not been well. I can ask him when I see him, though.'

'Let him know I'm thinking about him.'

'Why don't you just call him?' Imogen said.

'I have; he doesn't answer. I guess he is asleep or something.' Gary shrugged.

'How long until you get through all this lot, do you think?'

'It could take a few days, I reckon. More if I go through the contracts or look through past business deals. I want to make sure I don't miss anything. From what you have told me, this guy is a complete shit and deserves to be locked up. If we can't get him for domestic abuse or murder, then we will get him on something white collar. Who cares as long as he is put away?'

'I agree. Everything is a dead end at the moment and even if we could compel Angela to speak, I doubt she would say anything of use; she is too terrified of him. I think she would rather go to jail than bank on us putting him away.'

'Well, let's hope we can get her out of there some other way, then,' Gary said.

'Just quickly, can you see if there is anything on Reece Corrigan when he was younger, too? Like a juvey record or something. As an adult he's been clean as a whistle, but it all had to start somewhere. I can't help thinking we have missed something big.'

Gary tapped away at the keys for a few minutes and Imogen watched as he pulled up several documents at such a speed that it seemed impossible to glean any useful information from each one. Obviously, Gary knew what he was looking for.

'OK, so yeah, he was on the periphery of a few things but never directly involved. Looks like he spent a few years in Liverpool, where he got mixed up with the wrong people. He was cautioned twice but then nothing.'

'What was he cautioned for?'

'A couple of cases of common assault when he was seventeen years old, both wiped from his record after two years because of his age. In both cases the victims didn't speak out against him. There was a knife on the scene, but they couldn't prove it was his, hence the caution and not an arrest.'

'Sounds like our man.'

'He had an older brother who was killed in a street fight. His father was in and out of prison, too. Mother left when he was still in nappies, so no strong female influence in his life.'

'Get you, Mr Forensic Psychology. What was his dad in for?'

'Organised crime. Low-level, though. They didn't have much in the way of money and certainly no power.'

'Maybe that's his problem, then.'

'Sounds like being a manly man was a big deal in that household.'

'As usual, you are amazing. Can you send me over all the pertinent information? Can you check if there is anything else on him and the company? He told us he hired ex-cons before. Maybe see if we can get a list of those together and assess whether any of them could have killed Glover. I don't think Corrigan gets his hands dirty himself.'

'I'll see what I can find.'

# Chapter Fifty-Six

Seeing Dr Hadley had helped. The pain medication was good and Adrian could feel himself getting better slowly, at least physically. He wanted to get back to life now. He thought he could beat the PTSD by working hard to be normal again, to be the person he was before, maybe better. The doctor had said it could go away after a while and that's what he wanted. There had to be a way he could achieve that.

He was cooking dinner every night, resigned to the fact that Imogen was coming over. Her presence in the house did make him feel better – when he was alone, he was afraid. He ignored the fear as much as he could, pushed it to the back of his mind and got on with it, but it lingered like a shadow, attached yet apart. He was showering at least five times a day, but who was keeping count?

It had been a week since the attack. He still hadn't been sleeping very well, but he was able to sit on a cushion without wanting to scream in agony. The memory of that night was worse when he tried to sleep – that's when he was alone with his thoughts and his mind just wouldn't stop. He had watched hundreds of episodes of television shows, obsessively involving himself in character plots and fictional people's lives. Occasionally, something he saw on the television would bring a moment hurtling to the surface. He was angry and frustrated that he couldn't just put it behind him. Why did it have such a hold on him?

He had been in scary situations before but, admittedly, this was a few notches above anything else he had experienced. The physical reminder didn't help, though the pain was improving. At least his outward appearance was returning to normal, even if he didn't know what he could do about the inside. The bruise on his rib was dying; it had lost its vibrancy and was starting to fade.

Suddenly, he heard the key turn in the lock. He peered towards the front door, holding his breath.

'Hey, Dad,' his teenage son said.

Adrian was startled at seeing Tom. He was over-whelmed with shame and he felt sick again.

'I'll be with you in a minute. I don't feel so good.'

'You don't look so good, either,' Tom said as he went into the lounge, dumping his laptop bag on the ground.

'There's food in the kitchen if you want,' Adrian said as he hurried up the stairs into the bathroom.

He slammed the door and gulped for air. He leaned over the basin, ready to throw up again, saliva pooling in his mouth. Was he going to feel this way every time he saw Tom? He didn't even want to look him in the eye.

He had to compose himself; he couldn't let this beat him. He could do it – he could make himself better. He refused to be a slave to this. He wiped his leaking eyes again. Was this ever going to end?

He went back downstairs to find Tom scoffing a sausage roll. Adrian went and put his arms around his son. His rib smarted but he didn't care.

'I called your colleague, Imogen, and asked if I could come over; your phone was off. I didn't know how else to get in touch with you,' Tom explained. 'We've got the afternoon off because of some kind of problem in the sixth form centre. She said you would be happy to see me.'

'I am. It's good to see you. I didn't think we were seeing each other until next weekend,' Adrian said.

Tears hovered on edge of his lids again. He turned away and started to make a coffee before it began. Losing it in front of Tom was the last thing he needed. He had to be stronger now than he had been so far. He couldn't let Tom know he was hurting, for his son's sake.

'What happened to you, anyway?'

'Just a work thing, nothing major.'

'Can I see your rib?'

'It's faded a lot,' Adrian said, realising Imogen must have explained his injuries to Tom.

Adrian lifted his shirt and showed Tom the bruise – you could see his ribs outlined in a smoky grey and a cranberry cloud like bruising around the whole area. There were some green-and-yellow marks; it looked like a nebula. Beautiful in its own way.

'Wow! that must have really hurt.'

'Still does. A couple more weeks until I'm better.'

'Do you want to watch a movie or something?' Tom said.

Adrian could see that Tom was worried about him and it broke his heart. Even in Tom's sixth form attire of a dark grey business suit with a shirt and tie, he barely looked his seventeen years. Adrian couldn't believe that he was going to be eighteen in a couple of months.

'What did you have in mind?'

'I don't know; you can pick one of those eighties action movies you keep threatening to show me.'

'*Predator* it is, then,' Adrian said.

Tom sat at one end of the sofa and Adrian at the other. They didn't get far into the movie before Adrian fell asleep, another hurdle jumped. He hadn't considered how difficult it would be to see Tom again. Everything was difficult, everything was new. It was as though someone had flipped the world upside down and blindfolded him, still expecting him to know his way around. Being with Tom felt good, if uncomfortable, but then everything was uncomfortable. It didn't feel dangerous like almost every other situation.

He woke just as the end credits were rolling. Tom had nodded off too at some point. Adrian's phone vibrated and lit up; it was Dr Hadley.

'Hi.'

'I just wanted to give you a call and see how you were doing. Did your HIV test at the clinic go OK? I can swing by later on if you need me to, if you want a chat or anything?'

'The test went OK; I should get the results in a couple of weeks. And you don't have to come and see me. I'll come and see you soon.'

'It's no bother. I'm guessing you still haven't spoken to anyone about what happened.'

'Not yet, no.'

'There are people you can phone anonymously. Don't suffer through this alone. It won't go away on its own.'

'I know. Thank you. I will speak to someone.'

'If you need to speak to me about what happened that night, you can. I'm happy to listen.'

The idea of telling anyone he then had to look in the eye on a regular basis was not something Adrian could even consider without feeling nauseous. She was right, though. He did need to speak to someone. The guilt and shame were pulling him to pieces.

Tom took a deep breath and opened his eyes. Adrian couldn't cope with both of these states at the same time, victim and father – he could only just manage one and not even that convincingly.

'I can't really talk right now. I'll come and see you in a couple of days,' Adrian said and hung up the phone.

'Everything OK?'

'Yes, fine. I'm just tired. You're welcome to hang out here, but I think I need to get back to bed.'

Adrian poised himself to get up, mentally preparing himself for the pain. He wanted to have a shower; it had become a part of his routine to have one at this time of day. His routine was about the only thing keeping him together right now.

Tom stood and held both of his hands out to Adrian

to help him to his feet. Adrian was so proud of the person Tom was turning into. He couldn't cry, not now, he had done so well.

'Nah, I told Mum I would get back. Just wanted to make sure you're OK.'

'Satisfied?' Adrian smiled his best *I'm OK* smile.

'Can I hug you?' Tom asked.

'Gently,' Adrian said as Tom wrapped his long, slender arms around his shoulders, barely touching him.

'I love you, Dad.'

'I love you, too.' Adrian's voice cracked as he said the words.

Tom didn't look at his father; instead, he grabbed his bag and disappeared. Adrian didn't have time to think about Tom, about what his son might think of him if he knew the truth. That he might be ashamed of his father, that he might never look at him the same way again. Seeing Tom just strengthened Adrian's resolve not to report it.

He walked up the stairs and got into the shower for the third time that day. He never stayed in there for long, but there was something about the feeling of the water all around him that made him feel better. He liked the idea that all the skin he had inhabited that day was now gone, rubbed away and down the drain. He had shed his outer layer; there was no part of the skin he had now that had touched that man. A small comfort, but any comfort was good.

He found himself alternating between two tracksuits, washing one while he was wearing the other, obsessed with being clean.

Adrian hadn't been completely honest with Tom. He had no intention of going to bed just yet; he had something else to do first.

He walked out of the house and to the Sacred Heart Church on South Street. He hadn't been to church in a while, not unless he was there as a police officer to ask questions. His mother had insisted he be confirmed at the Sacred Heart and so going there would at least make him feel closer to her, if not God. He rarely missed his mother; he didn't allow himself to think about her much. Since the attack he wanted her here more than ever – she would know how to make it go away, wouldn't she?

She often took him to church. He would sit on the back pew during confessional while she disappeared inside the wooden cubicle for what felt like an eternity. When she came out, she always seemed better somehow, renewed. He wanted to feel that. Today, he was the one here to confess.

The times of confession were on the website; he had looked it up. He felt confident that he could disclose to a priest, even though he had almost forgotten how to make confession. It was strange to him that this would be the place he would come, but he didn't trust anyone else with his soul and that's what needed cleansing now.

The familiar smell of the church was reassuring. He touched the holy water and did the sign of the cross as he passed over the threshold. There was no one else in here; it was empty. He walked to the confessional and stepped inside.

'Forgive me, Father, for I have sinned. It has been over ten years since my last confession.'

'Go on.' The voice came from behind the panel.

Adrian took a deep breath. 'I have lied, I have engaged in self-abuse.'

'What do you mean by self-abuse?'

'I drink a lot and sometimes I get into fights on purpose. I have also been sexually promiscuous.'

'Why did you come here now after ten years? You know you're supposed to come at least once a year.'

'I know, Father. My faith has not always been strong. I feel further from God than ever and so I wanted to make confession.'

'Why do you feel further from God?'

'I can't tell you,' Adrian said, suddenly unsure of himself.

He came to confess but he didn't expect it to be so difficult.

'I'm bound by the confessional, you can speak to me,' the priest said.

'I was sexually assaulted. I can't help wondering if it's because I'm being punished for something, for losing faith, maybe.'

'For not coming to church? No. That's not why you were sexually assaulted.'

'I need to attach some meaning to what happened. I need for there to be a reason.'

'The reason belongs to the person who attacked you; they know why it happened. The fault doesn't lie with you. You mustn't blame yourself.'

Adrian caught his breath. He still had one more sin to confess.

'I've considered taking my own life.'

'Suicide is a mortal sin. It's important that you preserve your life, not just for God, but also for yourself, for the people around you who love and depend on you. Think about how your death would affect them,' the priest said.

'I know. It just comes over me, though. That I can't be here anymore, that I can't deal with this. I don't want to think it. I'm trying not to,' Adrian said, unsure of how to explain the way it had just suddenly become a viable option for him, as though it could be the answer to anything.

'If you have ever lost someone you love, or even if you love someone profoundly, you can imagine how their death would affect you. Do you want to be the cause of that kind of pain for the people around you?'

'No, of course not.' Adrian wiped his face.

'Then resist. You can conquer this. You have already been through the worst part. What comes now is healing and healing takes time. Be patient.'

'Thank you, Father. I am sorry for these and all the sins of my past life; for not loving others and not loving you. Help me not to sin again. Amen.'

Adrian recited the act of contrition the way he remembered it, the robotic repetition he had uttered so many times, the words feeling familiar but somehow both insincere and more meaningful at the same time. He hoped this would help, he didn't know what else to do. He had to get back to his real life. Maybe this would wipe the slate clean and let him start over again.

# Chapter Fifty-Seven

Imogen waited in the briefing room for the others to arrive. She had been feeling increasingly alone since Adrian hadn't been at work – her relationships with the other people at the station highlighted for what they weren't. She was worried about Adrian almost constantly. Sick with the feeling that there was something he wasn't telling her. She always knew when she was being lied to.

But Adrian wasn't like other people. He had more hang-ups and complexes than anyone she had ever met before, so this could all just be a side of him she had never seen before. She was already too dependent on him. They bounced off of each other well and without his voice there, she seemed unsure where to look next in terms of the case. She found herself having conversations with him in her head, but when she saw him, he never seemed to want to talk about the case.

The doors opened before she had a chance to wallow any further. Matt Walsh, Gary Tunney and DCI Kapoor all sat down and waited for Imogen to start.

'We've got nothing, basically. Nothing concrete, anyway. Lots of hearsay but no actual evidence of any wrongdoing. I am still trying to find Clive Osborne, but it's like he disappeared off the face of the earth,' Imogen said.

'Angela Corrigan had nothing else useful to say about him, then?' DCI Kapoor said.

'Just that they were meant to leave together and he never showed up. No one reported him missing,' Imogen said.

'Three guesses why,' Walsh said.

'Well, the old Corrigan Construction head office in Shropshire has been levelled and turned into a car park about three years ago. If anyone was buried around there they would have been found; the car park goes underground for three levels,' Gary offered.

'What about their previous residence?' DCI Kapoor said.

'The owners are away in New York on holiday at the moment. They come back in a couple of weeks. We don't have enough to compel a search warrant at this point, so we just have to wait,' Walsh said.

'No one else has access?' DCI Kapoor said.

'No. I spoke to the owner, asked him if there was anything unusual about the sale, and he told me the Corrigans were very eager to sell. Took way below the asking price and moved out before the sale was even properly completed. Allowed the Parkins to make alterations before they even got in there,' Walsh said.

'Why do we think that is?' DCI Kapoor said.

'They obviously needed to get out of town. Well, Reece Corrigan did,' Imogen said.

'What do we think is at the house?' DCI Kapoor said.

'I don't know. I wouldn't put anything past Corrigan, though. From what we have learned from employees and other acquaintances, he is a dangerous man,' Walsh said.

'The last time Clive Osborne used his debit card was in the newsagent's about a block away from that house. No trace of him after that,' Gary said.

'So, he went to visit them at home and then disappeared?' Imogen said.

They were all thinking the same thing. Osborne most likely fell foul of Corrigan's temper. Maybe he did turn up to take Angela away. Maybe Reece found Osborne before he got to her. Imogen felt a pang of sympathy for Angela again. All these years thinking that he had abandoned her when he hadn't at all. Still, speculation wasn't enough – they needed proof.

'Maybe he's still there,' Kapoor said ominously. 'When can we gain access to the house, then?'

'I already thought of that. I spoke to the owner and he said he would try and take an earlier flight. He is being very cooperative and has consented to a full search when he gets back even without a warrant,' Walsh said.

'Unusual,' Imogen said.

'His wife is a copper, so I guess that has something

to do with it. Also, he said that Reece Corrigan gave him the heebie-jeebies. His word, not mine. Considering we have no probable cause at this point, it's the best we can hope for,' Gary said.

'The body could be anywhere, though. How many jobs have they worked on since Clive Osborne disappeared?' Imogen said.

'Almost five hundred,' Gary chimed in helpfully. 'If you count the small jobs, as well.'

'Brilliant, 'DCI Kapoor said. 'Which one of you is going to head up there for the search?'

'I think we should both go, when the Parkins get back. DS Grey and I,' DI Walsh said.

'So, Osborne has never been reported as a missing person?' DCI Kapoor asked.

'He isn't in the system, no,' Imogen said. It was the first thing she had checked.

'That's a bit strange, isn't it? How long since anyone has seen him?' DCI Kapoor said.

'The Corrigans moved down here shortly after the last time he was seen, around ten years ago. As Gary said, there has been no activity on any of his bank accounts or credit cards. He has money in the bank, too. It hasn't been touched in over ten years,' Imogen said.

'See if you can speak to a member of his family and find out why he wasn't reported missing,' DCI Kapoor said.

'I'll try and find someone,' Gary said.

'Let's hope the search of the house turns something up because, as it stands, I don't see how we can stop this man. The lack of people willing to speak out against him is staggering. There must be someone,' DCI Kapoor said, frustrated.

'Simon Glover's sister called and asked about picking up the remains yesterday,' Imogen said.

She hated the word 'remains'; it sounded almost like 'leftovers', as though it was nothing more than the bits no one had any use for anymore.

'Unfortunately, that can't happen until this investigation is over. Any news from Jimmy Chilton yet? Do you think he'll come through with any information?'

'No news yet, Ma'am. He seems to be on the edge at the moment. I get the feeling that this has all got a lot more serious than he was prepared for. I don't think he thought murder was on the cards. I do believe that he has absolutely no power. I get the impression Corrigan keeps him around because he is weak and compliant. I think he will come through if we give him time,' Imogen said.

'Time is rarely ever on our side with men like Corrigan. OK, let's get on with it, then,' DCI Kapoor said with a heavy sigh.

They all felt heavy with this investigation. Reece Corrigan was obviously a complete scumbag but, unfortunately, you couldn't put all of that before a judge. With Angela unwilling to testify and everyone else claiming they suspected things but never actually saw him do anything, it really did seem like he was going to get away with it.

Imogen felt like she had to get Corrigan to prove Adrian wrong. Not to shove it in his face, but to give him peace of mind and show that the system can work. They needed to get this case behind them for so many reasons and as long as Reece was literally getting away with murder, the chances of them being able to move forwards and get past this knot in their relationship were slim.

## Chapter Fifty-Eight

It was fourteen days since Adrian had been attacked – fifteen since he had been at work. Driving to the station took a new kind of courage. He knew he would be inside, safe, but he didn't want to see his colleagues. What if they knew? What if someone figured it out just by looking at him? At least on the outside he looked the same as he usually did. His face was no longer bruised and his lip had completely healed.

When he arrived, Imogen walked across the car park towards his car, a genuine look of happiness to see him on her face. Did he even deserve her anymore? Did she deserve him? Didn't she deserve better?

He got out of the car and closed the door. His pain was manageable now; he just had to remember to move slowly so as not to set himself back again. Appearing to be normal was his goal for now.

'I missed you so much!' She beamed.

'I saw you this morning,' Adrian said, walking slowly towards the station.

He had drifted in and out of sleep on the sofa while she slept upstairs in the bed, alone. They had breakfast together, but things were difficult right now. Maybe Imogen thought working together again could fix the rift that was forming between them.

'I mean here – this place is shit without you.'

He smiled. 'Thank you.'

'I've been forced to eat proper lunches with Gary in the canteen every day.'

'I'll be deskbound for a while, so no drive-thrus just yet.'

'Killjoy.' Imogen looped her arm through his and whispered to him, 'I really wish I could kiss you.'

She opened the station door and Adrian sucked in a breath before stepping inside. Here, now, there was no escaping it. Life had to go on – it was going to go on whether he was ready or not. Time to get back on the wheel and try to get back to before the attack. Back through that railway arch.

They walked through the security door and into the main room. DCI Kapoor stuck her head out of her office.

'DS Miles, DS Grey. My office, please.'

He walked straight to the DCI's office without looking around at the faces to see if they were watching him or not.

'Hello, Ma'am.'

'Good to see you, Adrian. How are you feeling?'

'My rib still hurts a little, but I'm OK.'

'Imogen tells me you've been horribly ill. Are you sure you're ready to come back?'

'Absolutely. I've been going crazy at home.'

'Gary will do a run-through of what we know so far. He'll recap and you can see where we are. Maybe your fresh eyes on this will help us get this bastard. It's good to have you back.'

'Good to be back, Ma'am.'

'Did Imogen speak to you about the conversation we had the other day? About maybe having you working on different teams. Just to shake things up.'

'She did,' he said. 'But Imogen and I work well together. The incident the other day was completely my fault and had nothing to do with anyone else. I acted inappropriately; the nature of the crime is personal to me, Ma'am, and I lost my head a bit. DS Grey was attempting to defuse the situation.'

The truth was, Adrian didn't want to be partnered with anyone else, because he didn't trust anyone else. He knew where he was with Imogen, at least, and they did work well together. He didn't know Matt Walsh enough to want to spend time alone with him in a car. In fact, it made him angry even thinking about it. Angry because being alone in a car with another man wasn't something he would even have thought about a few weeks ago. Was this it, then? Was everything tainted by this one thing?

'And you agree, Imogen?'

'Absolutely. I trust DS Miles completely and I believe it was a minor blip,' Imogen said.

'Regardless,' DCI Kapoor started, turning to Adrian,

'until you pass your physical, DS Grey will be working with DI Walsh.'

'I don't need a babysitter,' Imogen said.

DCI Kapoor ignored her.

'Adrian, I don't know the exact circumstances that led to your injuries, but it's important to remember that you are always a police officer. It doesn't matter where you are, you represent all of us, whatever you are doing, whoever you are doing it with. My trust is not unconditional.

'When I was posted here it was with the primary objective of restoring this department's reputation. No one is above the law. I have had some discretion to deal with matters as I saw fit in order to minimise public distrust, but now the dust has well and truly settled we need to be above reproach. All of us.'

'It won't happen again, Ma'am,' Adrian said.

He had no desire to put himself in any more unnecessarily dangerous situations.

'Great. I'll be through to the briefing room in a moment.'

Imogen and Adrian both stood and walked back out into the bullpen. Adrian had to ignore his beating heart, desperate to focus on something else. This was his life now. He had to come here every day and so he needed to get used to it. He needed to calm the hell down and get on with it.

'OK?' Imogen said.

'I need the bathroom. I'll be through in a moment.'

Adrian rushed through the corridor as fast as he could. His rib ached but he didn't care. Inside the bathroom he quickly entered the cubicle and locked the door, pressing the weight of his body against it. *Keep it together*. He hadn't eaten breakfast and so there was nothing to come out of him, but the nausea passed.

It was a trade-off, being around other people and feeling sick and afraid, versus being alone and feeling sick and afraid. Both had their pros and cons. He felt safer with other people around, safer from physical harm, at least. What he didn't like about being around other people was the feeling that maybe they would be able to see past the thin veneer he had put in place, as though maybe somehow he couldn't act normal enough. It was impossible to decide which of these was worse.

His mind drifted back to suicide, just like that. If you can't exist in one place or another, then where do you go? Remembering what the priest had said to him about how his death would impact those who care about him, he composed himself. He stepped out of the cubicle and splashed water on his face. He left the men's room and walked to the briefing room.

*Let's do this.*

# Chapter Fifty-Nine

Imogen had noticed that Adrian still wasn't eating much. She had assumed that he was doing his eating in the day while she was at work, but since he had come back in, she hadn't even seen him eating here, either; nor drinking as much as he should be. It was becoming harder to ignore the concerns she had for his health. It was also getting difficult to pretend there wasn't a problem.

Was there something he wasn't telling her? It had been weeks and the bruising was almost completely gone, yet he still moved with difficulty. His posture was different – tense, somehow. Add to that the fact that he was distant and distracted.

Since she had started working with him, Adrian had always been open and warm, even when things were difficult in their own personal lives. He was the one who liked to put other people at ease. It was difficult to put into words the way Adrian was, but he always put others' comfort first, or maybe he was just like that with her. He was a considerate man, more than most she had met.

But the last couple of weeks he hadn't been like that. He was irritable and difficult to deal with. Maybe the case had brought something back about his childhood. Maybe it was the incident with Reece Corrigan, or it could be what she had said about Adrian being responsible if Angela got hurt. Perhaps he was finding the case even harder than she'd realised. Maybe when the pain in his ribs passed completely, he would be more like himself; after all, pain could be very dispiriting.

She put her worries on hold for now. He had reassured her several times and she had no reason to think he was still holding what she had said against her.

That evening, when she went to his place, he answered the door with a smile. She smiled back, but she could feel him pull away before she even approached. Small things like that did little to quieten the doubting voices in her head.

'I thought maybe we could do something tonight.'

'I'm still not a hundred per cent. I can't go roller-blading just yet,' he said.

'No, I thought maybe cinema. Or we could go out and eat.'

'I'm not really hungry.'

'You've lost a lot of weight, you know. I barely ever see you eating.'

'Did you come here to lecture me? Because I'm not in the mood,' he snapped.

'No. No, of course I didn't.' She looked down at her hands.

'I'm sorry. My ribs just hurt and I'm tired.' He smiled again, forcing his pained face away.

'Can we talk?'

'Sure.' He sighed heavily.

She noticed he didn't wince as his lungs filled with air. Were his ribs even still hurting him? Why would he lie?

They sat at the dining table in the lounge. Imogen tried not to look hurt right off the bat. It was a strange feeling for her, being worried about another person like this, being worried whether or not they still liked her. The fact that she was feeling like this just proved to her how much she really did care for Adrian. If anyone else had behaved the way he was behaving in a relationship with her, she would have dropped them.

'I think you're lying to me,' she said.

She noticed the faintest look of panic on his face as she spoke.

'About what?'

'I don't think you're OK with what I said to you at the Corrigan house.'

He let out a smile. 'I can't even remember what you said.'

'Then why the frosty treatment, Miley?'

'Miley, eh? Yikes. I must be in trouble.'

'You're not in trouble; don't be silly. I just don't understand what's going on with you. It's like an alien took over your body or something.'

'I'm just in pain, that's all. I'm not angry with you.'

'I feel like you are. We hardly touch at all.'

'I'm sorry. This pain is constant and annoying. I'm worried I'll damage it again or something. I can't—'

'I'm not talking about sex, Adrian. I mean you don't touch me *at all*. You only kiss me if I kiss you first. You haven't touched my hand or my shoulder or anything. I feel like there's some invisible barrier between us or something. I don't feel welcome here, either. It's like you don't want to be anywhere near me. You seem so far away.'

Adrian reached across the table and took her hands. He was tender and tentative.

'I'm sorry. I'm feeling much better than I was,' he said. 'I'll try not to be so moody.'

'Be moody if you need to be, Adrian, just don't shut me out. One of the brilliant things about you and me is how honest I can be with you. You can't know how difficult that is for me. I don't want to not trust you anymore.'

'Noted. In that case, if you want honesty, can we stay in tonight, please? We could watch a movie here.'

'OK.' She smiled.

'Will you stay the night?'

'If you want me to.'

'I would like that. I like this place better when you're in it. I do want you around. I'm sorry if I made you feel otherwise.' Adrian smiled again and squeezed her hand.

Was he just saying what she wanted to hear? If he was it was working. She felt the uneasiness disappearing. He seemed more like himself.

Imogen watched Adrian push the food she had

brought with her around the plate, trying to make it look like he had eaten more than he had. When he got up and took their plates to the sink, Imogen noticed the waist on his trousers was loose. She couldn't figure out why he wasn't eating but didn't want to risk an argument by mentioning it again.

They settled in on the sofa and chose a film to watch. He pulled her close and she leaned on his shoulder as they held hands. After a while she noticed he had fallen asleep and so she got up. The film wasn't particularly good and she was restless. She saw his phone on the table next to the sofa. *You can't.*

Staring at Adrian, she slowly reached for his mobile and picked it up. She knew the pattern he used to swipe across the front in order to unlock it; she had seen him do it a million times. He had made no effort to keep it a secret from her. If he caught her now, he probably would.

After unlocking the phone, she immediately looked at his contacts list and his recent calls. Mostly Tom and her, but there was also another name that kept popping up: Dr Zoe Hadley. Why had they been talking? Every couple of days, according to his phone. And not just for a minute or so. Occasionally, closer to ten minutes, which is a long time for a casual acquaintance. He had been on a date with her months ago, but nothing ever came of it. Had he changed his mind?

He stirred and she quickly closed the screen and put the phone back into sleep mode.

In the kitchen, she wiped down the units that were already spotless and washed the plates that were in the sink. She opened the fridge and noticed that the contents were exactly the same as yesterday – he hadn't eaten anything or got any more food in.

'What are you doing?' Adrian said, standing in the doorway to the kitchen.

'I was hungry,' Imogen said, not wanting to let him know she was checking up on him, terrified he knew she had looked at his phone.

'There's still some Chinese on the table.'

'I'll clear it up,' Imogen said.

As she went to push past him into the lounge, he grabbed her arm. She looked up at him, trying to hide the concern. He kissed her. The first real kiss in weeks. She breathed him in as he pushed her back against the doorframe. It felt so good to have his body pressing against her. She could hear his short, sharp gasps of breath as he pushed past his rib pain.

For the first time in a long time he was there with her. They were in this moment together. For so long now he had been elsewhere, preoccupied with his pain or maybe even his past. She stroked his arm and he pulled away.

'Sorry if I've been neglecting you,' he said.

'Sorry if I'm being needy. I don't know what's up with me. I just can't stop worrying about you, about us. Since that argument . . ' Imogen started but couldn't finish.

'I love you, Imogen,' Adrian said. 'I don't want you to doubt that at all.'

It was the first time he had said it and she didn't know how to respond. Though now she had been presented with the option, there was really only one thing to say.

'I love you, too.'

He kissed her again and she put her arms around his waist, gently, careful not to hurt his rib. Adrian squeezed her breast and kissed her neck, slowly at first but then biting her, drawing her skin into his mouth. She had to push him away before he left a mark on her, not willing to lie to the DCI about what it was.

He pushed back and kissed her even harder, the waistband of her jeans tugging as he tried to push his hand down the front. She grabbed his shoulders and forced him backwards, alarmed at his urgency.

'I thought this was what you wanted?' he said breathlessly.

'What *I* wanted? Don't you?'

'Of course I do. I'm just still in a bit of pain, that's all.'

'I can wait,' Imogen said, almost certain that she saw a look of relief on his face.

He pecked her on the cheek and went back into the lounge. As quickly as their moment of passion had started, it was over.

Maybe she was being paranoid. Maybe she wasn't, though. Maybe there was something very wrong.

# Chapter Sixty

Adrian was over halfway through the PEP pills the doctor had given him – three weeks already. He could hardly believe it. It seemed so long ago and yet sometimes it was like it was happening all over again. Whole chunks of time seemed to pass by without him noticing, usually when he was alone. Imogen being there at least kept him tethered to the present. The rest of the time he was lost inside himself, desperately trying to find his way back to the surface.

The physical pain had gone and Adrian missed it. It was as though he had no excuse anymore and he had to return to normality, whatever that was. He couldn't keep pretending he was in pain to avoid sex. It wasn't that he didn't want to be with her, he did, he just wasn't sure if he could. He was more terrified that they would start and then he would freak out. Then she would definitely know something was wrong. Maybe drinking was the way forward, or maybe that was a huge mistake. So much to consider.

This wasn't fair to Imogen at all. Every time she looked at him, he could feel her eyes, dripping with worry. Adrian knew that his weight loss was concerning her, but not eating felt like a way to control something; he felt so out of control with everything else. When he was brave enough to look in the mirror, he could see the hollows of his cheeks getting deeper. He had to find a way through this, to be himself again.

He had wanted to wait until he got the results of his HIV test at least. He was waiting for Dr Hadley to call him with the results, having given consent for them to be given to her. Dr Hadley told him she would call at some point today.

He had already decided that if the results were positive, he would break up with Imogen. The idea killed him, but then he couldn't put her in any danger. Not because of what he wanted or needed. He couldn't be selfish like that.

He had asked Dr Hadley to call before work if at all possible and so he waited. Sitting in the armchair in the lounge trying to think about nothing, which is an impossibility in and of itself. He concentrated on his breathing and tried to be aware of his body as he did so. There was no physical pain anywhere anymore. He had got so used to it that he didn't even notice it disappearing.

The phone rang.

'Hello. Dr Hadley?'

'Hi, Adrian. Good news! Your test came back negative,' she said, considerately skipping any small talk, which he really appreciated.

'Thank you.'

'I also got the results from the swab I took. The DNA isn't in the system. It's been logged and filed as a John Doe. I will email over the serial number in case you want to look at it yourself. As it's in the system, if any other cases come up then it should flag them. I have put a note on the file that if anything like that happens, I should be personally alerted.'

'OK,' he said.

He hadn't thought about it linking to any other cases. It made him feel sick.

'How are you getting on?'

'Not good. I mean, life feels normal, until I remember how I used to be and it's nothing like that. I'm constantly tense, scared of everything. I can't trust my own judgement. I keep forgetting things.'

'I think we need to look at therapy now. If you're willing to?'

'I'll have to think about it. I don't know if I can.'

'You don't have to talk about what happened to you. You can talk about anything.'

'I don't know. Thanks for everything, Doctor,' Adrian said, indicating an end to the discussion.

'OK. You know where I am.' She hung up.

So, there it was – one of the worries was almost gone. Although not a hundred per cent, it was as good as and Dr Hadley had explained that he should take it as a win.

He didn't feel much like a winner, though. Physically, everything was back to normal. Even the bruise on his rib was nothing more than a smudge of green now. He would have to undertake a physical exam at work before he was cleared for active duty, but he knew he could pass that. The question was, did he want to?

Those three weeks should feel like a long time and for the most part it did, except when the memory of that night was more than a memory, it was happening all over again. Part of him wanted to run away from his life, from the people he knew. He was constantly reminded that he had forgotten how he used to be around them. Every interaction required a level of effort that he just couldn't sustain. At least if he was somewhere new, he could be whoever he wanted and people would just accept that's how he was, who he was.

At the station, he struggled to focus, always concerned with who was behind him, who was walking past. Trying to keep his nerve enough not to give himself away. Imogen was at lunch with Gary when Adrian arrived that day. He had taken the morning to wait for the doctor's phone call. He didn't go to see them, something he would have done before.

He pulled up the case they were working on and decided to do what he had been doing every day since he had come back. Reading through interviews, looking at pictures, cross-referencing suspects. All the while wondering if the attack on him had anything to do with this case. Realistically, it could be any number of cases he had worked on in the past. But he didn't want to make any assumptions. It's not like he was actively looking for a suspect in his own assault, but his mind was always there, every photo, every interaction. He wondered if that feeling would ever go away. It certainly didn't feel possible now. Would he ever find peace until he knew who had done this to him?

He found himself looking through the list of Corrigan's staff. He had a lot of employees. Was one of these names the name of the man who raped him? It seemed highly likely. He found the list that Gary had compiled of workers at Corrigan Construction who had served time for one thing or another. The chances were that if the person who assaulted him worked for Corrigan, he would be on that list. He printed a copy. He would take it home and see if he could find the man himself.

He didn't know what he would do if he did find out who it was. Was he capable of killing? The idea of this man doing what he did to Adrian to anyone else was enough to make Adrian think that maybe he was. Then again, maybe he would get home and put the list in a drawer and never open that drawer again.

He pulled out his phone and looked at the serial number the doctor had given him. He typed it in to compare the DNA and see if it had flagged against anything else – they had different databases to the hospital. He felt sick even typing it in, worried that someone would figure out what he was doing.

There were no connected cases, but that could change. He closed it quickly as the thought that one day a name might pop up there crossed his mind. What would he do? He had no idea and just thinking about it made him feel sick; he could feel the colour draining from his face.

'What time did you get in?' Imogen said as she sat down.

He hadn't even noticed her approach.

'Not long now; about half an hour ago.'

He slid the papers out of the printer tray and quickly put them in his bottom drawer.

'Notice anything new? Anything jump out at you?'

'Sorry. Nothing yet.'

'Did you eat?'

'I grabbed a sandwich on my way in,' he lied.

'I'm just heading off to Shropshire with Walsh, but call me if you need anything.'

'I will,' he said, almost relieved that she wasn't going to be here watching him.

He could feel her watching him all the time these days. She knew something was wrong and he had to make sure she never found out what that something was. The thought of her knowing made him want to throw up. He remembered promising her that he would always be honest with her. In the past he had taken it upon himself to conceal the truth in order to protect her from his occasionally terrible professional decisions, but this was different. He had to keep this from her. There was no other choice.

# Chapter Sixty-One

Adrian took a deep breath before entering Gary's office, steeling himself for the inevitable physical contact and reminding himself that Gary was one of the good guys. As suspected, Gary's face lit up when he saw Adrian and he put his arms around him in a hug. Gary was one of the few male friends that Adrian had. He had transferred in from Plymouth after Imogen came to Exeter. They became friends almost instantly. Despite the hug, Adrian was surprisingly pleased to see Gary.

'Mate! You've been missed!' his friend said.

'I can tell. Sorry I haven't been in touch; really not been well,' Adrian said, pulling away.

'Imogen said you were properly ill. I think she was really worried you weren't going to make it.'

'A stomach flu coupled with a fractured rib are not happy bedfellows.'

'Well, it's been weird without you. DCI said I need to catch you up on the case.'

'Imogen's been keeping me informed for the most part.'

'Right, well, most of what we have is two dead bodies, a battered wife and a missing employee. I don't know how he is doing it, but he has managed to keep a pretty tight lid on whatever it is that he is up to.'

'What do you mean?'

'I mean in business terms, he seems to be just under the threshold to be investigated by the Monopolies and Mergers Commission. He throws the other contractors a bone every now and again, but it's not benevolence, it's purely to keep any kind of audit at bay, by the looks of things. This is purely speculation, of course. My guess is it's bid rigging – have you ever heard of that?'

'No.'

'Right, well, the way it works is that companies collude to enable the "winning" party to obtain contracts at uncompetitive prices – so, higher prices for sellers and lower prices for buyers. Typically speaking, the other contractors are compensated in various ways, either by cash payments, or in this case probably by not having their faces smashed in. They are also occasionally designated to be the "winning" bidder on other contracts, or hired as a subcontractor. This usually happens with government contracts and in past cases of bid rigging, the companies take it in turns to be the winners. From what I can see, Reece Corrigan's company has won every significant contract in the last few years. He doesn't take turns.'

'Couldn't that just be because they have a stellar reputation?'

'It's possible, of course, but for the other companies not to undercut him to stay afloat seems sketchy to me.'

'So, is what he is doing illegal, or not?'

'Not on paper. I wouldn't be surprised if the other construction companies have to offer him some financial incentive in order to get work though. I doubt there is any kind of paper trail, probably cash in hand. It's going to take more digging to find out what. If it's proven, each instance carries a prison term of up to six years. So, if they've been doing it for ten years on several contracts a year, then you are looking at some serious prison time.'

'What's the point of that for the other companies? Wouldn't they be out of pocket?'

'Not necessarily.'

'But if there is no evidence of this then what can we do about it?'

'It could take months of going through all of his personal expenditure and also looking at his assets and other things. I think if you can speak to one of his rivals, they might be able to give you some information. The next largest company is Hatfield Homes; they will definitely have crossed paths. Their company hasn't experienced the kind of growth you would expect given the current climate. In order for us to prove this by his accounts alone, he will need to be audited by a forensic accountant. It could take months and that stuff is a little beyond my capabilities.'

'I don't believe that for a second,' Adrian said.

'Well, I don't have time to do it and it would take someone else with the proper experience half the time.'

'Who can we speak to at Hatfield Homes?'

'The director there is Cameron Becker. I'll ping you the address.'

'How are things with you, anyway?' Adrian asked.

'Really good. Franka and I are going on holiday in about two weeks. Hopefully.'

'Where you going?'

'Croatia, to see her family. Meeting the parents and all that.'

'Oh, so her parents get to meet you before we get to meet her. I don't even know what she looks like,' Adrian said, half joking.

He wondered if there was something about his new girlfriend that Gary was trying to hide. It certainly felt like it; they'd been together for several months now and there was always a reason Gary couldn't introduce her to them. He couldn't be annoyed, though, because he hadn't even told Gary he was in a relationship with Imogen.

'She doesn't do photos, sorry,' Gary said.

'Well, she must be pretty special to have bagged a guy like you.'

Gary blushed and turned back to looking at his laptop screen.

'We should know a bit more after the search of the house at Oswestry. Hopefully, anyway,' Gary said.

'How long has this guy been missing?' Adrian said.

'Clive Osborne hasn't been seen in around ten years. Hard to pinpoint an exact date after so much time has passed. He last used his bank account about two weeks before the Corrigans moved into the area.'

'Who reported him missing?'

'No one; that's the strange thing. I have managed to locate his mother's phone number. She lives in Spain now.'

'Have you called her yet? I can do it after I speak to Cameron Becker,' Adrian offered.

'Great, I'll ping the number over to you.'

Gary tapped away at the keys furiously and just seconds later, Adrian felt his phone vibrate in his pocket to alert him that he had an email. Phone calls he could do.

# Chapter Sixty-Two

Sitting in a car with DI Walsh for almost four hours was going to be a challenge. Imogen was pleased at least that she was the one doing the driving, definitely preferable to being the passenger. She always found it hard to stay awake in the passenger side on journeys over an hour; she didn't much like reading in cars, either.

Beside her, DI Walsh was going through some information that Gary had given him, doing what they all did, looking for things they missed before. Sometimes you could look at something for the fiftieth time and suddenly it would make sense of something else. They only ever had fragments until they put the whole picture together.

She couldn't help thinking she should be back at the station with Adrian.

'I feel like there is some kind of problem with us, Grey,' Walsh said unexpectedly.

'What makes you say that?'

313

'Just a feeling I get.'

'I don't have a problem with you,' Imogen said.

'But?'

Imogen exhaled. He had brought it up, it was only fair that she tell him what was bothering her.

'I just don't know you. It's not like we chat about things. Knowing that you are close to the DCI also makes me wonder if I am constantly being evaluated, I guess. Plus, I don't like the way you speak about DS Miles sometimes. I think you have him all wrong.'

'But there is no problem between us . . .' He smiled and raised his eyebrow.

'Don't ask questions you don't want the answers to. I am not the girl who is going to lie to make you feel better.'

'Technically, I didn't ask a question.'

'The question was implied, or why mention it at all?'

'OK, then what do you want to know about me? You say we don't chat at all, but I am not one for small talk, Grey. As for DS Miles, I don't have a bad opinion of him, I just think he behaves unprofessionally sometimes.'

'You never put a foot wrong?'

'I didn't say that.'

'Let's start with an easy one, then,' Imogen said.

'Excuse me?'

'An easy question. You said I could ask you. Are you married?'

'No.'

'Have you ever been married?'

'I have.'

'So, you live alone now?'

'Totally and utterly, not even a goldfish for company.'

'How old are you?'

'I am forty-six years old. Before you say it, I know I look older. I went grey before I hit thirty.'

'OK. Why did you transfer down?'

'Mira called and said she had an opening and was looking for a DI she could trust. I have no ties and so it was easy enough to pick up and move to Exeter.'

'No other reason?'

'There are always other reasons. You transferred as well, you know how it is.'

'What's your opinion of me? Professionally speaking,' Imogen asked.

'I think you are holding yourself back and I don't know why. I suspect it has something to do with DS Miles, again. I think you two are too close. And I think your loyalty to him is both admirable and also professional suicide.'

'Thank you for being so blunt. My reasons for not wanting to put myself forward are more to do with the fact that I don't feel ready yet. I was never in this to become chief of police. Advancement is not something I crave. I like the role I am in. Do I seem like someone who would let another person hold me back?'

'I guess not and for what it's worth, I am not spying on you for the DCI,' Walsh said.

It was the first time she remembered him actually referring to their boss by rank and not her first name. Maybe he finally understood why there felt like a division between him and the rest of the team.

'What's your favourite band, then? What music do you like?' Imogen continued.

'Anything but jazz.'

'Amen to that.'

They talked about music for a while and Imogen felt the invisible barrier between them dissolve a little. They didn't have a great deal in common, but he was a serious man and she realised he just didn't speak when he didn't need to. Maybe she had had a problem with him, after all.

She noticed how he had braced himself before she started asking questions. She wondered what question he was most worried about. Everyone has one, that one question you can't lie or laugh your way out of, the one that exposes you for who you are. Her worries about Matt Walsh faded as they got closer to Shropshire. Maybe he wasn't so bad, after all.

# Chapter Sixty-Three

Adrian dialled Clive Osborne's mother in Spain. She answered almost immediately. He heard her take a long drag on a cigarette and exhale while she waited for him to introduce himself.

'Mrs Osborne, I am calling from Exeter police in the Devon constabulary to speak to you about your son, Clive?'

'It's Mrs Ortega now. Is Clive in trouble?'

'Nothing like that, Ma'am. We just wondered when the last time you heard from him was?'

'Did you say Exeter? Why is Exeter police interested in what Clive is up to?'

'He is a possible witness to a crime. We just want to speak to him about it. Can you tell me the last time you heard from him?'

'Why, yes, it was about two weeks ago.'

'You heard from him two weeks ago? Where is he?'

'Once a month he sends me some cash to keep me in ciggies, bless him. Lovely boy, my Clive.'

'So, you haven't actually spoken to him or seen him recently, then?'

'Like I said, he sends me money and Christmas cards and all that. He don't like flying, which is why he's never been out here. I haven't seen him in around ten years. He fell out with me when I decided to move to Spain with Xavi, my new husband. They don't get on. Xavi's a bit younger than Clive and he didn't approve. I understand, I suppose; it must have been strange for him.'

'Right, OK. Do you know a man called Reece Corrigan?'

'Yes, Reece, course I do. He's a very good friend to my Clive; sorted him out with a new job and everything after they left for Devon. He even set me up with a builder over here when we needed some work done on our place. Is this about Reece? Is that why you're calling me from Exeter?'

'No, we are purely trying to locate Clive. Do you have an address for him?'

'Sorry, no, I don't.'

'How much does he send you every month?'

'Three hundred euros.'

'How does he send that?'

'He sends me a card with the cash in it.'

'Thank you, Mrs Ortega, you've been very helpful.'

Adrian rung off, even more certain at this point that Clive Osborne was dead. Yet again, there was no evidence. Maybe they would find something at the house in Oswestry.

# Chapter Sixty-Four

The house in Oswestry was worth considerably less than the one in Exeter. It was a good size, but not quite as striking as the dream house Reece had bought with Angela Corrigan. The door of the modest 1940s semi-detached opened and a young man answered. He couldn't have been much older than twenty.

'I'm DS Grey and this is DI Walsh,' Imogen said, holding up her warrant card.

'You're here for the search? My dad has just gone down into the cellar with one of the police officers. Do you want me to get him for you?'

'Thanks, if you can just show us the way,' DI Walsh said.

'Sure, just follow me.'

They walked past a police officer doing a deep scan of the walls using a hand-held Doppler radar device. Reece Corrigan had the means to make a body disappear with relative ease. The chances of him leaving the body in the house he used to live in were slim; however, it was one of those things they couldn't ignore. The timing of him leaving the town and moving to Devon was suspicious, as though maybe time had run out for him there. Knowing what had happened to Simon Glover, they couldn't take a chance on this. No stone would remain unturned.

They followed the young man into the cellar, where his father stood looking over the room with concern.

'Hello, Mr Parkin. Thank you for letting us conduct this search. I am DI Walsh and this is DS Grey,' Walsh said.

'Anything I can do to help. My wife is on the force and so we are more than happy to assist.'

A man approached them.

'I am DS Ali Hasan. Welcome to our corner of the world. We've been going at this for a couple of hours but so far nothing. If the radar doesn't find anything then as a last effort, we will bring in the cadaver dogs. Sometimes they find things the radars don't and vice versa.'

'Thank you for having us,' Imogen said before turning to Mr Parkin. 'Is your wife here?'

'No, she stayed in New York. We were visiting her sister over there and I didn't think it was fair to ask her to come back when all you needed me to do was let you in. My son came back with me as well, to give his mother some alone time. She's had this holiday planned for months and you know what a pain it is switching holiday when you're in the police.'

'We really appreciate this. Did you ever meet Mr

Corrigan, before you bought the house off of him?' Walsh asked.

'I did meet him once, yes. I can't say I liked him much.'

'Did you meet his wife?' Imogen asked.

'No, I'm sorry. He showed me around the place and it was everything we were looking for. We snapped it up because of the lower asking price. My wife fell in love with the garden particularly.'

'Did you question why they were so desperate to move out quickly?' Imogen said.

'It was worth more than we paid for it. He wanted a quick sale. We even knocked him down a little and he still went for it. I'm afraid we didn't much care why he was doing it. He didn't even seem remotely fazed. My wife wanted to push it down even more, but I thought we had tried our luck enough. We paid about thirty grand under market price and ten years ago, that was a significant markdown.'

'Do you know if Mr Corrigan had had any work done on the place before he left?' Imogen asked.

'Well, this cellar hadn't long been done. Do you really think that there's a body here?'

Imogen shot DS Ali Hasan a look.

'We don't know. All we can do at this point is look. Your cooperation is definitely going to speed up the process,' Walsh said, trying to comfort the man.

'Will you have to dig up the foundations?' Mr Parkin said.

'Depends on the foundations. They start with ground-penetrating radar and then go from there. As long as it's thin enough, the radar can usually get a pretty good read on what's underneath. If there is any digging or drilling, you will be asked first and you will be compensated for any damage to the property. Apart from the cellar, is there anywhere else that you can think of?' Walsh said.

'No, I mean there is a sizeable garden out back, but it's very well established. The garage we had converted doubled the size of the kitchen. The builders had to reinforce the foundations; they would have found something then if there was anything there, I think. Whatever you need to do, you just go ahead. I would rather we knew for sure.'

Imogen nodded to Walsh to one side, indicating she wanted to speak to him away from prying ears.

'What do you think?' Imogen said.

'Sounds like Corrigan wanted to get out of here fast,' Walsh said.

'My thoughts exactly. Let's hope the radar gives us something we can nail this piece of shit on,' Imogen said.

# Chapter Sixty-Five

Adrian pulled up outside Cameron Becker's property, the director of Hatfield Homes, at DCI Kapoor's request. An old rectory house on the outskirts of St Leonards in Exeter. It felt strange to be conducting an interview without Imogen and even stranger to be alone.

He took a deep breath and knocked on the door, ignoring the anxiety that made him want to turn around and drive away. If he couldn't do something like this then what use was he?

The door opened a crack, the chain on. A man looked through the gap and Adrian pulled out his warrant card to show him. The door closed and Adrian heard the man remove the chain before opening it again.

'I'm DS Miles. I'm looking for Cameron Becker.'

'I'm Cameron Becker. How can I help you?' the man said.

'I need to speak to you about any dealings you may

323

have had with Corrigan Construction, namely with Reece Corrigan,' Adrian said.

'I'm afraid I don't know the man,' Becker said, clearly lying.

Adrian wasn't sure if he was projecting, but he could have sworn the man tensed as soon as he said Corrigan's name.

'We are currently investigating his business. I don't suppose you know anything about bid rigging?'

'I don't,' Becker said, clutching the door, seemingly desperate to close it.

'We've heard some rumours about Mr Corrigan, about people around him getting hurt. Do you know anything about that?' Adrian continued.

Cameron Becker peered up and down the road before leaning towards Adrian with a look of what can only be described as terror on his face.

A horrible idea formed in Adrian's mind. What if what happened in the back of that van wasn't the first time something like that had happened at the behest of Reece Corrigan? As if answering his own question, he remembered the look on Leon Quick's face as he took his own life. He dismissed the memory. He couldn't deal with this right now.

'Please, I can't tell you anything. You need to leave me alone,' Becker pleaded.

'Did he do something to you?' Adrian asked.

He could feel his brow furrowing as he said it. It seemed like a massive leap to assume that this man had been sexually assaulted, but somehow Adrian knew that's what had happened to this man. He could see it in his eyes.

'No. Just leave me alone. I don't know anything.'

Adrian took his card out and handed it to the man.

'If you think of anything, or if you want to talk, then call me. We can talk off the record if need be,' Adrian said, half trying to convey his understanding of the situation while still trying to remain professional.

He walked away from the house as Becker closed the door. His mind was on fire. He already knew Corrigan wasn't afraid of staging accidents against people he worked with. Was sexual assault part of his remit, as well? Was he using extreme sexual violence to gain power over people who got in his way? Even if Adrian's attack was connected to Corrigan, he had no idea if Corrigan had actually instructed the men to rape him. Maybe that was something the man in the van decided to do on his own.

This investigation wasn't even supposed to be about what happened to him and yet Adrian couldn't get away from it. He would have to face it at some point. He would want the answers one day, he knew that much. He just didn't know if he was strong enough to get those answers just yet.

His chest was heaving when he got back to the car. There was no hiding from this, was there? First, he had to concentrate on helping Angela out of her situation and then maybe he could think about himself. Everything was too much to think about at the moment. *Concentrate on one thing at a time.* He pulled away from the house, wondering how many other men Corrigan might have done this to.

# Chapter Sixty-Six

At the property in Oswestry several hours later, they had drilled a number of test holes in the garden and examined the dirt, soil and dust, with no trace of human remains. It had been a long shot, anyway. They couldn't go around digging up every place the Corrigans had lived or worked. The fact is, Reece Corrigan had ample opportunity and more than enough means to dispose of anyone he wanted. His company had been involved in so many construction jobs over the years that they could have hidden a body on any one of them. The chances were that they would never find Clive Osborne's remains. But it had been worth a shot. At least they'd tried.

Back at the car they waited for the Parkins to close the door before pulling away. Imogen looked at the clock: it was after ten. Walsh was driving this time. It was only fair and he insisted. Even though she preferred to drive, it was possible he preferred it, too. At least this way she might be able to get some sleep.

'What now, then?' Imogen said, trying to cram the work talk in before she nodded off.

'We'll have to put some more pressure on Jimmy Chilton, see if he can be a bit more forthcoming with the information.'

'Do you think that will work?'

'We already know that he never worked alongside Osborne and so I don't see how he can help us with that. He might have more information on Glover, though.'

'He definitely knows more than he is letting on. It always amazes me how many people are complicit in domestic abuse.'

'It's hard to get involved, I guess. You don't want to make things worse. It's one thing to suspect something and another entirely to out and out accuse someone.'

'Is that what it is?' Imogen asked. 'Or are people just more worried about looking after their own shit?'

'I suspect there is some of that, too.'

'It's so frustrating.'

'So, now I guess it's my turn to ask you a question.'

'What do you mean?'

'You asked me some questions before and now I want to ask you something.'

'What is it you want to ask me?'

'What do you think will happen when the DCI figures out that you and DS Miles are in a relationship together?'

At least that answered that question. Maybe she and Adrian weren't as discreet as they thought they were.

'Excuse me?' Imogen responded.

'That's assuming she hasn't figured it out already.'

'Did she say something to you?'

'Not to me, but it's obvious. Maybe she was waiting for it to peter out. These things happen a lot within the force. You're not the first.'

'Adrian has volunteered to transfer,' she said, almost like a boast, as though he should know that they had discussed it like adults already.

'So, he should probably do that.'

'Why doesn't she like team members dating? It's not against policy.'

'It's not my story to tell, I'm afraid, but if she knows you're together then she will partner you both up with other people. It just keeps things simpler on call-outs.'

'Have you ever been in a relationship with someone on your team?'

'This isn't about me,' Walsh replied.

'So that's a yes, then. You know what it's like – you work with someone day in and day out and you have no social life. Your world revolves around the job. People need other people. It's just a basic human thing. We certainly never intended for it to happen.'

'But it has happened. I just wanted to let you know that it hasn't gone unnoticed.'

Imogen wished this conversation wasn't happening right now. She was trapped in the car with DI Walsh and as friendly as this conversation was, it was almost certainly a reprimand.

'Is that why DCI Kapoor has suggested that I work primarily with you?'

'I told you, she hasn't said anything to me, but I would say that's a safe bet, yes.'

'Shit!' she swore.

'I'm just giving you a heads-up, DS Grey. You work with detectives, someone was bound to notice. As long as it doesn't interfere with anyone's ability to do their job, she will turn a blind eye. These last few weeks have been quite tense, though, and after the way this case is playing out—'

'That's got nothing to do with our relationship.'

'Maybe not, but if Adrian was working with another officer, maybe he wouldn't feel able to cultivate this anger of his.'

'So, it's my fault?'

'I'm just saying if he was with, say . . . me, he would remember he was working, that his personal feelings don't come into it.'

'Are you going to talk to the DCI about it?'

'Only if she speaks to me first. I'm not the enemy, Grey. I'm trying to give you some advice here.'

'OK. I appreciate you being honest with me. I guess DS Miles and I need to have another talk about the future. It doesn't feel like a fling, so we need to figure out a way to move forwards.'

'He could just move to another team and you would still see each other at the station, as well as at home.'

'I can't make the decisions for him, and this is a discussion for me and him to have, anyway. I'm sorry if we put you in a difficult position.'

'I'm not worried about me. Like I said before, these things happen a lot.'

'Well, I'm tired. I'm going to shut my eyes for a minute, if that's all right with you,' Imogen said before the conversation got even further away from her.

She should have known people had figured it out. Somewhere inside she already did. Would she even tell Adrian, or let him think that no one was any the wiser? She had hoped to keep it quiet until they had figured out what kind of relationship this was, it still felt too early to go public. She didn't want to keep secrets from him, but at the moment she had no idea how he would handle the news. He really wasn't himself.

She leaned against the glass and crossed her arms. It was cold in the car, but she didn't mind it that way. It occurred to her that maybe Walsh had started that difficult conversation to avoid talking to her for the rest of the journey. Was he that smart?

The catseyes on the motorway blinked past her like the tick of a clock, each around a second apart. She started to count in her head, mostly to stop herself from thinking about the dilemma she was faced with. Same shit, different day. The man or the job. She couldn't have both.

# Chapter Sixty-Seven

Imogen knocked on the door to Adrian's house, but there was no answer. She tried the spare key in the Yale lock, but the door wasn't budging. Adrian must have double-locked the door and she didn't have a key for the mortise lock. Maybe he thought she wouldn't be back and he was elsewhere, with someone else. She pulled out her phone and called him.

'Where are you?' Imogen asked, wondering why he hadn't answered the door.

'Is that you outside?' he whispered.

'Yes, it's me. Can you let me in, please?' she said, although he rang off before she even got to the end of the sentence.

He appeared at the door a few moments later and unlocked the secondary lock before letting her inside and closing the door quickly behind her.

'What's wrong?' he said.

'We just got back from Shropshire and I wanted to see you.'

'It's three in the morning.'

'Do you want me to leave?' she said, annoyed at him for not being pleased to see her.

She could have gone straight home. The way Adrian had been behaving lately, she should have gone straight home.

'No. No, of course not. Did you find anything?'

'Nothing at all. Complete waste of time. I'm starving, have you got any food?'

'I think there's some bread in the kitchen. I could make you some toast.'

'Thank you.'

She leaned forwards and kissed him – that flinch was there again, more pronounced than usual. She pushed it to one side and walked through to the kitchen.

Adrian followed behind and went straight to the toaster, busying himself with kitchen activities. She watched him closely and realised that he wasn't making eye contact with her deliberately. Was he feeling guilty about something? Imogen was good at reading people and she couldn't ignore her instincts anymore – she had to get the truth out of Adrian.

'Adrian, what's going on?' she asked.

'I'm making you toast, that's what's going on. Almost ready.'

'I mean with us. Something is wrong. I can feel it. Are you experiencing some kind of buyer's remorse or something?'

'I've told you before that there is nothing wrong with

us. I don't know what you want me to say. Do you want me to make something up? Will you leave me alone then?'

The toast popped up and Adrian got a plate to put it on.

'I thought we were being honest with each other.'

'Look, I'm tired. I don't have the energy for this. You know where the butter is,' he said, dumping the plate of toast on the table in front of her before leaving the room and going back upstairs.

She closed her mouth, realising that it was slightly open in shock. She had never known Adrian to behave like this before. She rushed upstairs after him, but when she reached the bedroom and opened the door, she saw that he was already back in bed and covered up.

'What the fuck was that?' she asked.

'Don't read too much into this, Imogen. I am just fucking tired.'

'I know you are lying to me about something, Adrian. One thing about you is that you have no poker face. Have I done something wrong?'

She could feel the neediness in her voice and she hated herself for it. She hated Adrian for it.

'No, no, of course not. Can we maybe talk about this in about four hours?' he said dismissively.

'I don't know if I can actually do this for much longer, Adrian. I hope this secret is worth what it's doing to us.'

'Grey, you're paranoid; there is nothing you don't know.'

'Grey? You're calling me by my surname and there's

nothing wrong? Is there someone else, Adrian? That's really the only thing I can think of.'

Adrian sat up in the bed and crossed his legs before running his hands through his hair. She could see he had the urge to grab clumps of it in frustration.

'Imogen. It's three o'clock in the fucking morning. I need to go back to sleep so that I can wake up for work tomorrow. I promise you that I am not sleeping with anyone else. I already told you I love you and I meant that, but if you really think I would cheat on you then you should leave.'

'Of course I don't. I'm just scared, that's all. I can feel you shutting me out. I don't know if we can survive that kind of relationship. I don't know if I want that.'

'So, one little problem and you want out, is that what you're saying?'

'I'm saying talk to me!'

'This is ridiculous! You can't just come here at three in the morning and demand . . . this. Is this about sex?'

'What? Of course it's not! I mean, don't think I haven't noticed that you don't seem to be interested in me anymore. I guess that's why I asked you if there was someone else.'

'Do you really think I would do that to you?'

He looked hurt at the suggestion this time.

'No, of course I don't, but I do know that you aren't talking to me. Did I do something wrong?'

'Look, you were right before. It's this case; it's getting to me. I'm sorry it's spilled over into our relationship, but I can't switch off. I am really trying not to dwell on it, but it's not letting me. I wish I thought talking things through would help, but I don't. Just be patient with me for a bit, please. I don't want you to go. I don't want to lose you, Imogen,' he said.

The softness had returned to his voice. The tension left her shoulders as she looked at him – he wasn't lying or pretending, at least at that moment.

'You know, that's the most you've said to me in weeks. I just don't like to think of you going through this alone when you don't have to.'

'I know, I'm sorry. I'll try harder.'

'You don't have to try at all, just let me be there for you.'

'You are. I would have gone crazy without you these last few weeks. I really don't deserve you.'

He held his hand out to her. She took it and he pulled her towards him, kissing her on the lips, soft and tender, reassuring her that all of her concerns were completely unfounded. Giving her exactly what she wanted.

# Chapter Sixty-Eight

Adrian had got four hours' sleep the previous night with Imogen turning up at three in the morning and making him feel like shit for making her feel like shit.

They lay together on the bed until the sun came up and it was time to get ready for work.

He had some thinking to do. He wasn't sure he was even fit to be in a relationship and so maybe he did need to let Imogen go, even though the thought killed him; she was more than his lover – she was his best friend, they were a team.

As it was, the situation was confusing. He wasn't doing the best job of getting back to normal and he was pulling Imogen down with him. If they broke up, he would be losing so much more than just a girlfriend. He briefly considered telling her the truth, but the thought of how she would look at him from that moment on quickly put an end to that idea. He washed his face in the sink of the station bathroom and went back to the team briefing he had asked to be excused from because he kept falling asleep.

He sat back down at the end of the conference table nearest the door, just as Gary finished explaining the company financials to the rest of the room.

'What did I miss?'

'I was basically telling everyone how, as far as I can tell, there is no way to get him through the business. Certainly not quickly. It's a dead end. Everything is just this side of legal and if there is anything untoward going on then I can't find it. No wonder he was so eager to give us copies of his files; they are in very good shape. I have handed it on to someone in forensic accounting, but it could be a while before we get anything back on that, if we actually do. They are the cleanest-looking books I have ever seen. He's clever; he knows how to cover his tracks. I'll give him that.'

'This is absolutely ludicrous. We are almost six weeks into a murder investigation and we know who did it but have absolutely no physical evidence tying him to the various crimes we suspect he is guilty of. Did you reach out to Cameron Becker?' DCI Kapoor asked Adrian.

'Another dead end. He didn't have anything to say about Corrigan at all,' Adrian said, his voice catching.

'Do you think he was telling the truth?'

'Yes,' Adrian lied.

If he was right about what had happened to Cameron Becker and the police investigated it, it could lead them to discovering what had happened to Adrian. He couldn't have that. Also he felt a little protective over

Becker, wanting to safeguard his privacy, understanding that coming forward was his choice and no one else's.

'So, we keep looking; there has to be something,' Imogen said.

'So far, we suspect he killed both Simon Glover and Clive Osborne. We also think he maimed a couple of people, as well. We think he attempted to murder his wife, Angela Corrigan. And not forgetting whatever drove Leon Quick to stabbing himself in front of two police officers out of the bloody blue. There was nothing in the house in Oswestry?' DCI Kapoor said.

'They haven't come back with anything, but they'd found nothing when we left. The cellar was newly remodelled when they moved in, but the Parkins permitted them to drill into the concrete to get to under the foundations and take soil samples. They are quick, simple tests on the ground and none of them threw up any trace of human remains. Forensics said that was their best bet at this point,' Imogen said.

'Feels a bit too much like a lucky dip for my liking. We are missing something or someone, I know we are,' DCI Kapoor said.

'Do you want us to take another run at his right-hand man, Jimmy Chilton? He must have some information by now,' Imogen said.

'You do that, DS Grey. Scare the shit out of him if you need to. He definitely knows more than he is letting on. Bring him in and make him sweat it out in an interview room. Go and speak to Quick's parents first, see if they can't tell you a bit more about why he left. I know you haven't been cleared for active duty yet,

DS Miles, but as these are grieving parents and not suspects, you should be fine. I think it needs to be the two of you who go and speak to them, not someone new. They've met you before,' DCI Kapoor said.

Adrian was thankful at least that he had been paired with Imogen and not someone else. The thought of leaving the station was not particularly appealing after what happened at Cameron Becker's. These days he divided his time between home, work and sometimes the church. He didn't want to deal with anything or anyone else. He knew he would have to get over all of that if he wanted to continue as a police officer. Before the attack he had never considered being anything else. His whole life had been called into question. He didn't even know who he was anymore.

Imogen tapped him on the shoulder and he realised the briefing had ended. His mind had wandered off again. Standing, he walked out of the room, because that's what he was supposed to do now. Just a few more hours of going through the motions and he could go home and shower, sleep and let go of the pretence for just a while.

# Chapter Sixty-Nine

Adrian got chills as they pulled back into the Quicks' driveway, remembering what happened the last time they were there. Adrian thought of who he had been then and it felt like a lifetime ago.

Imogen pushed the doorbell and Mrs Quick answered the door. She had that look still, grief, the hollow of bereavement. They had known they wouldn't be welcome after what had happened last time they were there, but nothing could prepare Adrian for the look of sheer hatred and betrayal Mrs Quick gave him.

'What do *you* want?' she asked.

'We just wanted to ask you a few questions about your son, Mrs Quick,' Adrian said.

'Can we come in?' Imogen added.

'I don't think so. Just ask me what you want to ask and then leave.'

'Do you know why your son moved back home?'

'He said he wanted to save some money, said he was

struggling to keep on top of his bills. I didn't really scrutinise his reasoning; I was just glad to have him home.'

'Did he say much to you about his work at Corrigan Construction?'

'No, but he was different after he worked there. It changed him, it did.'

'Changed him how?' Adrian asked, remembering that Gerry Thompson had said something similar about working there.

'He just became a total recluse. He was always late for things, or just didn't turn up at all. He cut himself off from almost everyone he knew apart from Simon.'

As she spoke, Adrian thought again of the idea that had come to him at Cameron Becker's residence. He remembered the look on Leon Quick's face as he plunged the knife into himself. There had been something he would rather die for than talk to them about.

A few weeks ago, Adrian had no idea what could have caused a young man to behave in such a way. As soon as the thought entered his mind it stuck. No proof, but Adrian knew. He thought of Leon's face and he knew. He knew what had happened to Leon because it had happened to him and, he believed, to Cameron Becker, too.

Reece Corrigan was behind the sexual assault on Adrian. Any doubt Adrian had of that fact was quashed by this realisation. He might not have done it himself, but he was the driving force. To distract him from the case? To teach him a lesson? To put him in his place? There were no boundaries. There was nothing Reece

Corrigan wasn't willing to do to protect himself. There was also no way Adrian was going to let him get away with it.

This meant that it was more than likely one of Corrigan's associates was his attacker. This narrowed things down and gave Adrian a sense of peace, knowing which direction the attack had come from, knowing the reason.

The adrenaline coursed through him with new vigour as he imagined getting his revenge, followed by the feeling that this was already more than he could handle on his own. He couldn't tell Imogen, though; he didn't know if he would ever be able to tell her. Keeping such a big secret from her didn't feel right, but there was no way Adrian could utter those words yet. He needed to get better first. Before taking any more action, he had to stop falling apart and put himself back together.

He remembered the list he had printed off and put in his drawer. He would start to investigate each name on it. He knew Leon's attack must have happened just before he'd moved home. It occurred to him that while Quick's attack was taking place, Adrian was just doing his normal Adrian things, oblivious to what was happening, oblivious to who Leon Quick was.

It seemed strange to think about that attack now, that if they had known, that if Leon had reported it then they would have investigated it. Maybe they would have found who did it. Maybe that person would have been in prison. Was it the same person who attacked Adrian? He almost hoped so, because the thought of someone else committing sexual assault at Reece Corrigan's bidding was too much to bear.

Adrian thought about all the people who were going about their business while he was being raped. A sense of guilt washed over him. He should report it. He should stop this animal from being able to do it again.

Imogen's hand on his arm pulled him from his thoughts again as Mrs Quick shut the door. He hadn't even realised he had zoned out again. Still fragile and undone from the attack, he knew his plans would have to wait until he could function vaguely normally again. He could beat this.

# Chapter Seventy

Since they had left the Quick interview, Imogen had noticed a change in Adrian's behaviour yet again. She was having trouble keeping up with his moods lately and it was doing her head in somewhat.

'That was a waste of time,' she said, slumping into her chair.

'We are just clutching at straws now,' Adrian said.

'What's left but clutching at straws? Angela Corrigan is too resigned to her fate to put up a fight. She absolutely won't tell us anything. She put her life in danger by even mentioning Clive Osborne to us and we have found nothing.'

'Self-preservation wins out in the end. She has no faith that we can deal with her husband and so she is making sure she is safe. If Corrigan did kill both Glover and Osborne for trying to get her away from him, then it's hardly surprising that she doesn't want to drag anyone else into it,' Adrian said, thinking of the price he had paid for trying to help Angela.

'She seems to be the catalyst for everything he does,' Imogen said. 'She's the key to all of this. We either need to get her to talk, or we need to get her away from him. His fear of losing her seems to be the thing driving him to all these vile acts.'

'Easier said than done,' Adrian said.

He didn't want to go anywhere near her house in case Corrigan was there. He had absolutely no idea what he would do if he was confronted with him. Would he fall apart, or would he try to kill him? In his mind, Adrian knew he wasn't ready for that conversation just yet.

'Let's get right into her background, then. She can't be completely without family. There is always someone, somewhere. I'll ask Gary if he can find anything.'

'What about Corrigan? Does he have any family anywhere?' Adrian asked.

'None that we have found. They both seem to exist in this little microcosm together and anyone who gets in the way ends up very badly hurt or worse.'

'We need to give her something before we can get her to talk to us properly. So that she knows we are doing everything we can. Some kind of hope that this time will be different, that he won't get away with it.'

'Except we have nothing of the kind. Every path we have is a dead end. Is he going to be the one who gets away?' Imogen said.

'Not if I can help it,' Adrian said.

She believed him.

Imogen's phone rang. She picked it up and looked at the screen.

'Detective Hasan,' she said as she answered, 'has there been a development?'

'Yes, actually, the dogs have found something.'

'A body?'

'Maybe. We haven't got to it yet. Mrs Parkins remembered that Corrigan's greenhouse was also installed a few months before they moved in. She said they were able to use the five-year warranty to get some of the panes fixed when a branch broke through it in a storm. We think there might be something underneath it. The dogs seem to think so, too.'

'How long until you know for sure?'

'They are disassembling the greenhouse now. Once that is done, we can start to dig. If there's a body, depending on how deep it is buried, it could be anywhere between one or four hours, I think, going by past incidents like this. It also depends on the condition of the body and whether or not it's been preserved or wrapped in any way, which will make it much easier to move in one piece. I will get it straight to the pathologist for analysis.'

'Thanks for keeping me updated. This could crack our case wide open,' Imogen said.

'Glad to help. I'll call you as soon as we know something.'

She hung up and looked at Adrian, who was just staring at the report in front of him; although he didn't seem to be reading it.

'They think they found something up in the house in Oswestry.'

'I thought that was a dead end?'

'Well, it was in the garden. The wife remembered that the greenhouse was almost new when they moved in. He's going to call back when they have something. You know what this means, though, don't you?'

'We need to verify and then get an ID on that body before we start counting our chickens.'

'Let's go and grab Jimmy Chilton,' Imogen said. 'He knows more than he is letting on. Walsh and I spoke to him before, and he told us he was going to tell us who was doing Corrigan's dirty work for him.'

Imogen wasn't sure, but she thought she saw the tiniest flash of something in Adrian's eyes. Was she being paranoid now? Was she seeing things that weren't there? She must have looked concerned, because Adrian offered her a weak smile.

'He was probably just stalling for time,' he said.

'Maybe. Let's find out.'

# Chapter Seventy-One

Adrian thumped on the door to Jimmy Chilton's house. It was afternoon and there was no indication that anyone was there. Still, Adrian had a bad feeling – not entirely unusual these days but still, something was off to him. He cupped his hands around his eyes and pressed them up against the glass part of the front door. There was no movement inside.

'The receptionist said he was home,' Imogen said.

'Apparently. Said he left a little while after ten this morning.'

'If he's not here, then where is he?'

'At the Corrigans'?' Adrian said.

'I doubt it; I think he was finally wising up to the fact that Corrigan wasn't going to be getting away with this for ever.'

'I'll check the perimeter.'

Adrian walked to the side of the house. The bins were leaning against the wall and he could see through the side gate into the garden. No activity there, either.

At the other side of the house he noticed the garage door was jutting out a little at the bottom, as though unable to close properly. He lay flat on the ground and looked underneath. The car was inside but it was sticking out further than it should and the garage door was closed down on it. The room was dark, so Adrian fished around inside his back pocket and pulled his phone out.

The light from his phone torch illuminated the floor. He could see paint pots in the corners, smashed glass on the floor. He thought he could see a boot by the front wheel. He couldn't quite tell if the boot was on a foot or not. There was barely any room to get in or out of the car. What was going on? There was enough space for him to slide underneath, but he would have just ended up under the car.

'Give me a hand with this,' he called to Imogen.

He grabbed the edge of the garage door and pulled upwards, trying to force it far enough so they could at least see inside the car. Imogen grabbed the other side and pulled with him. The mechanism groaned and creaked, but eventually the door was past the boot.

Adrian looked through the back and front windscreen to see Jimmy Chilton slumped over the bonnet. The windscreen had been smashed to let whoever was driving the car out and the door to the inside of the house was open.

'It's Chilton,' he called to Imogen. 'He's in there. Phone it in and call an ambulance. Someone's going to have to move this car. I'm going to go around the back of the house and see if there is another way into the garage.'

'Be careful,' Imogen said, pulling out her phone.

Adrian heard her on the phone to the station as he zipped past the bins on the other side of the house and opened the gate into the garden. He ran around to the kitchen door which, fortunately, was just a latch lock.

Adrian took his coat off and wrapped it around his fist before punching through the small pane of glass. Reaching inside, he unclipped the latch and let himself into the kitchen. Before venturing into the garage, Adrian opened the front door so Imogen could get inside the house; he didn't want to walk into that garage alone.

They found Jimmy Chilton pressed up against the wall, his legs invisible to them, his body sprouted from the headlamp.

'He didn't do this to himself,' Adrian said.

'Do you want to check his pulse or should I?' Imogen said.

'Either way, he's a dead man,' Adrian said quietly, in case by some miracle Jimmy could hear them.

Adrian had seen something like this when he had just joined the police, back when he was a PC. He had held the hand of the man until they moved the car, at which point he died instantly. Adrian reached across the bonnet, his fingers barely touching Jimmy's wrist. He wasn't sure, but he thought he could feel a faint pulse. It was a blessing that he wasn't conscious, at least.

This must be one of the worst ways to go, just waiting

and knowing that you are going to die – the car a part of your body and the only thing completing the circuit and allowing you not to bleed to death.

'How long do you think he's been like this?' Imogen said.

'I don't know. We know he left work at ten and it's a twenty-minute drive, assuming he came straight home. It's coming up to two o'clock now – around three hours, give or take. I hope he passed out soon after. His pulse is very weak, but it's there.'

'He's facing the car, so he saw it coming,' Imogen said.

'Someone might have seen something.'

'I doubt it. Corrigan is always so careful. We can get the uniforms to canvas the neighbourhood. I think we can safely assume this was Corrigan's doing. Maybe Chilton got those names for us in the end. Or Corrigan just decided he didn't trust him anymore.'

'It might be enough to persuade Angela Corrigan to speak to us,' Adrian said.

'Add to that the body they are digging up in Oswestry, she might,' Imogen said hopefully.

'Even if we can prove it is Clive Osborne's body, what are the chances of us being able to pin the murder on him? He is one slippery customer,' Adrian said.

He wasn't sure he even wanted Corrigan to go to prison. Men like that thrive on the inside.

'We should go and speak to Angela again, after we go back and brief the DCI. She said she wanted information on any major developments. I would say this is pretty major.' Imogen stood up. 'You coming?'

'Did they give you a time on the ambulance?'

'It should be here within ten minutes, they said. The uniformed police might take a little longer.'

'You want to go back and brief the DCI without me? I'll stay with him. I can get a lift back to the station with one of the uniforms,' Adrian said, hoping she would say yes.

He wasn't even cleared for duty yet. The truth was he didn't want to see Reece Corrigan.

'Actually, I might. I just need to pop home and get something,' Imogen said.

Adrian was alone in the garage with Jimmy Chilton's broken body. He had obviously outlived his usefulness. Could Corrigan feel the net closing in on him? Is that why his behaviour was getting more rash? He must have known this would come back to him.

Chilton groaned and started to stir. His eyes opened and Adrian could see the exact moment when he realised that he was going to die. He looked up and saw Adrian.

'It's OK, there's an ambulance on its way,' Adrian said, knowing that the ambulance wouldn't be able to save Chilton but wanting to give him some hope.

'I'm sorry,' Chilton said breathlessly.

Adrian had no idea what he was saying sorry for.

'Just hang in there.'

Adrian leaned across the bonnet and took hold of Chilton's hand. No one deserved to go like this.

'I tried to tell Reece to stop, told him I was going to tell you . . .' he trailed off.

'Tell me what?'

What was Chilton talking about? Was he talking about what happened to Adrian? Did he know something? Did Adrian want to know what he knew? Chilton wasn't going to live through this, Adrian knew that much, and so now might be the only chance he had to ask the question.

'Jimmy. What are you sorry for?'

'I should never have covered for him. Angela . . . she shouldn't be there . . .'

'What about Angela?' Adrian said, almost relieved that Jimmy had probably been talking about her all along. Glad he didn't have to confront his situation right now.

'I didn't know at first. I should have stopped him when I found out . . .' Jimmy whispered before losing consciousness again.

Was Jimmy talking about the domestic abuse or something else?

Sirens approached the house as soon as he had finished the sentence. The ambulance had arrived, although the chances of them being able to help Jimmy now were worse than slim.

Adrian stood up and took a deep breath before stepping away from Chilton's barely living body so the paramedics could get to him and see if they could do anything. He watched Imogen drive away and was immediately flooded with a mixture of relief and guilt. He knew he wasn't being fair to her. He just didn't know how to be any way else right now. He was trying to get back to the man he used to be.

The paramedic looked up and shook his head. There

was no hope for Jimmy. If they could just get Angela to testify, they could stop Reece Corrigan. Adrian daren't get his hopes up at this point, but there it was. It seemed as though they might actually have a chance to nail this shitbag.

## Chapter Seventy-Two

In the car, Imogen was grateful to be away from Adrian. Constantly second-guessing everything he said or did wasn't doing either of them any good. She was annoyed with herself for looking at his phone. He wouldn't cheat on her, she knew he wouldn't. So why did that nagging voice in her head refuse to give her a moment's peace?

Instead of driving down towards the station, she doubled back and drove to Wonford Hospital instead. What on earth did she think she was going to find there?

She parked in the car park nearest the ambulance bay, knowing that Dr Hadley was usually in accident and emergency. This was stupid. If Adrian found out about this, he would be really pissed off with her, especially as she already knew he wasn't cheating on her.

She *knew* it. Didn't she? But then, why so many phone calls between them over the last few weeks? Had he turned to Dr Hadley after their argument at the

Corrigan house? Is that where he went? Is that when it started? That seemed to be the moment when everything changed between them. Why couldn't she just keep her stupid mouth shut? She shouldn't be so paranoid about his history with the doctor; it was one date that Adrian had claimed was a real non-starter. Furious with herself, Imogen had to know for sure; she had to speak to Zoe Hadley for herself.

'Is Dr Hadley in?' Imogen asked the receptionist, showing her warrant card.

'I'll get her for you. Take a seat; she might be a few minutes.'

The row of plastic seating was empty, a quiet night in A & E. She sat on the last seat nearest the exit, in case she changed her mind and decided to flee before Dr Hadley emerged from the belly of the hospital.

Too late.

'DS Grey. What are you doing here?'

She hadn't even considered what she was going to say when asked that question. What the hell *was* she doing here? She stood up and walked over to where Dr Hadley was standing.

'I . . . There's no easy way to ask this.'

'OK.'

'Are you seeing DS Miles again?'

'What do you mean?'

'I mean, I heard some rumours around the office that you two were seeing each other. You know, like, dating,' Imogen said, unsure why she could claim that was any of her business even if it was true.

'No,' Dr Hadley answered. 'I don't know how much

he told you about when we went out that one time, but it was not something either of us wanted to repeat. But what if we were seeing each other? Would that be a problem?' Dr Hadley folded her arms and raised an eyebrow.

'No, no, of course not. I just wanted to let you know he was ill.'

'Yes, I know, thank you. He came into A & E when he fractured that rib. I saw to him then.'

'Of course, sorry.'

She could see a look of suspicion on Dr Hadley's face. It suddenly occurred to her that the doctor could easily tell Adrian that she had been in here, checking up on him. She really wished she had thought this one through. Adrian made her a bit crazy, she had decided.

'I was just passing, so I thought I would come and ask you. He's really been quite poorly. I wondered if you could give me any advice on how to help him recover faster.' *Good one, Imogen.*

'The usual, really. Plenty of fluids, plenty of rest, no alcohol. No great secret to healing a fractured rib.' Dr Hadley placed her hand on Imogen's shoulder and looked at her earnestly. 'Some things just take time.'

'Well, thanks, Doctor.'

Imogen shifted backwards, unsure as to why she was so uncomfortable, but something about the way the doctor had just looked at her made her uneasy.

'Don't worry; I won't mention this to Adrian if I speak to him,' Dr Hadley said.

That was also a strange thing to say, just to offer like that. What did the doctor know that she didn't?

'Thank you, Doctor,' Imogen said as Dr Hadley stepped back through the triage doors and into the hospital.

Imogen was sure now that there was no secret romantic relationship going on there, but why else would they be talking? It was true that Adrian didn't have an abundance of friends outside the police service – hell, he didn't even have that many inside the police service. He had a tendency to rub the men up the wrong way and the women kept their distance because of his reputation, unless they had already slept with him, in which case they avoided him like the plague.

Maybe it was purely about his injury, but this impromptu meeting with the doctor had done little to quash the voice in Imogen's head that was telling her something was wrong. Adrian certainly had no intention of telling her if he hadn't done so already, she knew that much about him. She also knew she couldn't take much more of this.

She left the hospital and got in the car alone. She felt alone a lot these days, even when she wasn't.

# Chapter Seventy-Three

Adrian got back to the station to find Imogen coming out of DCI Kapoor's office. It was getting late and he wanted to go home and shower. Seeing Jimmy like that made Adrian think about what had happened to him and whether he himself would have preferred to be pinned to a wall, conscious and knowing full well that he was going to die. Would he have preferred to go through that than what happened to him in the back of that white van? He didn't know. Surely being alive was better than being dead. Surely.

Reece Corrigan was evil – that much was true. Maybe even the worst that Adrian had ever seen, and he had seen some really fucked-up things.

'The DCI wants to see you,' Imogen said as she passed him.

The warmth between them was disappearing. He carried on walking directly to the DCI's office.

Being with Imogen both at work and at home made

it harder for him to pretend to be all right all the time. There was no respite and she was noticing the holes in his demeanour.

Adrian knocked on the DCI's door and she called for him to enter.

'Ma'am?' Adrian said.

'I just wanted you to know that I've had confirmation that you've passed your medical and are therefore released from desk duty.'

'Oh. Great,' Adrian lied.

'Also, DS Hasan called from Oswestry and confirmed that a body has been discovered but is as yet unidentified. We've almost got him. Let's press Angela one more time, now that we have some tangible evidence.'

DCI Kapoor looked back down at the paperwork on her desk and carried on working. Adrian pulled the door closed and walked back to his desk. Life goes on whether you're ready or not.

He went to the bottom drawer of his desk and pulled out the printed list – the names of staff from Corrigan's construction company who had spent time in prison. He folded the sheet of paper and put it in his pocket before Imogen came back.

One of these men most likely hurt him. He had spent enough time with Gary Tunney to know how to use the internet to his advantage. He already had plenty of information to start with: names, addresses and offences. What he really wanted was to see their faces and then eventually hear their voices. But that was also the part he was dreading the most, hearing that voice again.

He needed time to get over what had happened, but

360

he would find the two men from that night and he would make them pay for what happened to him, one way or another. If they wanted to operate outside the law then that was fine, as long as they knew there wouldn't be any phone calls to lawyers when Adrian eventually found out who they were.

He realised this was all a bit of a pipe dream. He was still too scared even to open the door. But he wasn't going to give up. They had already taken so much from him; they weren't getting everything.

He was greeted with that face of Imogen's again. She knew something was wrong; he really wished he knew how to be the person who could confide in her and tell her everything. Keeping a secret like this was taking its toll on their relationship. He needed to fix this somehow. He knew he couldn't tell her, though. Maybe one day he would be strong enough.

'Let's go see Angela Corrigan and tell her about Jimmy and the body; see if that changes her position,' Imogen said as she walked past, barely looking at Adrian.

He followed behind her, the dismissive look on her face making him feel like a disobedient dog.

# Chapter Seventy-Four

Angela Corrigan answered the door. The side of her face was red; the remnants of an open slap clung to her cheek. She took a deep breath when she saw them, no doubt preparing to find new ways of avoiding their questions. Walking into the house, Adrian could smell the gin on her before he even saw the half-empty bottle on the kitchen worktop.

'You just missed him. He's gone to the site.'

'I thought Friday was poker night?' Adrian said, looking at the clock.

It was gone seven. Not that he wasn't grateful that Reece wasn't here.

'We need to speak to you about Oswestry.'

Angela poured herself another gin and emptied a small can of tonic water into the glass, grimacing slightly as she took another gulp. Adrian and Imogen watched her and waited for her to respond.

'Don't worry, this is only my second one.'

She smiled before polishing off the last of the drink and tipping even more gin into the glass.

'We looked for Clive Osborne. I spoke to his mother,' Adrian said. 'She said he sends her money every month.'

'Did you find Clive? Has she seen him?' Angela said.

'She hadn't actually seen him for a long time, no,' Adrian said.

'He's dead. You know that, don't you? First him and now Simon. I thought he abandoned me, but no, he's dead. I kind of had a suspicion, but I gave Reece the benefit of the doubt, because who does that? But after Simon, I realise that I was naive. He's capable of so much more than even you know.'

'The police up there are conducting a search of the property and grounds where you used to live,' Imogen said.

'I hated that house.'

'Well, they think they found something,' Imogen said.

'A body? Clive's body?' Angela said.

'We haven't identified it yet, but it's possible. We should have a rough ID very soon,' Imogen said.

'Then what happens?' Angela drank some more.

'We build a case against your husband. There is enough circumstantial evidence to charge him,' Imogen said, knowing full well they would need more than what they had. They would need Angela's testimony.

'He'll get away with it. That's what he does. He does whatever he wants and no one can stop him. I certainly can't.'

'Maybe once they get under the greenhouse there will be more evidence there, as well,' Imogen said.

'It doesn't matter what you do. He won't be held accountable. He never is,' Angela said softly.

'I promise you, we will get him. He isn't going to get away with anything he's done,' Imogen said.

'There's something else, as well,' Adrian said.

'What now?' Angela asked.

'We just came from Jimmy Chilton's place. Have you spoken to him at all recently?'

'I don't really know him very well. I have stayed away from the site as much as possible since Simon left a few months ago. I have no friends there. Reece likes his lackeys and spies.'

'Well, he agreed to help us with our investigation,' Imogen said.

'That's surprising. I thought Chilton would take a bullet for Reece.'

'The walls are coming down around your husband and he knows it. With your help, we can make sure it happens a lot faster. We are going to get him. He's not going to get away with it,' Adrian said, avoiding telling Angela that Chilton was dead.

She smiled and nodded knowingly, reading between the lines, resigning herself further into her role as captive wife.

Adrian caught her eye. He wanted her to know that he was serious, that he meant what he was saying. Part of him wanted her to know that he understood what she was feeling, the powerlessness and the loss of hope. The circumstances were different, but the root of their pain was the same.

'Wait a minute,' Angela said suddenly. 'Did you say the body in Oswestry was under the greenhouse?'

'Yes, why?'

'Well, that can't be Clive. He was one of the men who put the greenhouse up. It went up a few weeks before he disappeared.' Angela's face became clouded in confusion, as if she was trying to remember.

'Are you absolutely sure?' Imogen asked.

'I am. I remember because he bought me an orchid to look after. He gave it me as a birthday gift to put in the greenhouse after it was finished.'

Just like that, the bewildered look on her face disappeared and she plastered on her phoney dutiful-wife face.

'Who else could it be if not him?' Imogen asked.

Angela shrugged then changed the subject.

'Can I get you a drink?'

'No, we're fine, thank you,' Imogen answered.

Adrian could see Angela's brow furrowing as though trying to remember something.

'We're going to get him, Angela, but it would be so much easier with your testimony,' Imogen said.

Angela seemed to be considering what she was saying.

'Fine, I'll talk to you. But first I need to go to the bathroom.'

'Thank you,' Imogen said, trying and failing to keep the surprise out of her voice.

'Take a seat. I will be right back.'

Angela walked into the hallway and then seconds later, they heard the front door slam followed by the thrum of an engine and tyres on the gravel path outside.

'Shit!' Imogen said.

They rushed to the window to see her driving away. She was gone.

# Chapter Seventy-Five

I squirm as he kisses me. He runs his fingers through my hair. He tells me he loves me and I smile, hating myself as I do so. Always well behaved, always doing what I am told. We are in the kitchen and the kettle has just boiled. I imagine picking it up and pouring it over his head, his puffy red skin peeling away from the face that I have grown to hate. In my mind, his scream is a high-pitched wail as his flesh blisters and burns.

I've had this fantasy before, but I never pick up the kettle, just like I never pick up the knife or any of the other things I think about killing him with. I am not brave, or maybe R is right, maybe trying that wouldn't be bravery at all, it would be stupidity.

He slides his hand under the hem of my skirt and between my thighs. I really don't want to and so I place my hand on his, stopping it from moving any further upwards. I know he won't be happy; he doesn't like to be denied anything. I remind him that he said he had to go to the new building site in the park because he left his phone there earlier today. I don't really care that he has lost his phone, but I don't want to have sex with him right now.

He looks down at my hand and I see the anger just seconds before he slaps me. He storms out of the house and I am alone. I call that a win.

I grab a bottle of gin; I am running out and so I make a mental note to get some more. I have already decided to finish this bottle before he gets home. I know he won't let me refuse him sex a second time in one day and if it's all the same, I would rather be drunk when it happens.

There is a knock at the door, and I know before I answer who will be standing there. DS Imogen Grey and DS Adrian Miles. I am relieved to see him at the house again. I thought R had done something to him and that's why he'd stayed away. Maybe I have overestimated R's reach.

There is no use fighting the police anymore. Even though they haven't got R yet, they seem determined. It's the first time R hasn't been able to weasel his way out of trouble with the police and I don't think he likes the loss of power. I have no doubt he will try anything to redress the balance.

DS Grey tells me she has been to visit the house in Oswestry. I have a mixture of emotions when I hear this. I have both good and bad memories of R in that house, before he turned into the monster he is now.

Although he was never quite right, when I think about our history I can't understand how I hadn't *realised what he had done. Now, the police have found a body. It's not a total shock, let's put it that way. I should have known sooner, or at least suspected.*

*I wonder what the house looks like now. I have no doubt it will have changed significantly in the past ten years. I only hope the family who moved in managed to build some happier memories than the ones I have. It was the beginning of the end for me. Then we moved here, a fresh start, I had no idea that it meant isolating me from everyone I had ever known. My whole life revolved around R and I was completely dependent on him for everything. He knew what he was doing.*

*The detectives tell me that Jimmy Chilton was assisting them. I knew from the first moment I met him that he couldn't be trusted. There was something intrinsically weak about him. Now, I feel like maybe I judged him harshly. I had no idea he was helping the police; I didn't think he would have the courage to do something like that.*

*Something the detectives tell me about the house in Oswestry jumps into my mind. I try not to think about those days when everything changed – they are too upsetting for me. I can accept what came after, but to go from feeling loved by a person to them making you feel so ashamed and disgusted with yourself, it's hard to come to terms with something like that. It's hard to remember them the way they used to be.*

*You wonder what you did wrong to bring about this change in them. But the greenhouse . . . I used to love tending to the garden. It was one of my great escapes in life and R bought me a greenhouse. I remember Clive* letting me watch him install it and so I know it wasn't Clive's body under the installation. It was then that Clive offered to help me get away. R must have found out. I wonder where Clive's body is now. I have no doubt that he is dead, as well.

There is only one other person I can think of who would be under the greenhouse. I am sure R found it hilarious, watching me potter about in there, looking after the flowers, knowing who I was walking on. I see how everything is a game or a power play to him. He doesn't care about me – maybe he never did. It's all about him.

If I am right, then the police will definitely be able to arrest him. That body will be conclusive proof of what he has done. I need to get to him before the police do, though. I need to get to him because, if it is who I think it is, I don't want him to go to prison. I want him to die.

# Chapter Seventy-Six

It seemed obvious to Imogen where Angela was going. She was going to confront her husband about the body; she must have an idea who it was. Beside her in the car, she saw Adrian clenching his fists until they were white. She really didn't think him being around Reece Corrigan was a good idea. He had attached too much of himself to this case and seemed to be forgetting that it wasn't about his life or his history with his parents. It wasn't about the domestic abuse his mother suffered at the hands of his father. In all honesty, it was more about murder than the domestic abuse, in any case. If Angela wouldn't speak up, then there was very little they could do about her situation. Murder, however, it was harder to get away with.

Imogen's phone rang. It was Detective Hasan again. She put it on speakerphone.

'Detective Hasan, do you have a positive ID for me?'

'Not yet, but I can tell you it isn't Clive Osborne.'

'How can you be sure?'

'Because it's a woman.'

'What? That doesn't make any sense.'

'It's definitely the skeletal remains of a female. She's been there around ten years.'

'Thank you for letting me know so swiftly,' Imogen said.

'No problem. I'll get back to you when I have more.'

'Thanks.' She pressed the red button and looked at Adrian.

Adrian looked as confused as Imogen. Whoever the female buried under the greenhouse was, she had never once been on their radar when it came to this case.

'She's gone to the site, to confront him,' Adrian said.

'Do you have any idea about what?' Imogen asked. 'Did she ever indicate who the woman at Oswestry could be?'

'When, exactly? She told me less than she told you, Imogen. You were the one she told about Osborne, remember?' Adrian said angrily.

'So, where the hell is he?'

'It was always a long shot when it came to Osborne's body – the house, the number of contracts they oversaw in Shropshire. Osborne could be underneath any one of the buildings they worked on.'

'I guess,' Imogen said then added, 'If Reece Corrigan is there, are you going to be able to keep your shit together?'

'What do you mean?' Adrian snapped.

'I mean last time you decked him and he could have brought charges against you, not to mention the fact that he cracked your rib. With everything we have heard about this guy, it sounds like you got off lightly.'

'I can keep my cool, don't worry,' Adrian said not entirely convincingly, his jaw straining as he clenched it.

'I just don't want you to get in any trouble. I don't want to give DCI Kapoor another reason to put you with someone else, or me with Walsh.'

'I know. I promise, I won't hit him,' Adrian said, his voice flat.

'We just can't give him anything, you know? We have to nail this prick, for Angela's sake,' Imogen said.

She knew that Adrian meant what he was saying at the time he said it, but all of that could go out of the window the moment they saw Corrigan with his wife.

Imogen felt the burden of having Adrian with her – in this particular case, he wasn't so much a partner to her as another variable she had to make sure didn't go to shit. Maybe Matt Walsh was right when he said she was ready for more responsibility. Maybe she was letting Adrian hold her back. She felt disloyal even thinking it.

'I should tell you that Walsh knows about us,' Imogen said.

'You told him?'

'No. He asked me about it on the way back from Shropshire. I couldn't lie when he asked me directly.'

'Is he going tell the DCI?'

'He says not.'

'Do you believe him?' Adrian asked.

'Well, he hasn't said anything so far. Plus, he reckons she already knows. He said it's kind of obvious.'

'What does he think we should do?'

'Nothing, by the sounds of it. If we tell the DCI, then she has to act on it. He thinks that's why she is ignoring it.'

'So why did he mention it?'

'Because . . .' Imogen paused and took a deep breath. 'Maybe it's messing up our ability to do our jobs properly.'

'He means me, though, doesn't he? Not you. Not perfect Imogen.'

'That's not fair,' Imogen said, hurt by his words. *Where did that come from?*

'Maybe that's what he wants. He wants you to either drop me as a partner or as a boyfriend so that he can swoop in and save the day; be your shoulder to cry on under the guise of protecting your career.'

'Are you taking the piss right now? What *are* you talking about?'

Imogen was taken aback. It was unlike him to be jealous. She might be angry with him if she didn't suddenly remember the fact that she had checked the call history on his phone without his permission.

'Sounds to me like Matt wants to spend some quality time with you.'

'So, he can't just think I am a good police officer? He must fancy me because I don't hold any value in any other capacity, is that what you're saying?'

'I didn't say that.'

'For what it's worth, he made a good argument for

why we shouldn't work together anymore. For a start, we'd be talking about the case right now instead of our own bullshit.'

'I'll follow your lead, Imogen. Whatever you think is best.'

'So, it's all on me? Wonderful.'

'Seems like no one talks to me about these things anyway,' Adrian said. 'You're the adult in this relationship, judging by the way everyone is always talking to you about what we should be doing.'

As irritating as Adrian's petulant behaviour was, at least this was a conversation.

'That's not fair.'

'So, let's talk about the case, then. Who does that body belong to?'

Imogen blew out her cheeks in exasperation before speaking again.

'We have reason to believe it's someone Angela knows, so we can assume she's connected to her in some way. A friend, maybe.'

'Do we know if Gary had any luck gaining information about previous contacts they may have had in Shropshire?' Adrian asked.

'Call him and find out.'

Adrian pulled out his phone and called Gary, putting him on speakerphone.

'Where are you guys?' Gary said.

'On our way to the Corrigan construction site. We think Angela Corrigan has gone there to speak to her husband about the body under the greenhouse. Any news on that?'

'Nothing yet; they are still getting it out, as far as I know. Officer Hasan called in to update us about fifteen minutes ago. The paramedics didn't manage to save Jimmy Chilton, I'm afraid. After Adrian left the scene, they got him out and put him in the ambulance, but he died before they even got to the hospital.'

'We didn't think there was much hope they would be able to,' Adrian said.

'What about the identity of the body under the greenhouse? Have you got any ideas about who it may be?' Imogen said.

'None, but I did find something strange,' Gary said.

'Go on,' Imogen said.

'Well, I was looking for any trace of family for Angela Corrigan and I was looking at her wedding certificate. I can't quite work it out.'

'What do you mean?'

'According to this, she married Reece when she was sixteen years old.'

'That's grim. How old was he?'

'Forty-four.'

'Wow. So, they got married just before they moved down to Exeter?'

'Looks like it.'

'Her father's name will be on the certificate, won't it?' Imogen said.

'Yep. His name was Joseph Purcell. I checked and both he and his wife died in 2006 within a few months of each other, two years before the marriage took place.'

'She really didn't have anyone looking out for her, did she?' Imogen muttered.

'I'll keep digging but that's as far as I have got right now.'

'Thanks, Gary,' Adrian said, hanging up the phone.

They drove into the brand-new as-yet-unopened business park and pulled up as close to the construction site as they could. Angela Corrigan's white Lexus was parked on-site. Reece Corrigan's Range Rover was also there, the boot open. But there was no sign of either of them.

Imogen took a deep breath before speaking, her hands quivering from either upset or anger, she couldn't tell which.

'I don't know what is with you lately, Adrian, but you'd better shape the fuck up.'

'I'm sorry . . . I didn't—'

'You ready?' Imogen said, getting out of the car and slamming the door before he had a chance to answer.

# Chapter Seventy-Seven

The business park wasn't due to open for another eighteen months at least and so the area was completely deserted. There were unfinished buildings and empty plots dotted throughout.

Adrian felt a rising panic as they approached a half-finished building, wondering where Reece Corrigan would be, wondering who else was here.

This was due to be the new site of Corrigan Construction, a flagship building. Adrian had so many thoughts fighting for attention. What if *they* were here? But also, knowing that Corrigan knew, what if he said something? Adrian knew he should be focused on the case, but it seemed impossible. He shouldn't even be here. He should never have come back to work.

He looked up at the building. The top two floors were incomplete; some of the floor-to-ceiling windows were missing. He looked across the front of the building at the rooms, but he couldn't see where the Corrigans might be.

'Are you OK?' Imogen said, 'You look a little pale.'

'Let's just concentrate on what we're here for,' he said.

'Sorry I asked.'

'We'll cover more ground if we split up,' Adrian said, hoping to be able to confront Corrigan on his own, unsure what he might do when he saw him.

Adrian couldn't have Imogen find out about what happened to him that way and if Corrigan really thought he was going down, there was no telling what he might reveal.

'I don't think that's a good idea.'

'I don't need a babysitter, Grey.'

'We both know what this man is capable of. I would rather not run into him on my own,' Imogen said.

He hadn't even considered that this might be difficult for Imogen; he was so consumed with himself and what happened that there was barely any room to think about anything else. He couldn't let himself get lost in his self-pity again. This wasn't fair. What he was doing wasn't fair. Was he willing to put Imogen in danger just to keep his secret? No, no, he wasn't. He was relieved to find a line he wouldn't cross; it made things easier somehow.

'I'm sorry. Of course we'll stay together. Any idea where they might be? This place is huge.'

They stood in the unfinished lobby of the four-storey building. The lobby was central and the east wing of the site seemed to be the most complete. The other side was still under construction.

'Does the lift work?' Imogen said, pressing the button.

The panel lit up and the arrow signalled the lift was returning from the fourth floor. That must have been where they went.

The doors opened and they got inside. Adrian wasn't a fan of lifts at the best of times; it was definitely worse in a half-finished building. He didn't know what the doors were going to reveal when they opened. The lift groaned as it climbed.

Adrian looked over at Imogen, who was staring at the panel and watching the numbers creep up. He had created a chasm between them by pushing her away. Reaching over, he took her fingers in his hand. She turned towards him, surprised.

Adrian didn't know what was going to happen in the next few minutes, but he knew that this might be the last opportunity he would have to kiss her like this, without her knowing what had happened. Even if she was annoyed at him now, it was better than pity, which was inevitable if she discovered the truth – he wasn't sure he could handle that.

He leaned towards her and placed his lips on hers, trying not to let his emotions overrun him. Adrian savoured the moment and forgot everything. He wouldn't let his anxieties put her at risk anymore. He had been selfish. Pulling away, he looked into her eyes for what felt like the last time. The doors opened and the cold air hit them immediately.

'What was that for?' Imogen said as she stepped out of the lift.

'I just wanted you to know, in case you didn't

already, that I love you. I hope you believe me when I say that.'

'I do believe you.'

'I'm really sorry if I have been difficult lately. I'm going to try to be better. I don't know why you have put up with me. I really don't deserve you.'

'I won't argue with you there. Let's get this bastard and then we can talk about how you're going to make it up to me.'

She smiled, the first time in a while, he noted. He really had messed everything up.

There was a dim glow at the end of the soon-to-be hallway; it was low, casting a stripe of light across the floor. Adrian supposed it was a torch. They walked towards it. As they got closer, they could hear talking, raised and fast, an argument.

Adrian turned to Imogen and whispered, 'They don't know we are here. Let me go and talk to them and you call this in. I think we might need back-up.'

He could see her weighing up what he was suggesting in her mind before nodding in agreement. She pulled out her phone and stayed where she was. Adrian moved forwards, terrified of what he might see when he walked into that room.

# Chapter Seventy-Eight

Hiding behind the wall to the left of the entrance, Adrian listened to the conversation between Reece Corrigan and his wife. She was distraught and her words didn't make any sense. Adrian wanted to make sure they were the only people here before entering the room.

He couldn't hear anyone else, so he pushed himself away from the wall and stepped inside. The first thing he saw was a missing window: the whole side of the room facing out over the car park was exposed, yet to have the glass installed. The second thing he saw was the gun.

'Angela, put the gun down,' Adrian said as he approached, palms face out in the air, so she would know he wasn't trying to hide anything from her.

As he moved forwards, he was wary of the gaping hole in the side of the room. He hated heights.

'Just let me kill him. You can't stop him; this is the only way to stop him. Why do you care if he dies?' she said.

Her hands were shaking and he could see that the safety was off.

'I really don't care if he dies, but this isn't about him, it's about you. I think he's taken enough from you. You shouldn't go to prison for him. He's not worth it.'

'Just pull the trigger, Angela. You know it's the only way to get away from me,' Reece hissed.

'Shut up, Corrigan,' Adrian said.

'She won't hurt me; she's got nothing without me and she knows it,' Corrigan said.

Adrian could hear the tension in his voice this time.

'Stand back, DS Miles,' Angela shouted as Adrian got closer. 'I'll pull the trigger. I know how to use a gun . . . my daddy taught me,' she sneered.

'You deserve to have a life. If you pull that trigger, you'll go to prison for a long time,' Adrian said softly. 'That's what he wants: to own you for ever.'

'Anything is better than this half-life I am living. I would be doing the world a favour.'

'We can take care of him now. We found a body. That's physical evidence.'

'He twists things. You don't know what he's like.'

'He knows exactly what I'm like,' Corrigan said with a smile.

Was that an admission of complicity in Adrian's assault? As much as Adrian wanted him to confess to what he had done, this wasn't the time or the place for it. He studied Corrigan's face for a moment. The smirk on it erased any final doubts he had about who was behind the attack in the van.

At the same time, Adrian realised that there was no

way he wasn't going to investigate who attacked him. He had kept the physical evidence, he already had a list of Corrigan's staff, possible suspects in his attack, safely stashed in his home. As much as he thought he was ignoring it, he wasn't. His training and instinct had already started looking for clues that he was behind his sexual assault. At some point, he would have to finish the job.

'What happened?' Angela directed her question at both of them before turning to Adrian, 'Did he do something to you? I told you he could get to you,' Angela Corrigan looked between her husband and Adrian, a new panic in her voice.

This is what Adrian dreaded; she didn't feel safe with him anymore. Angela had a vantage point that others didn't have and so maybe she could see those microscopic involuntary facial movements that others wouldn't notice. Maybe Adrian was giving the game away. He was glad Imogen wasn't here for this. If the truth got out about what had happened to him then no one would feel safe with him again.

'Who does the body at the house in Oswestry belong to?' Adrian said, steering the conversation away from himself.

'No one important,' Reece said.

No sooner had he said the words than the gun went off.

Reece Corrigan fell backwards onto the ground. He clutched at his arm and smiled through gritted teeth. Adrian thought he heard a chuckle as he made a move to help Reece.

'Stay back, Detective Miles,' Angela said before turning the gun on Adrian. 'Let him bleed.'

Imogen rushed into the room a moment after the gun had fired, her face panicked. She saw Angela with the gun pointed at Adrian and then she looked down and saw Reece Corrigan lying on the floor, blood oozing from between the fingers that clutched his arm. A bullet had grazed his shoulder.

'Angela, what are you doing? We've almost got him,' Imogen said softly.

'Who did we find at the house in Oswestry, Angela?' Adrian said.

'He said she left, that she found out about me and went away,' Angela said, her eyes filling as she stared ahead, her eyes not connecting with anything but a memory.

'Who found out about you?' Adrian asked.

'Because I made her leave, he told me that I had to look after him, that he was the only person left who loved me,' she said, turning to Corrigan. 'You told me the greenhouse was a gift. You're sick!'

'No one else would have taken you in, Angela, you know that. You have nothing to offer.'

'Just stop talking,' Adrian snapped at Reece.

'Angela, I'm going to call an ambulance for him. He's bleeding,' Imogen said.

'No,' Angela shouted, turning the gun and pointing it at Imogen. 'Don't call an ambulance. If you touch your phone, I'll shoot you. Throw it on the floor.'

Having a gun pointed at him was not a situation Adrian ever liked to be in. This wasn't the first time and even though it wasn't a regular occurrence, it happened more times than any police officer would like. Seeing a gun pointed at Imogen filled Adrian with a much more amplified sense of fear. He couldn't let anything happen to her.

Imogen pulled her phone from her pocket and threw it on the floor.

'Angela, you don't want to do this,' Adrian said, taking a small step forwards.

Maybe he could get to her before she did anything stupid.

'Stay where you are, Detective Miles.'

'Where did you get the gun?' Adrian asked.

'It was in his car, that's where he keeps it. He had it the night Simon and I tried to leave; he threatened us with it. The night I watched him beat Simon half to death on the floor of his bedroom. Simon begged him to stop, but he just wouldn't.'

'I thought you didn't remember?' Imogen said.

'I didn't, not at first. I saw the gun at Simon's place when they threw Simon and me in the back of the white van. He told them to kill us and dump us. It's all coming back to me now,' Angela said, turning to Corrigan. 'How could you? He was your friend. I bet you are so disappointed that I didn't die, too!'

Adrian heard the words 'white van' and felt a shock-wave go through him. This couldn't be a coincidence. It must be the same men.

'He was trying to take you away from me and I won't allow that, Angela. You're mine. If I can't have you, no one can!'

'You didn't have to kill him. We weren't having an affair. I would have stayed with you, if you just let him go.'

'I don't believe you. I bet he had his filthy hands all over you. I couldn't have that. You belong to me,' Corrigan snapped.

Adrian edged forwards again, but Angela didn't see him. She kept the gun on Imogen.

'Could you identify the men who took you? Did you know them?' Adrian asked.

'They wore masks. I didn't see them,' Angela said, almost to Adrian's relief.

'You still haven't told us who the body belonged to in Oswestry,' Imogen said.

'You won't believe me,' Angela said.

'It's him we don't believe, Angela. He's done. We have got him. He can't get to you again. With your testimony, he'll go away for a long time for the deaths of Simon Glover and whoever was buried under that greenhouse. You can get a divorce and move on.'

'I don't need a divorce; we aren't married.'

'We found a marriage certificate that says you were married in 2008,' Imogen said, surprised.

'That wasn't me,' Angela said. 'It was my mother's body under the greenhouse. He killed my mother. That marriage certificate was theirs.'

'What do you mean? Your name was on it,' Imogen said.

'Reece told me she left after finding out about what we were doing. She left me a note and everything. Told me she never wanted to hear from me again, that I was

387

disgusting and a disappointment. I was only fifteen.'
Angela wiped the tears from her cheek with the back
of her hand.

'Who was Joseph Purcell?' Adrian asked, remembering the slot in the marriage certificate for the father
of the bride's name, a horrible feeling creeping over
him.

Angela took a deep breath before speaking.

'My grandfather. Angela was my mother.'

'I'm sorry?' Adrian said.

This changed everything. The situation Angela
Corrigan was in wasn't just domestic abuse – it was a
whole host of other things that they hadn't even considered. Even on the darkest days working for the police,
this is not something you come across very often, thank
God. Add child abuse, neglect, murder, rape, incest and
God only knows what else to Reece Corrigan's list of
crimes. No wonder Angela was terrified of him. He'd
had her whole life to show her just how powerful he
was.

# Chapter Seventy-Nine

*As I stand here with the gun in my hand, I am scared to pull the trigger. It's as if even in death he will somehow still control every aspect of my life. The gun is heavier than I imagined. I remember seeing R swinging it with such force when he was hitting Simon that night. I have remembered everything. Funnily enough, it was coming back here to the building site that finally pulled all the jigsaw pieces together. We were here that night, Simon and me.*

*We met at Simon's place. R was conducting some kind of nefarious business deal in a pub somewhere and would then be going to his Friday night poker game. I sneaked out. I got a taxi into town and then a bus to Charmouth.*

*I remember a kiss. Kissing Simon was the first time I had ever kissed a man who wasn't R. It was sweet and tender, it was special, and in that moment, I would have been happy for everything just to stop, to go no further, like hitting pause on a movie. But it didn't. He found us and then he tried to kill us. To the end, Simon fought to get me away and look at what it cost him. Too much. I am not worth it.*

*My palms are sweaty. I have never held a gun before, but something about this feels predestined, as if we were always heading for this moment or some semblance of it. Maybe in an alternate universe it's him with the gun, but in this one it's me. Even with the weapon I know I don't have the power, it's always him. He can always say the right thing to shrink me to nothing.*

*But then I remember my mother, buried under the greenhouse, and I find my strength again.*

*As much as I hate this man, he is still the face of the man I grew up worshipping; it's hard to separate the two in my head sometimes. I have never really known what love is, I suppose. He made me believe my mother left and so her love never felt real to me. I thought that if she left me there was no way she could love me. I often wondered where she had gone, if she was happy, if she went on to have more children who she loved more than me, children who weren't a disappointment. I feel my finger tighten on the trigger.*

*I listen to R spinning his lies; although he doesn't try as hard as he used to with me anymore. He knows that he could tell me anything and I would stay. I am trapped. This, of course, gives me nothing to lose. Is that what he is banking on? He would never have the courage to take his own life, seeing it as a sign of weakness and letting me off the hook. If he gets me to kill him then I go to prison and he is out of the game, he will still have won. We are playing a different game, though. For me, his death is a win. I will feel no guilt. I am sure of that.*

*I hear Adrian Miles before I see him enter the room. He is trying to talk me into giving the gun up, but I won't; R doesn't get to walk away this time. I see that strange look of satisfaction on R's face when Adrian arrives; he says things that I know are secret codes. He gets that same look on his face when he says things to me in front of his men, things that only I understand, things that no one else would see as particularly upsetting or threatening. That's because we share those secrets. I can see he has a secret like that with Adrian Miles and I wonder what it is. I am more resolute than ever to put an end to this vile man.*

*Patricide, that's what they call it. When I go to prison, I will be the girl who killed her father and people will want to know why. I watch Adrian's face as he speaks, another good man my father has hurt. It will never end unless I end it.*

*Adrian asks me who the body belongs to in the house and I can't even bring myself to think it, let alone say it. My father speaks first and my finger presses down on the trigger. I see the red erupt from his arm as he falls to the ground. I don't want it to be over too quickly. I will only get to kill him once.*

*DS Grey rushes into the room and immediately searches for her partner. I see she is worried that I have hurt him. She cares for him, I can see that. My mind starts racing and I try to remember my mother; I was angry and upset with her, so I put her out of my mind.*

*I feel guilty for not knowing the truth, not realising what a psychopath he was. Would I have been able to get away sooner if I had? Probably not – just another layer of misery to add to my already miserable life. I am past caring about going to prison. My only goal now is to make sure he dies before I leave this room.*

*Both of the detectives talk to me, asking me questions I don't have the answers to. I see the look of disgust and pity on their faces as the whisper of the idea forms in their mind. I suspect there are other police coming to this location. I don't have much time if I want to make sure he is gone. They are going to try to stop me and I can't let them. I have to focus and stop thinking about my mother, about Simon, about how I ended up in the river.*

*My head is all over the place. I can barely concentrate on anything but the weight of the gun in my hand and how much easier it would be if I just turned it on myself.*

# Chapter Eighty

'I knew she wouldn't just leave me,' Angela said, tears streaming down her face.

Adrian moved closer still. This time she noticed and swung the gun back round to him, which made him feel strangely better than when it was pointing at Imogen.

'What are you talking about? He's not your husband?' Imogen said.

'I never married him, I can't. He's my biological father. My mother was called Angela Corrigan. I'm not the Angela Corrigan on the marriage certificate. My full name is Catherine Angela Corrigan. Not that anyone really checks them, anyway. When we moved here everyone made funny eyes about the age difference, but no one said anything.'

'Because no one cares about you but me,' Reece said.

'Shut your mouth,' Adrian hissed at Reece. He turned to Angela again. 'When did it start? When did he first . . .?'

'I am not sure exactly. I don't remember when. A few years before my mother died – three maybe. I remember finally telling my mother and she was so upset. Then she was gone. She left me a note saying how she never wanted to see me again. I wasn't as close to my mother as I was to him. Daddy's special girl, they always called me. I didn't understand until I got older how wrong everything was, until my friends at school talked about boys and things like that. Even though I knew it didn't feel right, what we were doing, I thought it was just normal in every family.'

'You were just a kid, you didn't do anything wrong,' Adrian said.

'I thought she left. I thought she hated me.'

'She threatened to take you away from me. I couldn't lose you, Angela. You're mine.'

Angela turned to Reece.

'So, she confronted you? Is that what happened? You bought me that greenhouse, told me it was to make me feel better, when really it was just an unmarked grave.'

As Adrian tried to process this information, Reece struggled to his feet; the wound on his arm was barely bleeding. Before Adrian had time to move, Corrigan lunged for Angela, knocking the gun from her hand. The gun went off as it fell to the floor. Adrian felt the bullet whizz past his ear.

Instinctively, Adrian clutched at the side of his head and pulled his hand away. No blood. Adrian looked behind him at the hole in the plasterboard – three inches to the left and the bullet would have hit his head. The way he felt at the moment, he wasn't entirely sure if he was relieved or not.

If the gun had fallen differently it could have hit Imogen. He looked at it lying there on the dustsheet. He wanted to point it at Reece and pull the trigger. He could pick it up now and claim it accidentally went off in the skirmish, killing Reece Corrigan. He could stop this man – a man who uses sex as a weapon, a way to gain power over people, people like Leon Quick, his own daughter and now Adrian, a police officer. Imogen would back him up if he pulled the trigger, he knew she would, especially if he told her why.

The temptation was strong, but there were other factors to consider, like the identity of the two men in the van. Reece was the only one who could tell him who they were.

He picked up the gun.

'Adrian!' Imogen shouted.

He had zoned out again.

He turned to see Imogen pulling Reece Corrigan back by his shoulders. He had his hands wrapped around his daughter's neck and was pressing his thumbs hard into the centre of her throat. She clawed at him and her legs flailed.

Adrian rushed over, realising yet again that he had left the moment and become preoccupied with himself. He wasn't fit to be back on the job.

He swung his arm with the full weight of his body, the gun still in his hand, the butt slamming into Reece's jaw. Corrigan let go of Angela immediately and fell to the ground. Adrian stood over him and hit him again and again with the gun. The sadness inside Adrian instantly transformed into anger and then some sort of perverse pleasure as the skin split and blood poured from Corrigan's face.

Corrigan stopped moving and Imogen grabbed hold of Adrian's wrist as he was about to hit him one more time.

'Stop! He's done. He's out,' Imogen said before calling behind her. 'Angela. Are you OK?'

Imogen looked at Adrian. He could feel the anger on his face and he could see how concerned she was. He nodded that she could let him go. She turned to Angela and helped her to stand.

'I know what you must think of me,' Angela said as she ran her fingers over the red marks on her throat.

'None of this is your fault,' Imogen said. 'Just hold tight. I have already called for some assistance and an ambulance.'

'You should have let him kill me,' Angela sobbed. 'Then he would definitely go to prison.'

'He will. They will confirm the identity of your mother and with your testimony against him for the years of abuse you endured, there is no way he can get away with it this time,' Imogen said.

Adrian turned to Imogen. 'Are you OK?'

The faintest blue lights pulsated against the ceiling. Their back-up had arrived.

Angela walked slowly over to Reece Corrigan's unconscious body and stood over him, a look of disgust on her face. No longer afraid. He was unconscious and blood trailed from swollen eye to the dusty floor.

'You don't know what he's like,' she said.

Adrian placed his hand on Imogen's shoulder to steady her. She looked shaken and confused by what they had just witnessed.

Before either of them had a chance to react, Angela picked up her foot and drove the heel of her shoe into Reece's eye. She was making sure he didn't get out of here alive. His body twitched as she pulled her foot up again before slamming it down one more time, this time in the other socket. There was no movement this time – he was already dead.

'Angela, stop!' Imogen screamed.

'I've got no one left. No one.'

Angela removed her foot again. This time the shoe stayed in place. She stumbled backwards until she was by the edge of the room, the full-length window that hadn't yet been installed.

'This is your chance to start a new life,' Imogen said.

'In prison?' Angela said, glancing behind her and appraising the fall.

'Given the circumstances and what you've been through, I don't expect you would serve a long sentence, Angela. Just step away from the window.' Adrian edged forwards with his hands held out. 'Come to me.'

'I can't,' Angela said, stepping backwards, a bloody imprint left where she had been standing.

Tears streamed down her face. She teetered at the edge.

Adrian was close enough to touch her now – he could grab her and pull her inside – but she could just as easily pull him out with her. He needed to talk her down. He spoke quietly to her.

'He's gone now. He can't hurt you or anyone else anymore. Just step forwards and grab my hand. Once the judge knows what he did, he will be lenient. I know it.'

'You can't know that.'

'Now that he is gone, I think a lot of people will come forward and testify as to what kind of man he really was. No one is going to blame you for what happened.'

Adrian moved forwards a little more and reached for Angela's cheek with his thumb, wiping her tears away, trying to ignore the sheer drop just inches away from him. He felt himself sway a little, his fear of heights getting the better of him. He still had his hand held out to the side in case he needed to grab the window frame to stop himself from falling.

'Come inside, Angela. You can trust me. I promise he can't get to you. He's dead. He can't get to anyone,' Adrian implored Angela with his eyes.

He could feel the tears of relief that Reece Corrigan was dead forming and he wanted her to know that he understood, that he was glad Reece was dead, too. Adrian remembered Angela's face tangled among the brush and how she had trusted him then. He could get her to trust him again. He hoped she could see everything he was trying to convey.

Angela stumbled forwards into his arms and sobbed into his shoulder. He held onto her tightly; he wanted her to know that she was safe from that man, that he couldn't hurt her anymore.

He turned his head slightly to see Imogen. The look

on her face was of complete fear. She didn't trust that he had a handle on the situation. He knew Imogen thought he was going to fall, that she thought she was going to lose him. *He* had done that. He knew he had to make a change. He couldn't put her through that again.

# Chapter Eighty-One

Six weeks earlier

*He comes into the bathroom and watches me as I shower. I try to shield the parts of myself that I don't want him to see. He removes his robe and climbs into the cubicle with me. Behind me, he kisses my neck and pushes me against the tiles. I draw my arms into my sides and wait for him to finish whatever it is he is doing.*

*He washes himself and then leaves. I continue washing, even though the water has gone cold. I scrub hardest at the parts where his body touched mine.*

*We have lunch together and he watches me eat. I feel like no matter what I do, he is watching me, even when I am alone.*

*After lunch, he suggests we go to London for a weekend away. I can go shopping and he can catch up with some business partners there. I smile and nod. I don't need any more clothes, but it's better just to accept his suggestions or he gets angry.*

*I never quite know what will make him angry and so it's better just to say yes to everything, or at least not to say no. I try not to look at the clock on the wall. He has already told me he is going out later on, so all I have to do is play happy families and wait. He will be gone soon enough.*

*I keep my gaze fixed on my book. My eyes scan the text and I turn the pages at the right times, but I can't tell anyone what this story is about. I am thinking about something else entirely. I am thinking about escaping.*

*I wait for ten minutes after he has left to make sure he is gone. I keep my book in my hand the whole time in case I have to get back into character.*

*I call a taxi. I have ten minutes to get my things together. I don't want to take much. I have a bag hidden in the back of the wardrobe with some clothes inside. Simon has got passports; I don't know where or how he got them. Still, I won't allow myself even to hope that I can get away until it has actually happened.*

*The taxi ride is short and it's only a short wait for the bus. Simon has given me a pay-as-you-go phone to contact him with. I made sure it was charged earlier this morning.*

*I try to suppress the excitement building inside me, but it's almost impossible. Is this really happening? Can I really get away? My mother got away and so it can be done. I heard him tell her countless times that she belonged to him and he would find her wherever she went – then when she finally did go, he did nothing. Could I be so lucky?*

*I get off the bus and Simon is waiting for me. I try not to run towards him, but the excitement pushes me forwards. We hug and he brushes my hair out of my face. I never thought I could ever feel love, but maybe this feeling I have for Simon is love. I don't know. I feel safe with him, something I am not sure I have ever felt before.*

*We go back to his apartment. As I cross the threshold to his flat, I get a bad feeling, as though someone is watching. I shake it off; there is no way R knows where I am. He wouldn't even be home yet. We have to get going before he gets back to our house, though, because I don't think it will take that long for him to find me here. I don't have friends.*

*Simon tells me we have to go and visit his friend Leon, who is holding onto the passports for him. He was worried that R would figure it out and do something to him. Told me that if anything happened to him then I could get the passport from Leon Quick.*

*Simon's bag is on his bed; he shows me the cash he has stashed inside. I don't care about money, but I know that we need it to get away. He tells me my father will never hurt me again. I want to believe him, I really do.*

*I reach up and touch Simon's face. I don't know how much time we have but it feels right. He leans forward and kisses me again, and I kiss him back. In the back of my mind, I don't truly believe we will escape. A part of me even wonders if I am awake and out of bed yet. Getting this far always felt like such an impossibility.*

*I push him onto the bed and climb on top of him,*

kissing his neck. We make love on the bed. I have never slept with anyone besides R. It's different, it's nice.

As we go to leave the apartment, I smell something; something familiar that makes my hair stand on end. R smokes these brown cigarillos. They aren't very common, and I just know he is close by and that he knows.

He told the truth about me never getting away. It took him less than three hours to find me. There is nothing I can do now. He is here and it's over. Does he have someone following me around? I wonder if Simon has realised we have been found. I should never have dragged him into this.

The front door bursts open with such force I let out a yelp. One of R's men has kicked it at the lock. R walks in and two men in black knitted masks follow behind. I smooth my clothes and hair instinctively, hoping my appearance doesn't displease him. As if somehow that will save me. I realise instantly how stupid that is. I don't feel like I recognise the men, but then I rarely go onsite anymore and of course I can't see their faces.

They each grab one of Simon's arms and restrain him as R approaches me. There is no point playing games anymore. R looks and sees the bags on the floor by the door; he knows we are running away together.

My cheek burns before I even notice R's hand as he swipes it across my face with such force it affects my hearing. My ear is ringing. I stumble, grabbing onto the doorframe for support.

R grabs a fistful of my hair and drags me into the

bedroom. The men follow, pulling Simon along with them. I wonder if R can tell we slept together.

I watch as Simon futilely begs for my safety, not for himself, which makes me sad; he doesn't deserve what's about to happen. I know if I say anything, if I defend Simon in any way, that it will just make things worse. When R is angry like this my protests never help.

R tells the other men to hit Simon and he instructs me to watch. R says he is making an exception for me. He doesn't usually get involved in the dirty work, but he wanted to see how this played out.

He doesn't look at Simon as they hit him – he looks at me. He wants me to know this is all my fault. He doesn't need to press the point home. I already know.

Within a few minutes, Simon is unrecognisable. That's when I first see the gun. R is holding it, pointing it directly in Simon's face. I can't help but let out a sob and he cuffs me across the face with his other hand.

I see the fear go from Simon, a look of acceptance on his face. I recognise that face – I have worn it enough times.

R lets out a belly laugh and then raises the arm that's holding the gun, allowing it to spin in his hand so that he is holding the barrel. He strikes at Simon, hitting him with the butt until Simon collapses on the floor, bleeding. His hand reaches out to me, either asking me to intervene, or just a final attempt to run away together – a delusion of hope.

My face is soaked with tears. I call R a bastard and he smiles. I tell him if he doesn't let Simon go that I will run again; if he does, I will stay. R tells me that he's done with me. That I am more trouble than I am worth. That I just don't listen. That I belong to him.

I spit in his face and he slaps me again. He tells me he has to go, but that neither Simon nor I will ever get the chance to betray him again. He uses his fist this time when he hits me and I fall to the ground.

R turns to the men and tells them to take us both to the site on the business park and put us in the foundations. I listen helplessly. I am not sure if I hear R correctly, but he takes one of the men to the side and tells him that he wants Simon to suffer when we reach our destination. He wants him to make Simon his bitch before he kills him. I know R well enough to know what this means.

Simon is looking at me and I see him mouth the word sorry, as if he has anything to be sorry about. I am the one who should be sorry. I caused all this.

Reece leaves and we are dragged to the back of a van and bundled inside. After a while the van slows and I realise we must be on residential streets judging by our speed. I can hear them saying they are bringing us to the building site. The foundations for the community rock garden are being laid in the week and they can put us there. We need to get away. I watch Simon drift in and out of consciousness, his face swollen and disfigured, gashes where the metal of the gun hit his temple and jaw and tore through the skin.

As we are driving, we go over a large bump in the road, maybe a stray log or tree, and I feel the van tilt and rumble as they try to carry on driving. The tyre has blown. The men in the van start to argue. They stop the van and get out, opening the side door. I play possum and pretend to be unconscious as they start working on the tyre.

I can hear them arguing at the front of the van. It's the front tyre. The back doors are ajar – it's almost as if they have forgotten what is in the back of the van. I jostle Simon until he wakes. He is punch-drunk, but he understands when I tell him we have a chance to go.

We get out of the van and run, the sound of the men's angry voices fading behind us. I vaguely recognise these roads: we are in Exeter. Maybe if we slip through the brush and walk along the river we can get to the quay and call for help.

It's dark and the temperature has dropped. I feel cold and dizzy. I don't know where we are anymore and Simon is barely moving behind me. I hear him fall in the water and I stop. He is too heavy for me to lift. I pull and pull but he doesn't move. I try to wake him, but he is gone. I don't have time to mourn and so I keep limping ahead, convinced that I can hear the men hot on my trail.

After what feels like forever labouring through the thickets along the bank on my own, I grow weaker without even noticing, the adrenaline wearing off and the pain kicking in. I am struggling but determined. I can see lights and try to get up a bank to get to the houses nearby and call for help.

I hear a car on the road and become convinced it's my father's men, come back to finish me. I crouch down as low as I can go to hide behind some bushes. I see *the roof of the van as they stop and look around. I hear them calling out my name playfully as though we are playing a game of hide-and-seek.*

*I huddle to keep warm and rest my head against the bank, the fog in my mind taking me over. I feel powerless to stop myself from passing out as the last drops of energy leave my body.*

# Chapter Eighty-Two

The ambulance took Catherine Corrigan to the hospital under police supervision. She was under arrest and would give a complete statement when she got back to the station, but Imogen could see a difference in the woman already. She looked happier – not happy by any stretch of the imagination, but there was an easiness to her that Imogen hadn't seen before.

When she was sure the other police officers were out of earshot, Imogen walked over to Adrian.

'What were you thinking?' she asked. 'I know what you were doing.'

'I don't know what you mean,' Adrian said, evasive as usual.

'When she had the gun pointed at me, you got her to turn it on you instead.'

Imogen just couldn't figure where Adrian's head was at at the moment. He walked towards that gun as though he didn't care if it went off.

'I don't like seeing a gun on you; I've seen it before, remember?' Adrian said.

'I don't need you to take a bullet for me, Miley. I need you to stay alive.'

'I need you to be alive, too.'

'I don't know what is going on, but tonight really felt like you had a death wish. The way you kissed me in the lift felt like a goodbye or something. You're really scaring me. You aren't the Adrian I know.'

'Now this case is over, I'll be able to think straight,' he said.

He walked towards the car and sat on the bonnet. He had that distant look on his face again. She struggled to know what he was thinking most of the time, but never more so than right now.

'What about the next case?' she asked when she caught up with him. 'And the one after that? You need to get a handle on this shit, Adrian. You can't go through life just exploding whenever anything reminds you of your past.'

'Don't give up on me, Imogen, that's all I am asking.'

'I wouldn't. I won't.'

'I think I need a little time off to get my shit together,' Adrian said. 'Tom's got study leave coming up; I might take him away for the week. If you don't mind?'

'Why would I mind? He's your son.'

He stood and kissed her tenderly on the cheek. She was taken aback, because there were still some uniformed police officers around and crime scene technicians processing both cars. Anyone could have seen them.

'You really are too good for me,' he said in a way that she didn't like at all.

# Chapter Eighty-Three

Adrian lay on the bed with Imogen. Reece Corrigan's death had brought him a modicum of peace, even though the actual perpetrator of the assault on him was still out there. At least he had a place to start when he decided to move forwards, when he decided to find the people who hurt him. He just had to concentrate on the positive here, which was that Reece Corrigan wouldn't get away with it.

Exhausted from the confrontation at the business park, they were both still in their work clothes. Neither one of them was ready to move.

They would interview Angela Corrigan in the morning and speak to everyone they had interviewed already with a hope that Corrigan's death might loosen some tongues. Now that Angela had agreed to give a statement and had confirmed that Simon Glover was beaten to within an inch of his life in his flat, they could put together a clearer picture of how it happened.

Adrian couldn't stop thinking about the list of names he had printed off – the ex-cons who worked for Corrigan. They would most likely be first on the list of people they would need to speak to. Maybe the police would find the two men who took Angela Corrigan and Simon Glover on that night. Adrian wasn't sure he could be a part of that investigation, not without putting Imogen in danger again. She needed a partner who would have her back, not fall to pieces in dangerous situations.

Adrian was tired of lying, tired of keeping secrets. He only had enough room in his life for one lie now and everything else needed to be less complicated. Going to work every day and lying about being with Imogen, lying about being OK to everyone he knew, lying to his boss about decisions he had made in the past. He just couldn't do it anymore. He had to simplify his life. There was no space for anything but that one big, ugly secret that he couldn't yet face telling anyone.

The longer he left it, the easier it got to tell that lie and the harder it got even to think about speaking it aloud. Maybe he could put those men to the back of his mind. He had even started ignoring Dr Hadley's calls. He had to pretend it never happened and that would take every ounce of his energy. He kissed Imogen on the forehead and then tilted her face towards him.

'Thank you for everything these last few weeks. You've been so good and I know I haven't been much fun to be around.'

'This sounds like another one of those big goodbyes, Adrian. What is going on?' Imogen asked.

He peered at her brown eyes and big black lashes, and it occurred to him that he hadn't really looked her in the eye for a while. He had been avoiding eye contact with anyone and everyone. Utterly consumed with himself. He didn't want to be that person anymore. This was another one of those life-defining moments and he had to make a choice. He kissed Imogen on the lips.

'I have given this a lot of thought,' he said.

'Given what a lot of thought?' she said, pulling away from him and propping herself on her elbow.

'I'm going to hand in my notice tomorrow.'

'Sorry, what?'

'I'm resigning,' he said.

'What the hell are you talking about?'

'Like you said, I haven't been myself. I think this has really taken it out of me and I don't like the way it made me behave. You are too important to me and I just need to take a breath, you know?'

'Just take your leave. See how you feel after that,' Imogen said.

'This has been coming for a long time, I think.'

'Are you breaking up with me?'

'No,' he said firmly. 'Unless that's what you want.'

'It's not what I want.'

'This way, we don't need to creep around. We can just be together.'

'I don't understand. Where has this come from?' she asked.

He couldn't tell her the truth and although this would change everything between them, he believed it could make them better. He couldn't keep walking into dangerous situations with her, never knowing when he was going to zone out or lose control. Never knowing who he was going to bump into.

He felt as though he was partially responsible for what happened to him, purely because he had antagonised Reece Corrigan. What if, instead of retaliating against Adrian, he had retaliated against Imogen? No. Adrian could live with a lot of things, but losing Imogen wouldn't be one of them. He had learned the hard way that you couldn't take love for granted, that it could be ripped from you at any moment.

'I love you, Imogen. That's all that matters. I just need a break from all this. With every case I seem to lose myself more and more. If I don't take control now, I don't know where I will end up.'

'What will you do?'

'I don't want you to worry about that. I just wanted to tell you,' he said, noticing that she didn't try to talk him out of it.

He saw tears gathering in Imogen's eyes. He knew it was a lot, what he was asking. He was changing her life as much as he was his, but he honestly didn't know what else to do. This was the only way to save himself, to save them. He kissed her again. She sniffled and pulled him in close for an embrace. For the first time in weeks they were really together, and he was thinking about her and not himself.

Adrian was going to be as honest as possible with Imogen from now on. He was going to put his attack behind him and get better. If that proved too difficult

413

then there was a box hidden in the back of the cupboard under his stairs. The box was full of photocopied police files relating to Reece Corrigan spanning several years. His clothes from that night were in there, too, and any other information that might be useful should he decide to find the man who raped him.

He wouldn't have the job getting in the way anymore. No one would be watching his every move, keeping him accountable. The idea of revenge and retribution stirred in the back of his mind and he found it impossible to ignore. He was almost excited at the prospect. He could make the man that assaulted him pay.

'What are you thinking about?' Imogen said.

'The future. Us.'

He kissed her neck and then her face again. He was ready to show her that he was willing to change everything, for her. The weight had lifted a little and he wanted this, he wanted her. This was the beginning of the rest of his life.

# Acknowledgements

First and foremost I would like to thank the men who spoke to me so openly about their experiences; I appreciate how difficult it must have been and I feel privileged to know you.

Thank you so much to all the readers. You really are the best. Also a huge thanks to the book bloggers and the blogging community – you are doing a great job!

Thanks as well to everyone at Avon Books who works so hard for their authors. Big thanks to Rachel, Claire and Tilda, who have done such a stellar editing job. Thanks Helen, Ollie and Sabah as well.

A special thanks to my former editor Phoebe Morgan; I miss you.

Thanks to my agents, Diane Banks, Hannah and James at Northbank Talent.

Thanks as well to my good friends in the crime writing community. You really all are the loveliest bunch of weirdos I have ever had the pleasure of meeting.

Thanks to Ed James for his advice and mediocre friendship.

Thanks to my husband and kids. Sorry you had to eat so much pasta throughout the writing of this book. Normal service will resume soon.

Thanks to the rest of my family. I know I am annoying.

# Author's Note

If you have been affected by the issues in this book, please know that you aren't alone and there is support out there for you.

Here are some resources you may find useful.

**Male Survivors Partnership – working for the good of male survivors of sexual assault.**
**Website: www.malesurvivor.co.uk**
**National Helpline: 0808 800 5005**

**Safeline – a non-discriminatory service to help survivors of sexual assault.**
**Website: www.safeline.org.uk**

**Mankind – supporting the 1 in 6 men affected by unwanted sexual experiences.**
**Website: www.mkcharity.org**

1in6 – support for male survivors of sexual assault.
Website: www.1in6.org

National Domestic Violence Helpline.
Website: www.nationaldomesticviolencehelpline.org.uk
Helpline: 0808 2000 247

Go back to where it all began . . .

The first smash-hit crime novel from
Katerina Diamond.
NOT for the faint-hearted . . .

**Everything you think you know
is a lie . . .**

'All hail the new Queen of Crime' *Heat*

# The
# Secret

Everything
you *think* you
know is a lie...

KATERINA DIAMOND

*SUNDAY TIMES* BESTSELLER

The Queen of Crime returns in her
second Miles and Grey novel.

**Some things can't be forgiven . . .**

'All hail the new Queen of Crime' *Heat*

# The
# Angel

Some things can't be forgiven...

THE *SUNDAY TIMES* BESTSELLER
## KATERINA DIAMOND

The Queen of Crime is back in
the third bestselling Miles and
Grey novel.

You make it. You break it.

**Katerina Diamond**

THE *SUNDAY TIMES* BESTSELLING AUTHOR

The Promise

Roses are red...
he wants you dead

The fourth Miles and Grey thriller
from the Sunday Times bestseller,
guaranteed to keep you up all night.

Sometimes the past comes
back to kill you . . .

'Diamond is the master of gripping literature'
Evening Standard

# Truth or Die

Sometimes the past
comes back to kill you...

## Katerina Diamond

THE SUNDAY TIMES BESTSELLING AUTHOR

NOT
FOR THE
FAINT-
HEARTED!

The fifth explosive, twisty Miles and Grey
thriller from the Queen of Crime.